V. A. STUART

V. A. Stuart is an acknowledged expert in British military and naval history, and is the author of more than sixty books and countless magazine articles. The excitement, authenticity and flavor in V. A. Stuart's writing is due in part to a colorful career as a world traveler and as an officer with the British Army in Burma, Japan, India and Australia during World War II.

The major part of V. A. Stuart's recent writing has been concerned with the periods surrounding the Indian Mutiny of 1857 and the Crimean War. It is in this latter area that this volume, the fourth in the saga of Phillip Horatio Hazard, continues what is planned as a series of at least twelve books.

The first book in this series, THE VALIANT SAILORS, was acclaimed by critics in England and America. *Publisher's Weekly* reported that "this meticulously recorded adventure novel is a worthy successor to the Captain Horatio Hornblower series, and make no bones about it." Here, then, is superb writing about the exciting days of iron men and wooden ships.

ALSO IN THE HAZARD SAGA:

The Valiant Sailors

The Brave Captains

Hazard's Command

Hazard of Huntress

by
V. A. STUART

PINNACLE BOOKS • NEW YORK CITY

HAZARD OF HUNTRESS

Copyright © 1972 by V. A. Stuart

A Pinnacle Book published by special arrangement with
Robert Hale Ltd., London, England.

ISBN: 0-523-00099-5

First printing, May, 1972
Second printing, August, 1972
Third printing, March, 1974

Printed in the United States of America

PINNACLE BOOKS, INC.
275 Madison Avenue
New York, N.Y. 10016

AUTHOR'S NOTE

With the exception of the Officers and Seamen of
H.M.S. *Huntress*, all the British Naval and Military Officers in this novel really existed and their
actions are a matter of historical fact. Their
opinions are also, in most cases, widely known
and where they have been credited with remarks
or conversations—as, for example, with the ficti-
tious characters—which are not actually their own
words, care has been taken to make sure that these
are, as far as possible, in keeping with their known
sentiments. The main events described did actually
take place but the "cloak and dagger" episode in
Odessa is a figment of the author's imagination . . .
although it *could* have happened much as described. General Canrobert did oppose Admiral
Lyons' plan to occupy the Sea of Azoff and the
first expedition, which sailed in May, 1855, was
recalled by the French Commander-in-Chief.

Letters from Captain George Broke of H.M.S. *Gladiator* to Rear-Admiral Sir Edmund Lyons, Commander-in-Chief, British Black Sea Fleet.
(later Sir George Broke K.C.B.)

(1)

Gladiator, off Odessa,
19th January 1855.

Sir,

I have the honor to acknowledge the receipt of your instructions of the 16th instant and to acquaint you that, in obedience to the same, notifications of the declaration of a blockade of Russian ports in the Black Sea, to commence on 1st of February next, was this day formally delivered at 10.30 a.m. by the Senior Lieutenant of this ship (in concert with an officer of His Imperial Majesty's French steam-frigate *Mogador*) to the Russian officer designated in the margin, who was sent to meet the boats of the two ships on their arrival off the Mole under a flag of truce.

The weather being foggy, the captain of the *Mogador* and myself deemed it advisable to make the communication at once. We therefore hoisted a flag of truce . . . and in order to call attention to it, I fired one black gun to seaward.

I beg to add, in consequence of the fog becoming

denser after the boats had left the ship, the officers sent in them found it necessary to approach within musket-shot of the Mole where, on a blank gun being fired, they stopped until the Russian boat came to them; with this one exception, your instructions were strictly carried out and under these circumstances I hope it will meet with your entire approval.

I have etc.,
(Signed) George N. Broke.

(2)

Gladiator, off Odessa
8th February 1855.

Sir,
I have the honor to inclose herewith a letter from the Spanish Consul at Odessa, which was sent out by a boat under flag of truce, at noon, on 6th instant, and delivered to Lieutenant Risk, of Her Majesty's steam-vessel *Wrangler*, acknowledging the receipt of the notification of blockade sent in by your directions on 19 ultimo. . . .

I have etc.,
(Signed) George N. Broke.

From: *Russian War*, 1855, Black Sea Official Correspondence. Edited by Captain A. C. Dewar, O.B.E., B.Litt., F.R.Hist.S., R.N.
Published by the Navy Records Society.

PROLOGUE

On the morning of 20th December 1854, a heavy snow-storm, driven by an icy off-shore wind, struck the British Fleet anchorage at the mouth of the Katcha River, to the north of Sebastopol. Very soon, the decks of the ships moored there were covered by an eight-inch carpet of treacherous white slush, on which men moved at their peril and which—like the moisture on yards and rigging —swiftly froze. A blood-red sun lent the scene a weird, seasonable beauty which few of the various duty watchers were able to appreciate, as they hacked half-heartedly at icicles and endeavored to clear the decks with brooms and shovels, blowing on their blue fingers and each man listening eagerly for the pipe that would summon him to his mess deck for breakfast.

In the stateroom of his 91-gun steam-screw flagship *Agamemnon*, Rear-Admiral Sir Edmund Lyons, at present second-in-command of the British Black Sea Fleet—who kept early hours—had just begun his own breakfast when his Secretary, Lieutenant Cleeve, entered and, with a murmured apology, laid a bundle of letters on the table beside him.

"I beg you to forgive my intrusion, sir, while you are still eating but mail from home has just been delivered by the *Banshee*. And—er—that is, sir . . ." the Secretary hesitated and then, gesturing to the envelope which lay on top of the small pile, he went on, his voice losing its impersonal correctness and betraying his excitement, "I felt sure, sir, that you would wish to see *this* letter immediately. The official dispatches have gone across to the

Furious but they won't have reached her yet and I thought, sir——"

"Thank you, Frederick," Sir Edmund acknowledged, cutting him short. He set down his coffee cup without undue haste and glanced at William Mends, his Flag-Captain, who was seated opposite, before picking up the letter to which Lieutenant Cleeve had drawn his attention. The envelope bore the Admiralty seal but was marked PERSONAL and was addressed to him in the familiar handwriting of the First Lord, Sir James Graham. Aware of what its contents were likely to be, the Admiral sighed and, again meeting the inquiring eyes of his Flag-Captain, answered the unspoken question in them with a brief inclination of his silver-grey head.

"Yes, Willie, I imagine the moment has come. And now that it has, I confess I'm not sure whether to be glad or sorry."

"The officers and seamen of the Fleet will be glad, sir," Mends assured him. "More than glad, every man-jack of them." His tone was enthusiastic, holding no hint of doubt.

The Admiral was silent, repeating his sigh as he broke the seal on the envelope. He had always known that Their Lordships had chosen him to succeed Vice-Admiral James Deans Dundas as Commander-in-Chief of the Black Sea Fleet, since it had been on this understanding that he had accepted his present subordinate appointment when the declaration of war on Russia had been imminent. Official notification of his promotion and his commission would, of course, be sent to the man he was to succeed, on board the steam frigate *Furious* to which, in readiness for departure, Admiral Dundas had recently shifted his flag. But his long friendship with the First Lord would, Sir Edmund Lyons knew, bring him news of the transfer of the command unofficially, in a personal letter delivered in the same mail bag as, in the past year, so many other personal letters had been sent, intended for his eyes alone. No other eyes had glimpsed them; he had respected the First Lord's confidence with scrupulous loyalty and had never

10

mentioned their correspondence to anyone save Lord Raglan, the British military Commander-in-Chief, and he found himself wondering now, as he looked down at the letter in his hand, whether his own Chief knew of the correspondence.

Probably he did, although he had never said so, never raised any objection, which suggested that he was indifferent to the fact that the First Lord had, throughout the war, asked for and frequently acted upon the advice and opinions of the Fleet's second-in-command, rather than those of its Chief. As indeed, Edmund Lyons reflected, had Lord Raglan. But Dundas had only himself to blame in this particular case, for had he not delegated what should properly have been his responsibility and left the necessary liaison between the Military Expeditionary Force and the Royal Navy to his second-in-command? Admiral Dundas never attended conferences ashore. He communicated with Lord Raglan, when he had to, by means of notes or messages which, as his subordinate, Lyons himself had been charged to deliver. The notes were usually brief, often discourteous and, at times, offensively critical of the military operations being conducted on shore and, Sir Edmund reflected wryly, they had made his task infinitely more difficult than it need have been.

It had taken all the tact he had learned, during the nineteen years he had served in the Diplomatic Corps, to smooth over the ruffled feelings which those notes had caused, particularly when he had had to deliver them to their French and Turkish allies. Lord Raglan had been the soul of patience, however. He was a kindly and considerate man, a gentleman in the fullest sense of that sometimes misused word, and he had refused to allow Dundas to ruffle *his* feelings. Even when his naval counterpart had stated, in writing, that the bombardment of Sebastopol's seaward defenses by the Allied Fleets on 17th October had been "a false action, which he declined to repeat and with which, as a naval officer of fifty years' experience, he was profoundly dissatisfied", Lord Ragland had not taken offense.

11

"In the Admiral's place, Sir Edmund, I fancy that I should have felt as he now does," the military Commander-in-Chief had said quietly. "He has suffered grievous losses and, alas! to no avail. It might have been a very different story had circumstances enabled us to launch a simultaneous landward attack but . . . they did not. So he is right—the action was a false one and I, too, regret it."

Sir Edmund frowned, remembering, as he slowly unfolded the letter from the First Lord and read its opening paragraph.

"We have sent orders to Admiral Dundas, empowering him to transfer the command of the Fleet to you and himself to return to England, unless some active operation be impending which it would not be consistent with his feelings and honor to leave unaccomplished in other hands. . . ."

He set the letter down on the table in front of him, permitting himself a brief and bitter little smile as he turned the last few words over in his mind.

Admiral Dundas, having served three years as Commander-in-Chief, was due, in any event, to haul down his flag in January but he had applied—several weeks ago—to be relieved on the grounds of ill-health. Not that his health was noticeably impaired; there was no reason why it should be, since he spent all his time aboard his comfortable, well-provisioned flagship, his second-in-command thought cynically. James Dundas had had no enthusiasm for the invasion of the Crimea, right from the outset, and still less for the Allied efforts to bombard the fortress city of Sebastopol into submission. As Naval Commander-in-Chief, he had supplied ships and men and guns—the two latter items with ever increasing reluctance—at Lord Raglan's behest, to aid the prosecution of the siege. With a Naval Brigade of over three thousand seamen and Marines manning the Upland batteries and many ships denuded of more than half their guns, the role of the British Fleet had become a secondary one. The Royal Navy now provided more troop carriers and supply ships than battle squad-

12

rons . . . an inglorious, although admittedly necessary service, the Fleet's future Commander-in-Chief reflected.

True, a blockade of the Russian Black Sea ports had
been maintained by a few overworked steam frigates but
this was effective only because the enemy Fleet lay immobilized in Sebastopol Harbor, imprisoned there by the
line of scuttled battleships which Admiral Korniloff had
been ordered to sink across its entrance, for the original
purpose of barring the harbor to the Allied Navies. But
as to any impending active operation . . . Sir Edmund
Lyons' mouth tightened.

He had wanted to attack Kinburn and Anapa, to capture Kertch and to lead his steam frigate squadron into the
Sea of Azoff, since it was mainly along these routes that
Prince Menschikoff, the Russian Commander-in-Chief,
obtained his supplies and his seemingly endless troop reinforcements. But Admiral Dundas had heard his suggestions, listened to his plans and had then ignored them.
Now, alas, it was too late to put any of them into the
active operation which Sir James Graham, in his letter,
optimistically envisaged. Winter was upon them and the
disastrous hurricane that on 14th November had struck
the Cheronese coast, had led to so appalling a loss in ships
and seamen—mainly off Balaclava—that a redistribution
of the Fleet had become a matter of urgent necessity.
The sailing ships-of-the-line, for which the gale had proved
there was no safe winter anchorage, were to be sent home
and replaced, as soon as possible, by steamers.

Already the *Britannia*, Admiral Dundas's flagship, had
left for the Bosphorous on the first stage of her journey,
in company with the *Trafalgar*, *Queen* and *London*—a
proportion of their seamen and all their Marines left behind with the Naval Brigade and borne on the books of
other ships. The *Bellerophon* would follow them, as soon
as sufficient Turkish troops had been convoyed from the
Bulgarian theatre to Eupatoria, to relieve the garrison
there. Henceforth, Admiral Lyons thought, aware of a
brief lifting of his spirits, Omar Pasha—the courageous
defender of Silestria—and the British General Cannon, on

13

loan to the Turkish Army, would undertake responsibility for the defense of Eupatoria. He would have to leave them two or three steam frigates but at least he would once more have the services of the invaluable Captain Saumarez Brock, who had been left in command there ever since the Allied landing at Calamita Bay in September. A foolish waste of an able commander and of one who was an expert on the Russina Black Sea ports and their defenses—whom Dundas had left to kick his heels in Eupatoria and. . . .

"Forgive me, sir . . ." the voice of his Flag-Captain broke into the Rear-Admiral's thoughts. "Shall I leave you to the perusal of your mail? Unless, of course, I can be of service to you?"

Sir Edmund Lyons shook his head, an affectionate smile lighting his tired, over-thin face as he looked up at the man who had been his right hand during the past seven months. "No, thank you, my dear fellow, there's nothing I need. I shall enjoy the luxury of sitting here in the warmth, with my feet up, for a change—instead of riding through a blizzard to confer with Lord Raglan. Possibly the Commander-in-Chief may require my presence aboard the *Furious* later this morning, I don't know." He waved a slim hand in the direction of the First Lord's letter. "But this *does* inform me that my commission as Commander-in-Chief has been sent out. And"—he quickly skimmed through the rest of the letter—"it also confirms that the *Royal Albert* is to receive my flag."

Captain Mends echoed his smile. "Then the moment has come, Admiral. Permit me to offer my congratulations, sir. No man on earth—or at sea—deserves it more and none is better able to undertake this command than yourself."

"You flatter me, Willie," Admiral Lyons accused. "But you're a loyal friend."

"I meant every word I said," Mends answered, with complete sincerity. "Believe me, sir, I meant it with all my heart. It has been a privilege to serve under you."

"Sir James Graham is taking it for granted that you'll transfer with me to the *Royal Albert*," the Admiral said.

14

"As I am, Willie. Sir Thomas Pasley is to bring her out and the First Lord says here that he is to succeed you in command of this ship. That's in order, is it not? You're happy about it?"

"Indeed I am, sir." William Mends's habitually grave face was wreathed in smiles now, his pleasure self-evident as he rose to his feet. The Admiral noticed Frederick Cleeve hovering inconspicuously in the background and nodded in dismissal. "I shall not need you either, my boy, for an hour or so. But"—he turned back to his Flag-Captain—"when the *Bellerophon* reaches this anchorage, I should like to see Lord George Paulet—and Captain Brock, if he's with him and any other Captain who's been engaged in convoying the Turks to Eupatoria. Keep me informed, if you please, Willie."

"Of course, sir."

"And perhaps," Sir Edmund went on, "you would have them make a signal to the *Miranda*. I should like my son Jack to dine with me—unless, of course, I'm invited to dine with the Commander-in-Chief which, in the circumstances, is not beyond the bounds of possibility. What do you think?"

Both Mends and Cleeve eyed him uncertainly for a moment and then both smiled, evidently sharing the same wry joke. "It's not beyond the bounds of possibility, sir," the Flag-Captain replied, his voice carefully flat. He and the Secretary went out together and, left alone, Admiral Lyons again picked up the letter from the First Lord. His steward, unbidden, brought him fresh coffee, poured out a cup for him and silently withdrew.

"I have offered to Admiral Stewart at Malta the post of second-in-command under you," Sir James Graham had written. *"I know not whether he will accept, but I am quite certain, if it take effect, that his appointment will be agreeable to you."*

It would indeed, the Admiral reflected. Rear-Admiral Sir Houston Stewart, as Admiral Superintendent in Malta, had given him splendid support when he had been compelled, at very short notice, to ask for an unprecedented

15

supply of small boats and pontoons in order to land the British Expeditionary Force, with its horses and guns, at Calamita Bay. Yes, as the First Lord had supposed, the appointment of Houston Stewart as his second-in-command was most agreeable to him; he could ask for no better man. And their relationship would be infinitely more cordial, he told himself, than his own had been with Admiral James Deans Dundas who—although aware of the imminence of his departure—had seen fit only to invite his successor to a dinner on board the *Britannia*, at which his farewells had been shared by all the senior Fleet captains. Sir Edmund shrugged his slim, slightly bowed shoulders and read on.

"In this case," the letter informed him, *"Admiral Stopford will go to Malta, and I wish to know with as little delay as possible if Captain Grey—now next for promotion as a rear-admiral—would be acceptable to you as Captain of the Fleet. When the command of* Hannibal *is vacant, this ship would be excellent for the flag of the second-in-command, though I have told Admiral Stewart that I cannot promise* Hannibal. . . ."

A frown puckered Admiral Lyons's smooth brow as he read the First Lord's inquiry concerning the appointment of a Captain of the Fleet—an undefined position that, under Admiral Dundas, had been filled by Montagu Stopford. Had not Stopford himself described it as so undefined a position as to be a false one? And he had added, with some feeling, that "few men capable of fulfilling what was expected of a Captain of the Fleet would remain long in the appointment." Even Nelson had found it very inconvenient when he had had his friend, Admiral George Murray, in this capacity off Toulon and had afterwards declined to appoint a Captain of the Fleet, although his Fleet had been increased to forty sail-of-the-line. Edmund Lyons's expression relaxed. What Nelson could do he, surely, would also be permitted to do; and Sir James Graham, judging by the wording of his question, was leaving the final decision to his new Commander-in-Chief. He knew Frederick Grey for an able but, perhaps, overambitious officer and guessed, although Sir James Graham had not hinted at this, that Grey, who possessed considerable influence in political quarters, had probably contrived to have his name put forward for the appointment.

Well, if there were no such appointment in his Fleet, then Grey could hardly complain if he weren't given it. The Admiral reached for his pen and, dipping it into the inkwell, wrote in the margin of the letter: *"No Captain of the Fleet. Quote Nelson for precedent."* He replaced the pen and read Sir James Graham's last two paragraphs.

"We must have some of the sailing ships long in commission brought home without delay," the First Lord warned. *"We have sent you some screw line-of-battle ships and will send one or two more. . . ."* The *Royal Albert, Hannibal, St. Jean d'Acre* and *Princess Royal* had all been promised to him, in earlier despatches, Admiral Lyons recalled and he hoped that Their Lordships would heed his urgent request for more light draught steam-screw frigates, of the *Arrow* and *Huntress* class but . . . there was no mention of gunboats. He read on.

"We have just heard of the fatal effects of the hurricane of the 14th, and have written to Admiral Dundas on the subject of a station for ships-of-war and transports during winter. I know not whether Sinope can, in present circumstances, be made available but I suspect that communication with the Army for stores, ammunition, provisions and its daily wants, must be kept up by a constant stream of steamers between Balaclava and the Bosphorus. This winter will tax all your skill and energies, but the prize at stake is worthy of more than ordinary efforts."

The letter ended with cordial expressions of goodwill and an assurance of the writer's full confidence in him, and Admiral Lyons smiled as he folded the two thin sheets of paper and placed them in his private letter book. His smile faded as he permitted himself to reflect what, in fact, the *"constant stream of steamers between Balaclava and the Bosphorus"* would mean in terms of men and effort—and not only between Balaclava and the Turkish capital.

There were nearly 40,000 Turks, with their arms, horses

17

and equipment, to be transported from Varna and Baltchik across the Black Sea to Eupatoria. Glad though he was to leave the defense of that place in the capable hands of Cannon and Omar Pasha, his resources were being strained to their limit, for the French naval Commander-in-Chief, Admiral Hamelin, had been able to offer only two steam frigates to assist him in his task. Admiral Dundas, on receiving Lord Raglan's request that he provide transport for the Turkish troops, had—typically—acceded to it and then delegated responsibility for the whole complex operation to himself, offering no suggestion as to how it was to be accomplished. That they had contrived to convoy some 9,000 Turks to Eupatoria already was, Sir Edmund decided, a miracle. The hurricane of 14th November had taken a greater toll of supply ships and troop transports than of the ships-of-war, it was true. But many of the latter had suffered severe damage and had, of necessity, to be sent to Constantinople for repair before they were fit for service. The repairs had taken weeks—some were not yet completed—and, as a result, he had been compelled virtually to abandon the blockade of all the Russian Black Sea ports except Sebastopol and use the warships as transports.

He drained his coffee cup and sighed as he refilled it, turning now to the rest of his mail. Most of the other letters he had received were family ones. His sister Catherine had written as usual, he saw, blessing her for her constancy. She had never married and he was coming to depend upon her more and more, he realized, since the death of his own beloved wife. No one could take Augusta's place in his heart. He missed her deeply, conscious always of an abiding pain whenever he thought of her but Catherine, good, kind soul that she was, did her best and kept him in touch with family affairs, seldom missing a mail.

The Admiral read her letter first, then a much shorter one from his elder son, Bickerton, which he put aside in readiness to show to Jack later on. Not that the boy had a great deal to tell either of them. His daughter, Minna,

18

had written a much longer epistle, which contained news of her daily doings, snippets of local and family gossip and an amusing account of some of the escapades of his eight-year-old grandson, who would one day be heir to the Duchy of Norfolk. This letter, too, he set aside for Jack to read, aware of an unaccustomed feeling of nostalgia.

His had always been a close-knit and devoted family. Even during the eventful years between 1835 and 1849, when he had been British Minister to the Court of King Otho of Greece, he and Augusta had seldom been parted from their children for very long. They had taken the two girls, Anne and Minna, out with them to Athens; Bickerton, after coming down from Cambridge, had been appointed to his own diplomatic staff and Jack, who had entered the Navy in 1829, had served as a midshipman on the station. Both his daughters had married well, the Admiral reflected fondly, and both had made the acquaintance of their husbands in Athens. Minna's wedding to young Fitzalan, eldest son of the Earl of Surrey, had taken place in London in June 1839, but pressure of political events in Greece had compelled him to remain at his post, so that only her mother had been present. The Admiral closed his eyes, remembering.

His elder girl, Anne, had fallen head over heels in love with a charming young Bavarian nobleman, Baron Philip de Wurtzburg, who had been brought up with King Otho and had accompanied him to Greece as his aide-de-camp. Although Philip de Wurtzburg was a favorite of hers and a frequent visitor to the Embassy, Augusta had been opposed to the marriage at first, fearing that, if Anne were the wife of a German national and permanently resident abroad, they would lose touch with her, but the young couple had been passionately in love and, in the end, Anne had overcome her mother's objections. The wedding, a magnificent affair, had taken place in Athens with the King and Queen in attendance, at the end of 1839. Both his daughters' marriages had turned out well, in their different ways, Edmund Lyons reflected. Both girls were ideally happy and Anne, although living abroad, did keep in touch—less so, perhaps, since her mother's untimely death in March 1852, soon after he had been transferred to Stockholm.

His sons, on the other hand, had not married, although Bickerton—named after his old Chief, Rear-Admiral Sir Richard Bickerton, under whose command he had first gone to sea in the *Terrible* in 1788—was thirty-seven and Jack only two years younger. In Jack's case it was understandable, since he was in the Navy and had only recently attained post-rank. He loved the Service and was dedicated to his profession but for Bickerton, who was in the Diplomatic Corps and who could well afford a wife and family, there was no excuse. Indeed, if he were to hope for advancement in his career, he would need the backing of an attractive, well-bred wife to entertain for him and. . . .

There was a brisk knock on the door of his cabin, he heard the Marine sentry on duty outside ground his musket, then the door opened and he looked up to see his son Jack standing there.

"Come in!" he invited, thrusting the rest of his letters aside. "Come in, my dear boy . . . I've been wanting to see you."

"Thank you, sir," said Jack in a deep pleasant voice. They greeted each other warmly, the Admiral regarding his son with conscious pride. He was both proud and fond of all his children, but Jack—who bore his own Christian name and that of the commander of his first ship, Richard Moubray—was his special pride and the one with whom, in their adult years, he had most in common. The boy looked like his mother and was coming increasingly to resemble her, he thought. He had her merry eyes, her smiling, sensitive mouth with its up-turned corners and curiously—since in all other respects he was very masculine—her slim, delicately shaped hands with their long fingers. Her hands and, he knew from earlier observation, also her fore-shortened life line, which crossed only half his palm. It was absurd to give credence to the gypsy superstition, which suggested that the lines on

20

a hand could foretell its owner's future, but Augusta, too, had had similar lines on her palm and she had been much too young to die. He bit back a sigh and forced himself to echo Jack's smile as his steward, without instructions, brought in fresh coffee.

"Ah!" the younger man exclaimed, with relish. "Hot coffee . . . just what I could do with, I must confess. It's foul, snowing hard and the snow freezing as it falls. My gig's midshipman had difficulty in finding your ship in the murk, believe it or not."

"I believe it," Sir Edmund Lyons assured him. He waved hospitably to the coffee. "Help yourself, Jack, and then sit down. The mail has arrived and I've letters for you to read."

"One in particular, sir?" his son suggested.

"What makes you think so?"

Jack Lyons laughed. "My dear Father, there was an atmosphere of such excited pleasure on the quarter-deck that I felt it before I set foot on board. Willie Mends looks as if a maiden aunt has just died and left him a fortune and he could hardly resist telling me the good news himself, without waiting for you to do so! And Fred Cleeve is dancing about like a dog with two tails. With all this snow piling up, he'll break his neck if he's not careful. Even your Jacks know there's something in the wind, so do not, I pray you, keep me in suspense. You *are* our new Commander-in-Chief, are you not?"

The Admiral inclined his head gravely. "I'm informed by the First Lord that my commission has been sent out. But"—he shrugged—"as you know, it is for Admiral Dundas to decide when I am to read it."

"The *Furious* is preparing to get under way, sir," Jack informed him. He held out both hands, the affection in his voice and eyes causing a lump to rise suddenly in his father's throat as he clasped the proffered hands and they smiled at each other for a long moment in silence. Then Jack said, a faint catch in his voice, "My most sincere congratulations, Father. I am truly glad, for your sake and that of the whole Fleet and, like every other officer and

21

seaman, I shall be proud to serve under your command. Now, at last, we shall be able to make plans for the future—plans for action that will justify our presence here and make a real contribution to the war we're supposed to be fighting, instead of seeing our ships used as glorified troop carriers."

"When the winter is over, not before," his father reminded him. "And when Their Lordships send me the steamers I must have, if any action whatsoever is to be possible. Sir James Graham visualizes our winter role as that of nursemaids to the Army, I may tell you!"

"Does he? Ah, well, even the Crimean winter cannot last for ever, praise be." Jack Lyons sipped his coffee appreciatively, his expression quizzical as he eyed his father over the rim of his cup. "And spring must follow it. But," he added, his tone wryly disrespectful but without malice, "I had last spring under Old Charlie Napier's command."

"Under his nominal command," the Admiral amended. "You weren't in the Baltic for long."

"True, sir. Needless to tell you, though, it was not *his* idea to send our detached squadron to the White Sea. He was quite staggered when Ommanney made his report on the venture but all he said was, 'Och, you'll all have made a tidy wee sum in prize-money, will ye no'?' and then, after thinking about it, 'But I don't doubt ye'll have cost Her Majesty a fortune in powder and shot and all to nae other purpose than tae line your ain pockets.' Ommanney, who had expected a pat on the back at least, was quite speechless." Jack grinned wryly. "In spite of his famous 'sharpen your cutlasses' signal when war was declared, Old Charlie didn't exactly encourage the ships under his command to engage the enemy if it could be avoided."

His father sighed. "Poor Charlie Napier is an old man," he defended. "But in his day there weren't many to touch him, you know. As a Member of Parliament he's done a great deal to improve the pay and conditions of our seamen and with complete altruism, for he did not endear himself to Their Lordships when he spoke up on behalf of the lower deck, as you may imagine. Perhaps he wasn't the right man for the Baltic command, perhaps he's too old for it, too disillusioned—but who else was there? Cochrane's nearly eighty, Parker well into his seventies and Seymour was in the West Indies when the appointment was made . . . the Cabinet hadn't much choice. Sir James was against him, of course."

"I should have preferred Cochrane, even at eighty," Jack stated with conviction. "And he was willing to accept the command, if rumor is to be believed."

"Too willing, I'm afraid." His father shrugged. "But Old Charlie is a fine seaman. Did you know that he was the first man actually to fit paddle-wheels to a naval vessel? Harry Keppel served under his command in the *Galatea* in about 1830 and I recall his telling me that Napier started using paddle-wheels then. They were his own design and were propelled by iron winch handles attached to stanchions on either side of his main deck, operated by hand."

Jack smiled. "He and Keppel aren't on such friendly terms now, sir. You know what a fire-eater Keppel is . . . well, he and Lord Clarence Paget worked out a splendid plan for an attack on Cronstadt, I was told. They even made a reconnaisance of the harbor in Lord Lichfield's private yacht and submitted their plan, with sketches of its defences, obtained at not inconsiderable risk. But Old Charlie would have none of it." Jack's smile widened. "He said it couldn't be done. When I was ordered home, I heard that Keppel, Paget and Elliott were being referred to as 'the Three Mutineers', because they voiced their disappointment rather strongly when Old Charlie also turned down a scheme they had for an attack on Sweaborg."

"H'm . . . the *St. Jean d'Acre* and the *Princess Royal* are, I hope, to join my flag sometime in the spring," the Admiral said thoughtfully. "I trust that Harry Keppel and Lord Clarence may yet find opportunities for the action they crave but . . ." he spread his hands in a resigned gesture. "To be honest, Jack, I am not at all sure that they will."

Jack regarded him with raised brows and asked incredulously, "Under *your* command, Father? Surely——"

"Yes, under my command. You have not been here very long but you must already have heard and seen enough to realize that mine will hardly be an independent command. Oh"—as Jack started to protest—"I don't mean that I have to take orders from Lord Raglan, far from it. And he is, in any event, the most considerate of men, always ready to discuss his strategy and share his problems with me. I like and admire him immensely and our relationship could not be better but his main problem is the same as my own—that of obtaining the support and the full co-operation of our French allies. That is a problem which—confidentially, Jack—neither of us has yet been able to solve."

Jack looked frankly puzzled. "But surely, so far as you are concerned, it will solve itself, will it not, when Admiral Bruat becomes the French naval C-in-C? You used to tell me, in your letters, that you and Bruat saw completely eye to eye and that it was Hamelin who was obstructive."

"Yes, that is so," the Admiral admitted. "But the French naval command *is* subordinate to the military command and Canrobert refuses to consider anything save the siege and the immediate requirements of his land forces. He appears to be convinced that the only way to capture Sebastopol is to batter it into submission by means of a continuous bombardment by heavy guns. I have endeavored, again and again and with Lord Raglan's full support, to persuade him to agree to a combined naval and military attack on Kertch but he always turns a deaf ear to me. For such an attack to succeed, we should need troops and he insists he can't spare any from the siege. Look. . . ." Sir Edmund crossed to his desk and took from it a rolled map, which he spread out on the table. "You may recall that when we discussed our plan for a naval expedition to the Sea of Azoff in the spring, I pointed out the enemy supply routes. The so-called siege of Sebastopol is a farce, so long as these remain unmolested. The north side of Sebastopol is completely open and Menschikoff is able to receive a constant stream of troop reinforcements at Bakshi-Serai, together with fresh supplies of arms and munitions and food, which he can send into Sebastopol as and when they are needed. By the same token, he has built up a large and well-equipped force in the Valley of the Tchernaya which could, at any time, attack and even capture Balaclava. The way to defeat him and to take Sebastopol is, I have always maintained, by attacks upon his supply routes. Here and here and here. . . ." His forefinger stabbed at place names on the map in front of them. "Attacks he is not expecting and for which he is not prepared, on strongpoints whose garrisons are now depleted and which he would be compelled to reinforce." The Admiral's voice rose as he talked on, outlining the strategy he and Lord Raglan had wanted to employ and pointing more than once to the narrow Isthmus of Perekop, by which the Crimean peninsula was joined to the Russian mainland.

Jack listened in silence, but with ever-increasing dismay. Although they had talked several times of the plan for a naval task force of light draft steam frigates to operate in the Sea of Azoff, of which he himself had been promised command, his father had never, until now, voiced the frustration he felt or given an explicit reason for the Navy's apparent failure to cut the enemy's vital line of communication with the mainland which—on the map, at any rate—looked so vulnerable.

"On my insistence, Captain Spratt of the *Spitfire* made a survey of the Gulf of Perekop three weeks ago," Admiral Lyons went on, his voice now sounding weary. "A course I had urged upon the Commander-in-Chief virtually since we set the siege trains ashore. Spratt's report confirmed what I had heard—the gulf is too shallow to be navigable, even by gunboats, within fourteen miles of the road across the isthmus. It is therefore unassailable from the sea but if troops could be set ashore here"— again his forefinger jabbed impatiently at the map—"it would be a very different story. Lord Raglan, in very truth alas, has no troops he *can* spare and all our Marines, as well as the Naval Brigade, are required for the siege. But General Canrobert . . ." he sighed. "Canrobert *could* let us have five or six thousand men without endangering his position, at least for the limited time that we should need them . . . yet he will not. He has also refused French support for an attempt—which I have every reason to suppose would be successful, since the Circassians have promised us their aid—to take Anapa. The only naval action he seems prepared to agree to is a second bombardment of Odessa in the spring which, in my considered view, would be a waste of powder and shot. . . . Odessa has sent all the troops and supplies Prince Menschikoff asked for and sent them, under our noses, last summer! So we have reached stalemate and winter is upon us. I shudder to think how many poor fellows will die of sickness and from exposure on the Upland before we see the spring—more, I gravely fear, from these causes than as a result of enemy action. And all because General Canrobert refused to advance on Sebastopol when the Allied Armies, after their victory at the Alma, could have walked into the place with scarcely a shot fired! And, furthermore, when we could have supported the advance from the sea, before Korniloff sank his line-of-battle ships across the harbor entrance. Sebastopol was ours for the taking!"

Jack smothered an exclamation. "Did not Sir George Brown volunteer to take the town with his Fourth Division alone and Lord Raglan urge the advance?"

The Admiral inclined his head. "They did, but to no avail. St. Arnaud was dying at the time, of course, and Canrobert had only just been appointed to the French Supreme Command so that then, I concede, perhaps his caution was understandable. But not later. He has always turned a deaf ear to Lord Raglan's requests to give his support to an assault on Sebastopol. Even when he has *not* refused—as on the occasion of our ill-fated naval attack on the harbor forts which, it was agreed by all the Allied commanders, was to have been the prelude to a landward assault—Canrobert has failed to keep his promise. Oh, he's had excuses, sometimes quite valid ones by his standards, but I venture to suggest that Lord Raglan would not have made them. Canrobert is a strange man, always in a state of agitated uncertainty, and his whole concept of war is at variance with ours. He'll never commit himself to any attack, unless his troops can be assured of massive artillery support and, although he's not lacking in personal courage, his doubts and fears on behalf of the troops under his command cause him—even when he *has* been persuaded to commit himself—to change his plans and revise the agreed time-table. All of which makes him"—the Admiral shrugged—"well, let us say, an ally I'd never have chosen and . . ." he hesitated, as if fearing that—even to his son—he might have spoken too plainly and added emphatically, "What I've told you is strictly *entre nous*, Jack. It must go no further, you understand."

"Of course not, sir. I'm glad you told me, though." Jack's hand rested for a moment on his father's. "I'm beginning to understand your predicament. Let us hope that General Canrobert will place no obstacles in the way of our Sea of Azoff operation. Do you think he will?"

"It is a possibility which, I fear, cannot be ruled out," the Admiral answered, his tone clipped. "Despite the fact that he has given his approval to our preliminary plans. These, as you're aware, call for him to furnish a minimum landing force of six thousand French troops—and we must have at least that number, Jack, or we shall achieve nothing."

"Yes, sir," Jack agreed. "But would not Omar Pasha provide us with a Turkish force, if the French will not help? Or Lord Raglan might be willing to release enough Marines for our purpose, temporarily, of course, and——"

"No," his father said. "Lord Raglan is most insistent that we must have French support . . . and he is right, we must. Yet when we endeavor to persuade Canrobert to give us a firm promise, he counters with the suggestion that our spring offensive should be directed against Odessa. If only I could convince him that Odessa is no longer contributing anything to the war!" He sighed. "You can see, can't you, my dear boy, why I am no Cochrane? As Commander-in-Chief, I fancy I shall come closer to emulating poor Charlie Napier, however little I desire to."

"Never!" Jack denied. "You have always had the Nelson touch, sir. And are you not the Admiral who stole the headlines in *The Times*, when you took this ship into shoal water, right under the guns of Fort Constantine? Aye, and stayed there, exchanging shot for shot with the enemy, with less than two foot of water under your keel? You can't deny it, sir. Why, a dozen people sent me the cuttings and Aunt Catherine showed them to me when I went home. I could recite the whole report to you from memory."

"God forbid!" Admiral Lyons spoke with a touch of asperity but, relenting, went on with a dry flash of humor. "And *that* was Canrobert's doing, believe it or not. The original plan of attack was mine but Canrobert insisted on one *he* had worked out being adopted in its stead. Imagine that, Jack—a naval plan of attack devised by a military commander! Bruat and I attended a conference on board the *Mogador* on the morning of 16th October and argued against it until we were hoarse. Admiral Dundas was horrified by the whole misconceived plan and even Admiral Hamelin did not like it but told me, with tears in his eyes, that he could not go against Canrobert, to whom his command is subordinate, as I mentioned. And Canrobert made it quite clear to us all that, unless his plan was adopted, he would refuse to permit the French Fleet to take part and would not support the land attack. So we had no choice, we had to accept what amounted to an ultimatum."

"But that was monstrous, Father!" Jack was stunned.

"Indeed it was," his father agreed. He reached for pen and paper and made a rough sketch. "And, as you can see, Canrobert yielded, as usual, to his obsession for supporting his troops with guns. In this case, with naval guns . . . even if it rendered the entire seaward attack on the forts ineffective. He had the French Fleet in line from Streletska Bay to the center of the harbor entrance—here, where

28

the Russians sank their line-of-battle ships, you see? Their sole purpose was to back up his land-based assault which, in the event, was never launched. And, in order that Hamelin might do so, *we* had to sweep round to south'ard, thus"—he pointed to the sketch—"to form up on the French van and prolong the line to the north. Our sail-of-the-line were all lashed to steamers, to bring them into position—and that position, on Canrobert's plan, was such as to require them to engage the forts at a range of eighteen hundred yards. Eighteen hundred yards, at extreme elevation! The *Britannia*, for example, our French military strategist placed here"—his finger indicated the flagship's position—"where she was exposed to the fire of several enemy batteries on the cliff-top, with all save her lower-deck guns out-ranged." Again the Admiral's voice held a note of bitter frustration, as the memory of that abortive and costly action returned in all its vivid, heartbreaking clarity. Yet it had been an action that, had it been carried out as he had originally envisaged, might have achieved its objective brilliantly.

Instead it had cost the combined British, French and Turkish Fleets over five hundred killed and wounded and had gained nothing, because General Canrobert had declined to order the land-based attack to which he had agreed and Lord Raglan had been unable to proceed without him. Canrobert's decision had been reached *before* the combined Fleets had steamed into position but the naval commanders had been left in ignorance of it, and the French Commander-in-Chief had decided to break his promise after a shell had exploded in the principal magazine on the Upland . . . Edmund Lyons expelled his breath in a weary sigh. What, he wondered, would the famous Cochrane—Lord Dundonald—have done in his present situation? How would *he* have dealt with Canrobert?

Jack was studying the sketch of the engagement with frowning concentration and, with a murmured, "This is not quite complete," his father took it from him to add a

29

curving, dotted line which followed the shoreline north-wards from Fort Constantine.

"That is the shoal," he explained. "Which was the reason why I had to indulge in what *The Times* correspondent exaggerated into heroics in his report. He's a civilian, of course, and does not understand the first thing about naval or military tactics. But as you can see, Jack my boy, the safest and most effective maneuver I could make, in the circumstances, was to lead my inshore squadron so close to the fort that its guns were unable to bear on any ship. By the same token, for our ships' guns to have even a remote chance of damaging stone walls at least six foot thick, our broadsides had to be fired at close range." He went into brief technical details and Jack nodded, still frowning, as he followed the Admiral's explanation by means of the sketch.

"You've seen Fort Constantine," his father went on. "It stands thirty-foot high and is horse-shoe shaped, mounting two tiers of guns in casemates, with additional guns *en barbette* on its summit—a total of almost a hundred pieces of ordnance, of which half command the approach and the channel. Behind the fort, on the north side, there's a ridge, terminating in a cliff about a hundred and fifty feet high. Here"—he leaned forward, to mark the location on his sketch—"the enemy placed a battery of eight guns, *en barbette*, to command the seaward approach where there's a bend on the north side of the shoal, with fairly deep water. They had observed us sounding it, of course, and were well aware that a line-of-battle ship could only approach Fort Constantine thus. We gave that particular battery the name Wasp, for obvious reasons. Further along, the cliff, towards the harbor mouth, they threw up several earthwork batteries —here and here—between the fort and the telegraph station. When I drew up my original plan of attack, I timed it for early morning, hoping for the usual sea mist and banking partly on stealing up on the enemy unobserved and partly on the fact that, due to their height, the guns of the cliff-top batteries would not, initially, be

30

able to depress sufficiently to sweep the water immediately beneath them. But. . . ." He sighed again.

"But . . . ?" Jack prompted, looking up from the sketch. "What happened, sir?"

"But General Canrobert saw fit, not only to alter my plan of attack but also to defer the whole operation by four hours," his father supplied harshly.

"Yet you still attacked, Father?"

The Admiral inclined his head regretfully. "Yes, we still attacked . . . in the belief that, if we failed to do so, we should endanger the success of the land-based assault on Sebastopol and its probable capture. An assault which, may I remind you"—he spread his hands in a despairing gesture—"had already been called off, at the eleventh hour, by Canrobert! We were not informed that he had countermanded his orders to his troops—even Admiral Hamelin wasn't told. No signal had been arranged to cover such an eventuality because it was considered to be beyond the bounds of possibility—Canrobert had given his word that he would throw his entire force into the attack. So . . . both we and the French Fleet steamed into action, convinced that we were doing so in support of the armies on shore."

"I find it . . . dear heaven, Father, I find it almost impossible to credit." Jack stared at him, shocked and bewildered. "The reports in the English press gave no hint, they——"

"Nevertheless, it is true," his father assured him.

"I am appalled, sir," Jack confessed. He listened in silence as his father gave him a brief and bitter account of what had happened during the action. "The real hero was Mr. Codrington Ball, Second-Master of the *Circassia*, who piloted us in, sounding as he went. We reached our position virtually unscathed, in company with the *Sanspareil*, which anchored on our starboard quarter. The rest of the squadron were less fortunate, coming under heavy fire from the Wasp and Telegraph batteries before they could get close enough inshore to place themselves out of danger. The *Albion* was set on fire and was compelled to haul off, followed an hour later by the *London* and the *Arethusa*, both set ablaze by red-hot shot. The *Albion* alone had eighty men killed and wounded. We ourselves began to come under very heavy fire, the guns of Fort Alexander, on the south side of the harbor, got our range and raked us . . . but you've read the newspaper reports. They were reasonably accurate in regard to the rest of the action, so I need not repeat it all. You know that poor Jope, my valet, lost an arm, don't you?"

"Yes, Aunt Catherine told me. She said you had ordered him below but he refused to leave your side."

The Admiral's expression relaxed. "Yes, poor fellow. But he was obeying my order most reluctantly when he was hit. We were fortunate, you know, to suffer only thirty casualties. Of our upper-deck guns, we could only use our bow pivot, we had so many gunners ashore with the Naval Brigade." He described the bombardment in detail, his firm mouth tight with remembered despair as he confessed that—for all their three hours of heroic toil—his gunners had been able to silence the guns of Fort Constantine for only ten minutes, when a lucky hit blew up some stored ammunition.

Jack's concern grew as he listened to the account of the lives which had been needlessly thrown away, of good men wounded and fine ships dismasted and set on fire . . . and all, his father told him, with a swift flash of anger, to no purpose because, once again, Canrobert had gone back on his word.

"We almost lost the *Rodney*," the Admiral said, the anger fading from his voice. "Graham brought her most valiantly to our succor, when we and the *Sanspareil* were sorely pressed by four of the cliff-top batteries and our upper deck was ablaze. At the critical moment the *Sanspareil* forged ahead of us and Graham, determined not to swerve from his resolution of drawing some of the fire from us, backed astern and ranged past the *Agamemnon* obliquely. When the *Rodney*'s bow was parallel with ours, Graham let go his anchor but, as the ship swung with her stern a few yards nearer the forts than ours, she tailed on to the shoal. The smoke was so thick, I did not see that she was aground but, fearing that she was about to come aboard of us, I ordered *Agamemnon* to haul astern to clear her and then—still unaware of poor Graham's predicament—I made a sweep in order to get another lick at two batteries that had been cutting us up all day. We had to slip our bower anchor, because the *Rodney* was lying athwart our hawse and, for one rather tense moment, our jib-guys were touching. Kynaston of the *Spitfire*, who had the *Rodney* in tow, was compelled to follow our example and haul astern, also with the loss of his best bower—but if he had not, he would have got himself on shore with Graham, as he told me afterwards."

"Yes, he told me that too," Jack confirmed.

"The newspapers reported it all, of course and, if you've talked to Kynaston, I'm probably telling you what you know already. But"—the Admiral looked up, smiling, to meet his son's gaze—"did you know that your young friend Phillip Hazard was commanding the *Trojan* which, with the *Spitfire* and *Lynx*, played a very gallant part in getting *Rodney* off the shoal?"

"No, I did not." Jack returned the Admiral's smile. "I've seen Phillip a couple of times but he never mentioned it. I knew he had the temporary command of *Trojan*—he was commanding her when we met in Constantinople, early in November, but I haven't seen him since. You gave him the *Huntress*, Algy told me. I'm very glad, sir. Phillip is the best of fellows."

"He deserved his promotion," Admiral Lyons answered. "He brought the *Trojan* quite unscathed through the hurricane and he was at sea when it struck, so he displayed seamanship of a high order. And he further distinguished himself during the recent attack on Eupatoria—Captain Brock sent a glowing report of his conduct after that affair. I could do no less than recommend him for his own command. As it chanced, the *Huntress* lost her commander, Francis Willoughby, on passage from England—the unfortunate fellow was accidentally drowned—so that I was able to give Phillip the vacancy. Not entirely with the ap-

proval of Admiral Dundas, I may say in confidence, Jack
. . . he wanted the command for one of his own protégés.
But I contrived, in this instance, to get my way."

"I am truly delighted to hear it, sir." Jack spoke with
genuine warmth. "Phillip will do well, I'm quite sure. I
trust you'll permit the *Huntress* to join my squadron when
—or perhaps I should say *if*—we enter the Sea of Azoff
in the spring. She's engaged in convoying the Turks to
Eupatoria at present, isn't she?"

The Admiral nodded. "Yes. I thought it would afford
Phillip the opportunity to shake down with his new crew,
few of whom are trained seamen . . . but she's due to return to this anchorage sometime today. It's a waste
of a new steam frigate to use her as a troop transport and
we've few enough, heaven knows, but what choice have I?
The Turks must be ferried from Bulgaria." He shrugged.
"I've heard from Sir James Graham that the *Royal Albert*
is on her way out to receive my flag. Did Willie Mends tell
you?"

"He mentioned it, yes, sir, and said he would be going
with you when you shift your flag. He is overjoyed at the
prospect—and so he should be!" Jack smiled at his father.
"I saw the *Royal Albert* on the stocks at Woolwich when
we were fitting out for the Baltic, and one of the shipwrights told me, with immense pride, that she'll be the
finest ship of her class in the world. Certainly nothing I
saw caused me to dispute his claim. In fact . . ." He
launched into enthusiastic detail but was interrupted by a
tap on the door.

The Admiral sighed. "Come in," he said resignedly
and, in response to his invitation, his nephew and Flag-
Lieutenant, Algernon Lyons, entered the cabin, to an-
nounce formally that the Commander-in-Chief requested
his presence aboard the flagship.

"Ah!" Sir Edmund Lyons exchanged a quizzical glance
with his son. "That is all, is it, Algy? I'm not to be offered
dinner?"

The Flag-Lieutenant permitted himself an expressive
shrug. He had succeeded the recently promoted Com-

mander Cowper Coles as Flag-Lieutenant, after serving with distinction in the attack on the Sulina mouth of the Danube in June, when his Captain, Hyde Parker of the *Firebrand*, had lost his life.

"Well, sir," he returned apologetically, "the *Furious* has steam up and is preparing to weigh, so I . . . that is, sir, I——"

"You do not anticipate that my leave-taking of the Commander-in-Chief is likely to detain me for very long?" Admiral Lyons suggested, again glancing in Jack's direction, a gleam in his very blue eyes, which lingered there in brief resentment and then, as swiftly, faded. "Very well, Algy, you may call away my barge." His steward appeared, bringing his boat-cloak and cocked hat, and he rose, stifling a sigh, to don them. "You'll await my return, I hope, Jack?"

"Yes, of course, sir." Jack assisted him into his cloak and let his hand rest affectionately on his father's shoulder for a moment as he added quietly, "This is the day we've all been waiting and hoping for, sir, throughout the Fleet, believe me. And I imagine that Admiral Dundas is aware of it."

"It's to be hoped he's not. Well, Algy, what are you waiting for? The Commander-in-Chief must not be delayed, least of all by his successor, if he's in a hurry to depart."

"Two steam frigates have been sighted approaching the anchorage, sir," Algy Lyons informed him diffidently. "It is hard to be certain in this visibility but one of them looks like the *Huntress* and I understand, from Captain Mends, sir, that you wished to be told of the arrival of any ships from Eupatoria."

"Yes, indeed I did." The Admiral brightened, as he turned again to his son. "We'll entertain Phillip Hazard aboard *this* ship, eh, Jack, my boy? You can play host to him until my return."

"That will give me great pleasure, sir," Jack assented readily.

"Good. I imagine the second frigate will be the *In-*

flexible—she was due here yesterday. I'd like both captains invited to dine with me, as soon as they come to anchor. See to it, Algy, if you please."

"Aye, aye, sir." The Flag-Lieutenant departed on his errand and Admiral Lyons went on thoughtfully, "The *Huntress's* arrival is well timed—I have a special mission in mind for her, as soon as she can be spared from ferrying the Turks."

"One better suited to her commander, sir?" Jack asked curiously.

"One for which he is uniquely suited." The Admiral's tone was brisk and he was smiling as he settled his cocked hat firmly on his head and moved towards the door of the state-room which his steward was holding open for him. "Phillip Hazard and his brother were prisoners-of-war in Odessa last summer and, if General Canrobert requires proof that there are better targets for our spring offensive, then I fancy that, given the right opportunity, they could provide it." He emerged into the passageway, acknowledging the salute of the Marine sentry on duty there. "You may tell Phillip, when he arrives, Jack my boy, that I'll give him two of the officers he has asked for, from the *Trojan* and the two midshipmen . . . but I cannot, at present, replace his First Lieutenant. Tell him, though, that I shall be sending his brother to him, as acting-Master."

"His brother . . . not Graham Hazard, surely, sir?" Jack's dark brows rose in an astonished curve. "Didn't he run the *Comet* aground at the mouth of the River Plate, about ten or eleven years ago? If my memory isn't at fault, he was charged with neglect of duty and dismissed the Service, wasn't he?"

"He was, yes," his father confirmed. "But since then I understand that he has served as an officer in the mercantile marine. At the outbreak of this war, he volunteered as a seaman and served in that capacity, in this Fleet, until he was promoted—on merit, I'm assured—Second-Master of the *Tiger*. He was commended for gallantry when the *Tiger* was set on fire and captured off

36

Odessa . . . and by the *Tiger*'s First Lieutenant, not by Phillip, who was also present, of course. That was how both the Hazards came to be prisoners-of-war in Odessa —Phillip, who was severely wounded in the *Tiger* affray, as a guest of the Governor, Baron Osten-Sacken, and nursed back to health by his captors." His eyes were lit by a swift, significant gleam and Jack nodded in understanding.

"Is it at all likely that Graham Hazard will have his commission restored to him, sir?"

The Admiral shrugged, moving towards the entry port, where the side-party had already assembled, preparatory to piping him, with due ceremony, into his waiting barge.

"The matter is one that only Their Lordships can decide . . . and I fear they may not view my recommendation very favorably. But I have made it because I consider that Hazard has earned a second chance, though what the outcome will be I have no idea. So, in the meantime, I shall send him to the *Huntress* as Master, which is the best I can do. Well"—the Admiral's thin hand rested briefly on his son's shoulder—"I must go, my dear boy . . . but I shall see you later."

"Aye, aye, sir." Jack Lyons stood aside to permit his cousin to take his place, as the side-party came to attention.

The new Commander-in-Chief of the Black Sea Fleet stepped into his barge, to the shrill twitter of the ceremonial pipe and, as he did so, a spontaneous, full-throated cheer rose from the men of the duty watch. Despite the bitter cold, both watches gathered on the upper deck and the cheering continued, growing in volume, until the barge vanished from sight into a cloud of swirling snowflakes.

1

PHILLIP HAZARD was in a mood of quiet elation when he left the *Agamemnon* to return to his own ship. It was pitch dark and very cold and he shivered as he took his place in the sternsheets of the *Huntress*'s gig and, wrapping his boat-cloak about him, nodded to the boat commander to cast off.

The Admiral's hospitality had been generous, as indeed it always was, and he had enjoyed his four-hour stay aboard the flagship immensely, not least for the unexpected opportunity it had afforded him to talk at length to his friend and one-time Captain, Jack Lyons. With his fellow guests at the well-found table, he had drunk the health of the new Commander-in-Chief after witnessing, from *Agamemnon*'s quarter-deck, the departure of his predecessor, whose flag had been flying for the last time from the steam frigate *Furious*. He had seen the courteous exchange of signals between the two Admirals, their earlier differences—of which the whole Fleet had been aware—forgotten as each wished the other well in a hoist of coloured bunting, seen dimly through the falling snow as the *Furious* steamed away from the anchorage and set course for Constantinople. Later, as he ate, he had listened with growing eagerness to the plans for future naval operations which the new Commander-in-Chief had lost no time in outlining to his guests and staff—plans that would be implemented as soon as the dread Crimean winter gave place to spring—if Sir Edmund Lyons had his way.

As surely he must, Phillip told himself, now that Admiral Dundas had gone . . . and in spite of Canrobert.

As Sir Edmund had remarked, a short while ago, Sebastopol could hold out indefinitely so long as its lines of communication remained open and reinforcements and supplies continued to pour into the town from the Russian mainland, with its vast resources of men and the materials of war. The siege guns on the Upland, upon which the French pinned their hopes, could pound the city's walls and forts day after weary day without bringing their defenders any nearer to defeat. And those defenders were housed and properly fed, spared the cruel rigors of winter under canvas, which the Allied land forces must endure.

The Fleets were, on the other hand, in undisputed command of the sea, as the Admiral had reminded his listeners. Once the enforced inertia of winter came to an end and when the ships of war were released from their inglorious role as transports, then they could and would make a major contribution to the successful prosecution of the siege of Sebastopol by attacking and cutting off the defenders' supply lines and starving them into surrender. Once the ice-bound Sea of Azoff became navigable, a squadron of light-draft vessels like his own could be despatched to carry the offensive to the enemy's back door. In the meantime . . . Phillip had permitted himself a bleak little smile.

His own orders, issued privately and in confidence by the Admiral himself just before he left the flagship, had given him much to think about. "It is possible that I may not require this service of you," the Admiral had said. "If I am able to convince General Canrobert on the information I have available, rest assured that I shall do so. But, if I cannot, then you will receive sealed orders, the precise nature of which you are to divulge to no one except your brother. In the meantime, prepare to sail at once to relieve the *Highflyer* in the Bay of Odessa."

Phillip frowned. On the face of it, he would only be exchanging one unrewarding duty for another and the *Huntress* would, in future, maintain a lonely vigil off the port of Odessa instead of beating back and forth from Varna to Eupatoria, with every foot of space below deck occupied by seasick Turkish soldiers, whose discipline—by Royal Navy standards—left a good deal to be desired. But at least there would be some chance of action when he sought the information the Admiral had asked him to obtain and, he reflected with satisfaction, he would be free of his passengers. True, he had been warned that, when the time came, he must accomplish his mission without unnecessary risk to his ship and her company, but the warning was superfluous since he was unlikely ever to forget the *Tiger*'s fate.

He was pleased to learn that he was to have his brother Graham as Master, and that young Anthony Cochrane was also to be appointed to the *Huntress*. A pity, though, that Cochrane wasn't more senior, so that he might have taken over as First Lieutenant. The two midshipmen who had been promised to him—Grey and O'Hara—would bring his complement of officers up to strength and put an end to a keenly felt deficiency which had tried him sorely ever since he had been given command of the *Huntress*.

Phillip's brow cleared. One major cause for dissatisfaction still remained in the person of Ambrose Quinn, his present First Lieutenant but . . . Admiral Lyons had been more than kind in acceding to his request for his brother's transfer from the *Trojan*, as well as Cochrane's, and in permitting him to have the two midshipmen. He could expect no more and, indeed, might well have had to be content with less. . . .

He raised his head, looking about him. It was still snowing heavily, he realized, as his gig pulled away from the temporary shelter of the towering *Agamemnon* and a biting off-shore wind drove a flurry of snow into his face. Beside him a shrill young voice exhorted the straining oarsmen to put their backs into it and he turned, in some surprise, recognizing the voice, although he hadn't at first recognized the muffled little figure crouching at his elbow.

Sensing his Captain's eyes on him and anticipating the question he was about to be asked, the boat's commander offered diffidently, "It's me, sir—O'Hara, late of Her Majesty's ship *Trojan* and now———"

"And now, it would seem, my gig's midshipman once more! Well, I'm extremely pleased to have you aboard, Mr. O'Hara." Phillip held out his hand and the midshipman wrung it enthusiastically. "How are you?"

"Fine, sir. And if I may be permitted to say so, sir, I'm awfully glad to be serving under your command again."

Imagining the grin he could not see in the darkness, Phillip permitted himself a brief smile. "I applied for you, you know," he said, in explanation.

"*Did* you, sir? Thank you, I . . . I very much appreciate your having done so." The boy's voice was vibrant with sincerity. He was a good boy, Phillip thought, with all the makings of a first rate young officer, reliable, keen and, because he could always win the respect of the men he commanded, well able to take responsibility. By comparison with the willing, but inexperienced, youngsters he had had to make do with up to now, both O'Hara and Grey would be worth their weight in gold to the *Huntress*.

"When did you come aboard?" he asked.

"An hour ago, sir," Midshipman O'Hara answered promptly. "As soon as the signal from the flagship was received Mr. Grey came with me—Mr. Cochrane and Mr. Hazard are to follow shortly, sir. And—er . . ." he hesitated. "I brought Able-Seaman O'Leary with me, too, sir. He somehow got wind of the Admiral's signal and put in a request to be transferred to the *Huntress* also. Captain Crawford granted his request and he was in my boat before it was called away."

"O'Leary!" Phillip exclaimed, feeling an odd tightening of his throat. He and O'Leary had gone through a great deal together and, he reminded himself, he owed much to the big, raw-boned Irish seaman, who had been his orderly during the battle for Balaclava and later on the Heights of Inkerman. "Is he fully recovered and fit for duty now, Mr. O'Hara?" he enquired doubtfully, recalling the severe injuries O'Leary had suffered when the *Trojan*, under his own brief command, had ridden out the Novem-

41

ber hurricane at sea, on her way to Eupatoria. "The last time I saw him, Surgeon Fraser was uncertain whether or not his leg would have to come off."

"Well, sir, the Surgeon saved his leg but he's not had an easy passage," O'Hara replied gravely. "And I can't truthfully say that he's fit. Captain Crawford wanted to send him to Therapia, to the Naval Hospital, but he contrived to avoid that. I fancy, sir, that the Captain was quite pleased to be rid of him. He's been in trouble a time or two, you see, sir, and well. . . ." The midshipman shrugged. "You know what he's like, sir."

He did, Phillip reflected wryly. Able-Seaman Joseph O'Leary had always had the name of a "Queen's Hard Bargain." Like many of his kind, he was at his best when he was in a tight corner or when there was fighting to be done; inaction drove him to drink and. inevitably, into trouble which was why, after nearly eighteen years' service, instead of being a petty officer, O'Leary was still rated A.B. He could imagine why Captain Crawford, who was reputed to keep rather a taut hand over his men, had been glad to see the last of him; but—he smiled to himself—Midshipman O'Hara had a weakness for his husky fellow-countryman and so, Phillip was forced to concede, had he. But it was hoped that the *Huntress*'s patrol would provide O'Leary with sufficient action to keep him happy or perhaps the responsibility of rank might have the desired effect. Heaven knew, his crew were raw enough. . . .

"Sir——" O'Hara ventured uncertainly. "You don't mind, do you, sir?"

"Mind? What should I mind, Mr. O'Hara?"

"Well, sir, I'm afraid that I backed up O'Leary's request to Captain Crawford," the midshipman admitted. He spun the tiller expertly, shouting a brisk order as, a ghostly white wraith in the gloom, the *Huntress* came into sight ahead of them. "I took the liberty of telling the Captain that you'd be pleased to have him, you see, sir. But he's not really fit for active service, I must confess, and I feared you might think that I'd . . . that I'd taken too much of a liberty. But O'Leary begged me to put in a word for him and . . . well, we're both Cork men, sir. I couldn't bring myself to refuse."

"I am very glad you did put in a word, whatever your reasons," Phillip assured him. "O'Leary is a good man and I *am* pleased to have him, fully fit or not. My present ship's company, with very few exceptions, are inexperienced seamen, with quite a deal to learn . . . and that applies to some of my officers also. Not to all, of course, but the two whom you and Mr. Grey will replace are naval cadets, at sea for the first time in their young lives. They'll be better off aboard a ship-of-the-line, which carries a chaplain and a schoolmaster and half a dozen mates, who'll have time to attend to their instruction." And, he thought grimly, where the poor little devils would be safe from the sadistic bullying of his First Lieutenant, from which—for all his vigilance—he hadn't always been on hand to protect them.

Ambrose Quinn was careful and he did not lack experience; he has chosen his time and his victims well. The two cadets, mere children of twelve and thirteen, were scared and submissive; they had borne the harsh treatment meted out to them without complaint and—Phillip frowned—on all too many occasions the youngsters' silence, and their stoical acceptance of punishment for alleged breaches of discipline, had made it impossible for him to intervene on their behalf, much as he had wanted to, for he detested bullying.

But at least Patrick O'Hara and the intelligent Robin Grey were lads of a different caliber, toughened by war and professionally equal to the adult seamen they commanded. They would know exactly how to deal with Ambrose Quinn. To make sure of this, he would make Grey up to Acting-Mate—he was old enough—and put him in charge of the midshipmen's berth, Phillip decided, and his expression relaxed a little. Then, as a sudden, uneasy thought occurred to him, he turned again to Midshipman O'Hara.

"Tell me, Mr. O'Hara, how did you contrive so quickly

43

to have yourself reinstated as my gig's midshipman? I left no instructions, since I was not aware until I reported to the Admiral, that my request had been granted and you would be joining my ship's company. Hitherto Mr. Lightfoot has been in command of the gig and I did not relieve him of his duties."

"Yes, sir," O'Hara agreed. Like the efficient boat commander he was, he kept his eyes alertly on the ship he was approaching and, judging his distance exactly, sang out a sharp, "Way enough! Ship oars!" His crew thankfully obeyed him; he put the tiller up and nodded to the bowman to stand by. Then, his tone cautiously noncommittal, he replied to Phillip's question. "Mr. Lightfoot had displeased the First Lieutenant. I don't know in what way, sir, I wasn't told. All I can tell you, sir, is that I was ordered to take his place."

"By the First Lieutenant?" Phillip asked coldly. It had not escaped his notice—nor, he was sure, O'Hara's—that there had been no hail from the *Huntress*'s deck and that, as the bowman deftly secured his boathook to the midships chains, there was no sign of a side-party assembling to receive him. Quinn had the watch and . . . His mouth tightened.

"Yes, sir," O'Hara confirmed flatly. "By the First Lieutenant, sir." He flashed a puzzled glance towards the entry port above his head. "Shall I hail the deck, sir?"

The thud of bare feet on the deck planking heralded the belated appearance of the side-party and Phillip shook his head. With the ease of long practice, he swung himself on to the ice-encrusted accommodation ladder and up this to the entry port, as a red-faced boatswain's mate raised his call to his lips. There was no sign of Quinn on the quarter-deck when he reached it and—harbor watch or no, Phillip thought angrily—his Captain's return on board should have ensured his presence there. Instead, one of the cadets, of whom he had spoken to O'Hara a short while ago, came scuttling nervously to meet him.

"Sir, I'm sorry," the boy stammered miserably. "I

44

didn't see or hear your boat until you'd secured, sir. I do beg your pardon but I——"

Phillip cut him short. "Are *you* in charge of the deck, Mr. Finch?" he asked, not unkindly. "Where is the First Lieutenant?"

"He—he went below, sir." A pair of frightened brown eyes looked pleadingly up into Phillip's face and he saw that they were filled with tears. "He went to attend to Johnny—that is, to Mr. Lightfoot, sir. But I'm afraid it's all up with him, sir. He—he was smashed to . . . to pulp when he hit the deck. And he couldn't speak, sir. I ran to him but he couldn't speak, not even to me. He didn't know me and——"

"Steady, lad," Phillip bade him, hardly able to believe the evidence of his own ears. The boy was sobbing openly now and he put an arm round the bowed shoulders, holding the small, shaking body firmly against his own. "Try to pull yourself together and tell me exactly what happened. How did young Lightfoot come to hit the deck? Surely he hadn't gone aloft, had he?"

"He . . . yes, he had, sir. And he fell, he . . . oh, it was horrible. I heard him cry out and. . . ." Finch's sobs were redoubled.

Phillip glanced upwards into the steadily falling snow, unable even to see the mainmast cross-trees from where he stood. Yards, rigging and shrouds were thickly encrusted with ice. For this reason, he recalled, on Admiral Dundas's own orders, the Fleet had dispensed with the ceremony of manning yards on his departure. Yet Lightfoot had, apparently, gone aloft . . . not, surely not, of his own volition? For a half-trained, frightened thirteen-year-old, a climb to the masthead would be fraught with peril, even in daylight. In darkness and during a snowstorm . . . he drew in his breath sharply, sickened by the picture his imagination conjured up. Had Quinn, was it conceivable that Quinn had seen fit to punish the unfortunate boy thus? O'Hara had said that Lightfoot had earned his displeasure but . . . he was jumping to conclusions, Phillip reproached himself, and he could be

45

wrong. At all costs he must not allow his dislike and mistrust of his First Lieutenant to cloud his judgment.

The mastheading of midshipmen had been officially prohibited in the Royal Navy for more than twenty years, although it was still carried out by a few die-hard captains of the old school, as he knew from bitter experience. The *Trojan*'s first commander, Captain North, had resorted to the practice on more than one occasion but not in conditions like these.

"Mr. Finch," he said crisply, "calm yourself, if you please, and tell me *why* Mr. Lightfoot went aloft. Was he ordered aloft for some reason? You understand, I——"

"Mr. Lightfoot was skylarking, sir." The harsh, grating voice of Ambrose Quinn came from behind him and Phillip spun round to face him, smothering an exclamation of mingled anger and disbelief. The First Lieutenant stood, cap in hand, in an attitude of simulated respect, the expression on his round, red face anything but respectful. He was a big man, with thinning dark hair, a good ten years Phillip's senior, whose strong, muscular body was starting to go a little to seed. Quinn had volunteered from the merchant marine, having previously served as Chief Mate of an East Indiaman, the aged and ailing Captain of which had left the day-to-day running of his ship in the capable hands of his second-in-command. And he *was* capable, Phillip had to admit; he had served with few better seamen than Ambrose Quinn but, on the other hand, with few on whom he had felt less able to rely.

From the moment he had taken command of the *Huntress*, he had been aware of his First Lieutenant's hostility and, guessing that this stemmed from the fact that Quinn had himself expected to be given the vacant command, he had endeavored to make allowances for his understandable disappointment. Indeed, Phillip reflected, as he met the older man's challenging stare, he had tolerated much, for this reason, that he would not otherwise have done . . . too much, perhaps, for Quinn had lost no opportunity to humiliate him and, where possible, to undermine his authority. His insolence was not open; he was very careful to pay lip service to his new commander, taking orders with alacrity but frequently failing to carry them out or, worse, putting his own interpretation on them. And, of course, he was a bully.

Phillip drew himself up to his own full and not unimpressive height and asked coldly, "How is the boy, Mr. Quinn?"

The First Lieutenant shrugged. "Dying, in my opinion, Commander Hazard. The young lunatic brought it on himself but"—he repeated his shrug, his indifference to poor little Lightfoot's suffering evident in both voice and gesture —"but there," he added, "boys will be boys—or perhaps I should say young gentlemen will be young gentlemen."

Phillip kept a tight rein on his temper. The sneering reference to "young gentlemen" was, he knew, intended to be offensive but he refused to be provoked. Ambrose Quinn was of comparatively humble birth and he had gone to sea, initially, as a boy in the Royal Navy, serving for ten years on the lower deck. He made no secret of this fact and at times, in speech and manner, deliberately drew attention to it, professing to despise the Service which, he claimed, chose its officers exclusively from the privileged upper classes and, when promoting them, set greater store by their social connections than on their merits. Which might be true, Phillip reflected cynically but, if it was, then Quinn himself offered no inducement for a change in the system. He turned, remembering that young Finch was still within earshot, and sent him below.

"Turn in, youngster," he advised and, meeting Quinn's gaze, added pointedly, "Mr. Quinn has the watch and he can manage without you. You're excused duty until tomorrow morning."

Quinn seemed about to offer an objection and then changed his mind. "As you remind me, sir, I have the watch. Will that be all? Shall I carry on?"

"That will *not* be all, Mr. Quinn." Phillip's voice cut like a whiplash. "I have a few questions to ask you concerning this unhappy affair. But first—you've sent for a surgeon, of course?"

"It wasn't necessary . . ." the First Lieutenant began, with his usual thinly disguised attempt at provocation, but a glance at Philip's ominously set face caused him once again to change his mind. He launched into an explanation, his tone placatory, "As luck would have it, you see, sir, we had a surgeon on board when the accident happened. The surgeon from your old ship, the *Trojan,* in fact—Surgeon Fraser. He had called to pay his respects to you and——"

"And he's with the boy now?" Phillip put in, relieved. Young Lightfoot could not be in better hands than Angus Fraser's, he knew.

"Yes, sir," Quinn confirmed. "Although I doubt whether there will be much he can do, except ease the poor lad's passing. We took him below, of course, but he wasn't conscious. All the same, I imagine you'll wish to see him as soon as you can."

Fraser would send for him if he was needed, Phillip thought. He moved towards the charthouse, motioning his second-in-command to accompany him and ignoring the suggestion that he should go below. There was nothing he could do for Lightfoot and the question of how the boy had met with his accident had to be cleared up, now, at once, while Quinn was still shaken by it and before he had had time to think up a plausible excuse for what had occurred.

"Step inside, if you please, Mr. Quinn," he invited, opening the door into the chartroom, his voice level and controlled. The chartroom was small and cramped but it offered privacy and shelter from the driving snow, as well as a chance to study Quinn's face by the light of the lantern hanging there.

"There's very little more I can tell you, Commander Hazard," the First Lieutenant objected, when Phillip closed the door behind them and seated himself at the chartroom table. "It was an accident. The boy was skylarking and he fell—it was the irresponsible act of a lunatic and, unhappily for himself, Mr. Lightfoot paid the inevitable penalty for such folly."

"Do you seriously expect me to believe that?" Phillip challenged icily. There was only one stool in the chartroom and Quinn was compelled to stand beneath the lantern, since his commanding officer was occupying the stool, and his expression betrayed his resentful discomfiture.

"I have told you the truth, whether or not you choose to believe it," he asserted, with a fine show of indignation. For all his vehemence, his words carried no conviction and Phillip watched him in deliberate and calculated silence, before continuing quite mildly, "I understand that you relieved Mr. Lightfoot of his duties as my gig's midshipman this evening. Is that so, Mr. Quinn?"

"I did, sir, yes," Ambrose Quinn admitted without hesitation, his tone still resentful, but his eyes wary. On firmer ground now, he proceeded to list Lightfoot's recent misdeeds, his recital—although lengthy—little more than a catalogue of the pranks of any high-spirited thirteen-year-old, as yet a stranger to the harsh discipline of a ship-of-war. "I've always known he was an insolent, slack little devil," the First Lieutenant qualified. "Spoiled and headstrong. . . . I know his type only too well. But I had not imagined him a thief."

"A thief, Mr. Quinn?" Phillip stared at him frowning. "Have you proof of that?"

Quinn inclined his head. "Indeed yes—I caught him smoking, with a couple of the other young gentlemen, shortly after you left the ship. They had a cigar, which they were passing from one to the other. . . . I'd missed some cigars from my cabin and, when I questioned him, Lightfoot admitted taking them. He——"

"And so you punished him?" Phillip's tone was still even.

"Certainly I did. I could hardly suppose that you would wish me to condone petty thieving on board this ship. But," Lieutenant Quinn added quickly, the wary look again in his eyes as they met Phillip's cold gaze, "I considered that it would be sufficient punishment to put Mr. O'Hara

49

in charge of your gig. Young Lightfoot took great pride in acting as your gig's midshipman, as no doubt you were aware."

Yes, Phillip thought wryly, he had been keenly aware of the boy's pride in his first command. Poor lad, he had had much to learn but he had tried hard and the gig's crew, because they had seen the real effort he was making, had covered up his mistakes and good humoredly tolerated his inadequacies. To replace him with O'Hara had been, as Ambrose Quinn said, more than sufficient punishment for any minor crimes he might have committed. But *had* that been the only punishment inflicted on him or had there been a threat of worse to come, some promise of retribution so unendurable that, in order to escape from it, poor little Lightfoot had fled in terror to the one sanctuary available to him? A precarious sanctuary in conditions like these, even for an experienced, fully trained topman, heaven knew, and for the unfortunate cadet, blindly seeking refuge, it had been dangerous indeed. But Lightfoot must, surely, have known the risk. Why, then, had he taken it? Because, as Quinn had suggested, he had suddenly taken leave of his senses? Phillip's frown deepened, in renewed disbelief. Or . . . because he had been ordered aloft? No, no, that was unthinkable, even for Ambrose Quinn who, for all the sadistic pleasure he derived from bullying the "young gentlemen" had always, in the past, been careful to keep within the letter of the law.

But he had to know, had to be certain. The questions, little as he relished them, had to be asked, but he must be careful not to phrase them as accusations which Quinn —aware that he could have no proof—would simply deny. Phillip sighed. As he sought for the right words the First Lieutenant, noticing his hesitation, took this as a measure of his own unassailable position and observed, with more than a hint of complacency, "I have nothing with which to reproach myself in this matter, I assure you, Commander Hazard—nothing whatsoever."

"I am glad to hear that." Phillip's eyes never left the older man's face and, under his relentless scrutiny, Quinn reddened. "I can take it, then, that relieving Mr. Lightfoot of command of my gig was the only punishment you ordered?"

"It was," the First Lieutenant answered promptly. "As I told you, I considered that this would suffice in Lightfoot's case. I warned him, of course, of what he might expect if he didn't mend his ways and——"

"And his reaction was to go skylarking in the rigging at the height of a snowstorm, with visibility cut to a few yards?" Phillip put in, an edge to his voice. "How do you account for that, pray?"

"I cannot account for it. But nor can I be held responsible if the boy choses to behave like a lunatic. He gave no indication of what he intended to do—I should have stopped him, naturally, if he had." Quinn shrugged indifferently but his earlier complacency was no longer quite so evident and Phillip decided to seize his opportunity.

"I presume, therefore, that you did not masthead him, Mr. Quinn? Or even threaten that you might do so?"

"Masthead him, Commander Hazard!" Ambrose Quinn exclaimed, now white with pent up fury, the color visibly draining from his normally ruddy cheeks as he, in turn, sought for words. "You have no right—no right whatsoever, even if you do happen to be in command of this ship—to make such an accusation against me! I demand that you withdraw it, I——"

"I have made no accusation. I have asked you a question . . . one I am bound to ask, before I log this accident. And I should like an answer, if you please, so that I may record it." Phillip met his angry gaze calmly. "It is for your sake, Mr. Quinn, as much as for mine and the boy's. If he dies there is a possibility that we may have to face a court of inquiry, as you very well know . . . and the court would have no hesitation in asking you this question, so you would be well advised to answer it now."

He had spoken quietly and reasonably and Lieutenant Quinn, belatedly seeing reason, made an effort to control himself. "The answer, of course, is no, Commander Hazard—categorically no, and I should be obliged if you would log that."

"I shall do so," Phillip assured him. He was almost convinced; Quinn's outraged denial had seemed genuine and, conscious of a sick feeling of relief, he added formally, "Thank you, Mr. Quinn. That, I think, will be all. Carry on, if you please."

Taken momentarily off his guard by the unexpected suddenness of his dismissal, the First Lieutenant hesitated, the color returning slowly to his heavily-jowled face. Then he began blusteringly, "I'd have you know, sir, that I do my duty at all times, conscientiously and to the best of my ability. And I've been at sea for considerably longer than you have. You are new to command and, with all due respect, sir, you. . . ." He broke off, warned by Phillip's expression not to go too far, and, after a brief pause, he tried another tack. "Perhaps we don't quite see eye to eye where discipline and the best means to enforce it are concerned, I'm ready to grant that. But I'm given a crew of plowboys and counter-hoppers and a few coastguards and fishermen, officered by pampered mother's darlings like Lightfoot, who are still damp behind the ears and can't be trusted out of my sight. As First Lieutenant it's my duty to turn them into seamen . . . which is what I'm endeavoring to do, Commander Hazard, and what I presume you're expecting me to do, as quickly and as efficiently as I can. As I said, I've a good deal of experience of licking a raw crew into shape and I can give you a smart ship—if you'll permit me a free hand."

Ambrose Quinn had not previously spoken his mind so frankly and, hoping that it might be possible to meet him at least half-way, Phillip let him have his say without interruption. But the faint hope had faded as Quinn, emboldened by his silence and once again mistaking this for weakness, talked on with growing arrogance. There could be no possibility of accepting the olive branch—if such it was—that he now appeared to be offering, on his terms.

Phillip continued to listen attentively to a stream of grievances but his patience began to wear thin. He could not compromise with a man like Quinn, he knew, or indeed with any man in whose integrity he had so little confidence. And he could not allow his second-in-command the free hand for which he had asked, in the present circumstances, while poor young Lightfoot's life still hung in the balance and the cause of the boy's accident remained in doubt. In addition, he thought glumly, Quinn's methods of instilling discipline were of the kind that he had always deplored—they smacked too much of the late Henry North's methods and he would not countenance them, least of all in a ship under his own command. Discipline might at present leave something to be desired but the *Huntress's* crew did—as Quinn had said—consist largely of men who were unaccustomed to service at sea, and they had barely had time, as yet, to shake down properly. Troopship conditions hadn't helped; nor had his youthful, inadequately trained officers, but now. . . .

"Well, Commander Hazard?" Quinn's voice broke into his thoughts. The First Lieutenant's eyes, narrowed and speculative, were fixed on his face, as if in an effort to assess the effect of his words. Evidently deciding that he had achieved his object, he continued, his tone confident, "I can handle men, if I'm allowed to . . . but ever since you took command of this ship, you've seen to it that I couldn't do my duty as it ought to be done. A good officer can't handle his crew with kid gloves; they don't respect him if he does. They're scum, sir, most of them, and they have to be taught who's master. I know—I've served on the lower deck, don't forget. And I——"

Phillip cut him short. Slowly and with deliberate purposefulness, he rose to his feet. "I, too, have had experience of licking a raw crew into shape, Mr. Quinn," he pointed out pleasantly. "And in the case of this ship's company, I prefer to do what is necesssary to smarten them up without too much coercion."

"Coercion, sir? I don't think I follow you."

"Then let me put it quite plainly, Mr. Quinn. I do not believe in unduly harsh punishment for minor misdemeanours, particularly those which are the result of youthful high spirits. Discipline must be enforced, we both know that, but I do not believe in punishing what are often honest mistakes or errors born of inexperience."

"I *had* observed that you don't believe in flogging either, sir." There was a faint but unmistakable sneer in the First Lieutenant's voice. "But that, no doubt, is because you are new to command. You——"

Phillip eyed him coldly. "I flog only for serious crimes, Mr. Quinn, or when I consider the offender incorrigible by any other means and I should be obliged if you would remember it. As to my being new to command, as you have twice remarked, it has evidently escaped your notice that I held the acting command of a thirty-one-gun frigate, in this theater of war, for over three months before being appointed to this ship."

"You mean you commanded the *Trojan*?" Quinn was no longer sneering and his astonishment appeared genuine.

"I mean that I commanded the *Trojan*," Phillip confirmed. He did not enlarge on this but went on, "I have not been blind to the fact that this ship lacked experienced officers, I assure you, but that is now to be rectified. The Commander-in-Chief has granted my request for four *Trojan* officers to replace four of our present youngsters, who will be transferred to the *Agamemnon* first thing tomorrow morning. Two of our new officers are midshipmen, Mr. Grey—whom I shall promote to Acting-Mate, in place of Mr. Cotterell—and Mr. O'Hara. Both, I understand, have already reported aboard and the other two are to follow."

The First Lieutenant nodded, stony-faced and clearly taken aback. "Two *Trojan* officers did accompany the surgeon," he said. "But I did not realize that they were to be appointed to this ship. There was no opportunity for me to talk to them; they had just come aboard when young Lightfoot fell from the mainmast and I . . . well, I suppose I took it for granted that, like the surgeon, they had merely called to pay their respects to you. I . . ." he hesitated and then, in a belated attempt to reassert his authority, added, "I'll see that they report to you at once, sir."

"No, don't trouble," Phillip bade him. "I am going below and I'll pass the word for them myself, after I've seen Mr. Lightfoot. But you may instruct Mr. Cotterell, Mr. Jones, Mr. Finch and the Assistant-Master to make ready for transfer to the flagship and invite them to take breakfast with me tomorrow morning, if you would, please. Thank you, Mr. Quinn—carry on, if you please."

"Aye, aye, sir," Quinn acknowledged reluctantly. He stood aside to permit Phillip to precede him from the chartroom, his mouth a hard, bitter line. "If I may say so, sir, I think it's a pity that you've decided to let Mr. Cotterell go—he has the makings of a good officer."

An officer of his own stamp, Phillip thought, who, as Mate, had acted as his informant and an all too willing instrument of justice, when the high spirits of the occupants of the midshipmen's berth had led them into childish breaches of discipline or—as in Lightfoot's case—thoughtless acts of defiance. However, once removed from Ambrose Quinn's influence, young Cotterell probably would make a good officer, given time and the right example. He was intelligent and not by nature a petty tyrant, any more than Lightfoot was a thief.

Phillip nodded curtly but did not reply to Quinn's parting remark. As he slowly crossed the snow-covered deck and started to descend by the after hatchway, he reviewed what had passed between them, brows knit in a pensive frown. He had, he supposed wearily, made it clear to his First Lieutenant that, having been appointed Captain of the *Huntress*, he intended to command her and to delegate none of his authority, until he was certain that it would not be abused.

Quinn, on the other hand, taking the opportunity he had been given to express his feelings and air his smouldering grievances, had made it equally clear that his loyalty was nonexistent and his support unreliable. He was evidently yearning for the conditions he had enjoyed aboard his East Indiaman, at sea for long months at a time under a figure-

55

head captain, who had been too ill or too indifferent to question anything he did and who had been satisfied simply to complete each voyage in good time and without trouble. Yet surely even Ambrose Quinn could hardly have expected to find such a situation—and such a Captain—in the Royal Navy in time of war? He had never talked of the *Huntress*'s first captain, the Honorable Francis Willoughby, who had brought the ship out from England and died just before reaching Constantinople, but, from all accounts, Willoughby had been several years older than Quinn and something of a taut hand. He would have got no change out of Willoughby, of course, but he might well have over-estimated his own chances of being given the vacant command. He might indeed still be hoping for this and . . . Phillip gave vent to an exasperated sigh.

If he were, then obviously a showdown between Quinn and himself had been inevitable—although whether this had improved matters remained to be seen. It had cleared the air, perhaps, and given each of them the measure of the other, but he doubted if it had done much more and even this, to his infinite regret, had only been achieved as a result of Lightfoot's tragic fall. He had failed poor little Lightfoot, Phillip told himself bitterly, by allowing Quinn too much rope and because, until now, he had tried to handle him with consideration and—how had the man himself put it?—with kid gloves. He drew himself up, conscious suddenly of a cold, hard anger. There would be no more kid gloves, where his second-in-command was concerned, he decided. Ambrose Quinn, whether he realized it or not, had come to the end of his rope.

2

"Ah, there you are, Commander Hazard! I was just on my way to report my patient's progress to you."

Phillip recognized the familiar portly figure of Angus Fraser coming towards him and, thankfully thrusting the problem of Quinn to the back of this mind, he greeted the elderly Scottish surgeon warmly. "It was a most fortunate chance that you were on board, Doctor. Needless to tell you, I am immensely grateful for your presence and for your timely aid to my poor little cadet. Step into my cabin, won't you, and tell me how he is faring? Better, perhaps, than I'd feared if your expression is anything to go by."

"Well, I think maybe we shall pull the wee lad through." Surgeon Fraser looked about him approvingly as he followed Phillip into his day cabin, accepting a chair and a generous tot of neat whisky with murmured thanks. "This is a grand snug ship," he observed, raising his glass in smiling salute. "And I confess I should not have minded being transferred to her myself, for the *Trojan* has become a mite too taut for my liking. But . . ." he shrugged his ample shoulders, still smiling. "As to your lad, he has a truly amazing constitution and more spunk than many a man of twice his age. I'd be rash if I promised you that he'll recover completely but he has a better than even chance. His injuries are fairly extensive, as might be expected—a fractured leg and arm, two or three broken or badly bruised ribs and an almighty lump on the back of his head. I've set his fractures and trussed him up but he's still badly shocked, so I'd not advise moving him tonight."

57

"We're under orders to sail tomorrow morning," Phillip told him. "And we carry only an assistant-surgeon, who is young and not very well up in his duties."

"Aye, well then, I'll bide with him for tonight," Angus Fraser offered. "If that's agreeable to you? Then tomorrow we can shift him to the *Trojan*, where I'll be able to keep him under my eye until he can be transferred to Therapia . . . if that is necessary. It might not be—young bones mend quickly and, as I told you, this wee fellow of yours has a most enviable constitution and plenty of spunk. He may heal as well as young Durbanville and, it's to be hoped, with both his legs. Anyway, Commander, he has regained his senses and has been asking for you." The surgeon drained his glass, eyeing Phillip quizzically over its rim. "I rather fancy the laddie has something on his conscience, for which he is anxious to apologize to you."

"Apologize to *me*?" Phillip echoed. "Then he shall, if that's what he wants, poor little chap . . . although, between ourselves, Doctor, the boot is on the other foot, I'm afraid. For various reasons, I——" he made to rise but Angus Fraser shook his grizzled head.

"It can wait a while, Commander Hazard. The boy is sleeping now. And I've been wanting a word with you."

"Of course." Phillip resumed his seat. "Is there something else you wish to tell me concerning the boy?"

"To ask you, rather," the surgeon amended. "If you will indulge my curiosity. Ah, thanks." He permitted his host to refill his glass. "I needed this, it's a miserably cold night. Much worse, though, for the poor fellows in the siege batteries and trenches on shore than it is for us . . . or so I remind myself, when I'm tempted to complain of my lot. But damn it, Hazard, I'm not a young man and this infernal cold penetrates my very bones! You maybe wouldn't think so, with all the flesh I have on me, but it does, I give you my word. The devil take this ill-omened war! If it did not feel so like desertion, I'd apply to be sent home." He sipped moodily at his whisky and Phillip watched him, without impatience, knowing both his courage and his worth. Angus Fraser might grumble—he frequently did—but he never spared himself no matter what the conditions he had to endure.

"And how is that leg of yours?" he demanded, after a short, contemplative silence. "Eh, Commander Hazard? The truth now, if you please."

"It scarcely troubles me at all, thanks to you, Doctor," Phillip assured him, not entirely truthfully.

"Small thanks to yourself, anyway, if it does not," Fraser returned dryly. "You neglect that old wound shamefully and I observe that you still limp." He set down his glass, shaking his head to the offer of another tot. "No, that will suffice . . . I still have work to do, and I should like to take a look at your leg before I go." Sensing that Phillip was about to object, he changed the subject. "About that boy Lightfoot . . . do you know what possessed him to attempt to climb to the main topmast, on a night like this? The laddie's not soft in the head, is he?"

"No, not by any means. He . . ." Phillip hesitated.

"Your First Lieutenant—Quinn's his name, I understand—insisted that he was skylarking," the old surgeon put in, frowning. "But I've my doubts on that score, since one of his messmates told me he had a bad head for heights and had never previously gone aloft by himself. As luck would have it, he'd barely got half-way up the mainmast when he fell, but the whole business seems a mite odd, don't you agree?"

With so old and trusted a friend as Surgeon Fraser, there was no need to hide his own misgivings and Phillip nodded, tight-lipped. "Yes, I agree," he admitted. "And I questioned Mr. Quinn as soon as I came aboard. But he swears he didn't order the boy aloft—nor, he says, did he punish or threaten to punish him, apart from taking him out of my gig's crew." He repeated the gist of his interview with his second-in-command and then asked uneasily, "I suppose Lightfoot said nothing to you?"

"No, not a word. He's not the kind to blab, I would imagine, and if he'd been caught smoking, maybe he. . . ." The surgeon's shrewd grey eyes met Phillip's with a question in them. Then he shrugged and went on, "I do not much care for the cut of your First Lieutenant, if I may be frank. This, coupled with the fact that Captain Crawford mentioned your having asked for Lieutenant Laidlaw to be transferred to this ship—in addition to your brother and young Anthony Cochrane—well, it gave me food for thought, shall we say?"

"I'm not to have Laidlaw," Phillip informed him regretfully.

"Aye, so I heard. A pity, for it would have meant a well deserved step-up for him . . . he's still only the *Trojan's* senior watchkeeper. I take it that, since Their Lordships have not yet seen fit to restore your brother's commission, you were hoping that Duncan Laidlaw might replace your present First Lieutenant?"

"Yes," Phillip confessed. "I was. I'm very short of experienced officers, you see, and I cannot make young Cochrane up, he's too junior. But I'll be glad to have him, all the same. Needless to tell you, though, the one person I'd give anything to have with me now is Martin Fox." He sighed, thinking, as he often did, of the man who had been his First Lieutenant when the *Trojan* had been under his command and who, since their midshipmen days, had been his closest friend. But Fox was dead, his valuable life thrown away in defense of Eupatoria, the Tartar town which was now to be handed over to the Turks. Poor Martin! His, it seemed, like so many others in this war, had been a wasted sacrifice.

Surgeon Fraser grunted sympathetically, as if guessing his thoughts and, rising with unexpected speed for one of his bulk, he gestured to Phillip to pull up his trouser leg. "I'll just take a wee peek at that tibia of yours," he said. "Since I'm here. I don't much like to see you limping, Commander Hazard, and if you're leaving this anchorage in the morning, it would be as well, don't you think?"

Phillip shrugged resignedly and submitted, with a good grace, to his examination, which was swift but thorough.

"You keep a dressing on it, I see," the surgeon remarked, blunt fingers gently probing.

60

"Well, yes, there's still the occasional splinter coming through. But——"

"So I observe. But it is not in bad shape, for all that. You're fortunate to have kept this leg, Commander—yon Russian surgeon made a grand job of it, believe me." Fraser sat back on his heels, nodding his approval. "Do you have some fresh bandages or shall I send for my medical bag? I'd like to strap this up for you properly."

"I have some in my night cabin, Doctor," Phillip answered reluctantly. "But there's no need for you to trouble. I can dress the leg myself; I'm used to doing it. Besides I ought to go and see young Lightfoot. Didn't you say he was asking for me?"

"Aye, I did," the surgeon agreed placidly. "But I also told you he would be sleeping. It will be best for him if he does, poor laddie. His apology can wait till morning, can't it?"

"Of course, if you say so. Only I was hoping——"

"That our young friend may tell you what he has failed to tell me?" Fraser suggested. "Aye, well, he may though I take leave to doubt it. He did not utter a sound when I was putting his broken bones back into place, so. . . ." He smiled. "Be so good as to fetch me those bandages, will you please, Commander Hazard? In any case I've something more to say to you—something relevant, I believe, to the problem which is exercising your mind just now. When I left the *Trojan* with Mr. Cochrane and your brother, I hadn't quite decided whether I might be doing more harm than good, if I brought the matter to your attention—although I was asked to do so. My meeting with your First Lieutenant and this unhappy accident finally made the decision for me." He sighed. "I think it's something you should know, if you aren't already aware of it." His tone was unusually grave and Phillip, after studying him thoughtfully for a moment, brought him the bandages he had asked for and resumed his seat.

"Well?" he invited curiously. "What is this matter of which you think I may be in ignorance? I presume, from your preamble, that it concerns Mr. Quinn, either directly or indirectly. Am I correct?"

Angus Fraser picked up one of the bandages and started to apply it. "Aye," he confirmed. "It concerns Mr. Quinn and your predecessor, Commander Francis Willoughby. But what I'm about to tell you is second-hand, though I've no reason to doubt the truth of it and, as I said, you may know all there is to know better than I do."

"I know very little about Commander Willoughby," Phillip replied. "Except that he died on the voyage out from England and Quinn had to take command. He brought the ship to Balaclava and held acting-command until I was appointed—an appointment which, strictly between ourselves, he did not welcome."

"Then you did not hear in what circumstances Willoughby met his death?" Angus Fraser was busy with his bandaging, his face hidden as he bent over his task but there was an odd, almost accusing note in his voice as he added, "And you did not inquire?"

"No." Phillip stared down at his balding grey head, frowning in perplexity. "No, Doctor, it was never mentioned and, now that I come to think about it, I never inquired. With so many deaths from disease out here, I suppose I took it for granted that he contracted some infection or other. . . ." Indeed, looking back, he could recall no member of his crew, officer or seaman, who had talked of their late commander in his hearing, although possibly they had talked among themselves. None, certainly, had spoken of Willoughby's death to him, but the *Huntress* had been at sea continuously since he had assumed command of her. She had been packed with Turkish troops and there had been little time for him to converse with his officers—save occasionally with Quinn—on any subject that did not pertain to the running of the ship or the well-being of her miserably overcrowded passengers. Even the Marines they had brought from Eupatoria had been crammed in like cattle and, he remembered, such spare time as he himself had had with his junior officers had been spent in giving them instruction or supervising them on watch. He had entertained none of them to breakfast—the traditional manner in which a captain established social intimacy with his juniors—since his own meals had been snatched hastily, or even dispensed with altogether, due to more pressing demands on his time. He drew in his breath sharply.

"What are you driving at, Doctor?" he asked. "How *did* Commander Willoughby die?"

"According to the court of inquiry, his death was accidental," Surgeon Fraser told him. His bandaging completed, he looked up to meet Phillip's puzzled gaze, his own expression oddly blank. "Apparently he vanished overboard in the Greek Archipelago, when the ship was approaching the Doro passage, off Cape Kafirevs, in darkness. No one saw him go."

"That area is notorious for sudden squalls and shifting winds," Phillip reminded him. "We ran into a very nasty example in the *Trojan* on the voyage out. Surely you haven't forgotten? I confess, after that experience, I'd think twice before I tried to run the Doro under sail and in darkness. It can be tricky enough in daylight, God knows."

"There was no squall when Commander Willoughby approached the passage, according to witnesses, and the ship was under her engines. Lieutenant Quinn attempted to suggest to the court that a sudden strong gust of wind did strike the ship but. . . ." The surgeon lumbered heavily to his feet. "No one else remembered it and it wasn't logged, so Quinn withdrew his suggestion. Pressed by the court, he finally had to admit that Willoughby had been drinking heavily. The court congratulated him on his loyalty to his late Captain and brought in a verdict of accidental death—a face-saving verdict, in view of Commander Willoughby's exemplary record in the Service." Again there was a strange note in the older man's voice and, as he seated himself, Phillip turned to him in frowning question.

"You said that you obtained this information—of which

63

I knew nothing—at second-hand, did you not? May I ask from whom you obtained it?"

Fraser sighed. "From two members of the court of inquiry," he returned quietly. "One of them was Captain Jonathan Clark of the *Rockhampton*—it was he who told me about it first. I was interested mainly because *you* had just been given the vacant command."

"I see." There could scarcely have been a more reliable source of information, Phillip thought, or a more considerate verdict, in the circumstances. And Quinn, whose loyalty to himself he had doubted, had not been lacking in loyalty to his former commander. Quinn had, in fact, emerged most creditably from the ordeal of the inquiry, even though his attempt to whitewash Francis Willoughby had failed. His silence on the subject was also to his credit and yet, from Surgeon Fraser's manner, it seemed that there was more to come.

"You're not disputing the court's verdict, are you, Doctor?" he asked incredulously. "In my view it was a generous one, and Mr. Quinn appears to have behaved very well."

"I'd have accepted that verdict and the reason for it, as you have, Commander Hazard. But. . . ." Angus Fraser gave him a wry little smile. "I chanced to be seated next to another member of the court at dinner on board the *Queen*, prior to her departure for home. The junior member, Henry Lucas, who had only recently gained his promotion. You know him, I think?"

Phillip inclined his head. "Yes, I do. He's a most likeable fellow."

"Aye, well, he served under Commander Willoughby on the China station for three years, and he told me, with complete conviction, that he had never known Willoughby to take a drink throughout that time. The poor man suffered from some severe digestive ailment for which alcohol, in any form, was an irritant." The surgeon paused, eyeing him expectantly.

"But . . ." Phillip was still sceptical. "If Henry Lucas

was actually a member of the court, couldn't he have convinced the others?"

Fraser shrugged. "He assured me that he did his utmost to convince them, but the fact that he hadn't seen Willoughby for almost a year weakened his case considerably. And he was, after all, the junior member of the court; he could not persist beyond a certain point. He said he thought it possible that his efforts did, to some extent, influence the verdict but he was most unhappy about the way the inquiry was conducted and the witnesses questioned."

"Who were the witnesses, did he say?"

"Aye, he did. There were apparently only three—Lieutenant Quinn, the quarter-master of the duty watch and a yonng Mate, whose name I cannot recall. Could it be Cotton?"

"Cotterell, I imagine," Phillip supplied.

The surgeon nodded. "Aye, that was the name. Neither he nor the quarter-master had much to say; Quinn did all the talking and Henry Lucas was certain that, for reasons of his own, Quinn was lying. He was unable to suggest a reason, though, and he could, of course, have been mistaken."

"But you don't think he was, Doctor?"

"I am in no position to judge." Fraser spoke flatly. "But for what reason does anyone lie? Because the truth might be damaging, I suppose, or because a lie might bring the liar some advantage. You know Mr. Quinn better than I do. Do *you* trust his veracity?"

Did he, Phillip asked himself, did anybody aboard the *Huntress* really know Ambrose Quinn? To the junior officers and seamen under him he was a tyrant, of whom most of them—with the possible exception of Cotterell—went in terror. And as to his veracity . . . Phillip expelled his breath in a troubled sigh. The man was capable of lying and, he strongly suspected, had lied his head off this evening about poor little Lightfoot but, even so, that was scarcely proof that he had lied about his late Captain. Indeed, most of what Angus Fraser had told him seemed to leave room for doubt, too much doubt, if he were to be fair to Quinn . . . and he had to be fair, if for no other reason than because he disliked his second-in-command so wholeheartedly.

Henry Lucas of the *Queen* was, on the other hand, an officer of proven integrity. It would be quite unlike him to blacken any man's character unless he had good reason to do so. True, he had been a friend of the late Francis Willoughby and it was, perhaps, a trifle strange that he should have chosen to confide in Surgeon Fraser, who was a medical man and not a seaman but . . . as if he had read his thoughts, Fraser answered his unvoiced question.

"Commander Lucas only told me what he did because he knew I had served with you and because he was anxious to warn you to watch your step with Quinn. Those were his exact words. He would have spoken to you himself, had he remained here, he assured me, and he *did* try to broach the subject to Captain Crawford without success. Crawford is, I know, a brother Scot, but he's an awful dour fellow and he seldom puts himself out for anyone. And, for some reason, he's not one of your admirers."

"I can guess the reason," Phillip admitted wryly.

Angus Fraser smiled. "And so can I! However, to return to Henry Lucas . . . he was most insistent and he even extracted a promise from me that I'd tell you, word for word, what he'd said. As I mentioned I was in two minds, when I set out to call on you, about whether or not to adhere strictly to my promise. But I came with the intention of putting you in possession of all the facts, in case you were not aware of them, which would enable you to form your own judgment. Having served under your command"—his smile widened—"I was confident that, whatever I said to his detriment, you would judge Mr. Quinn on his merits and without prejudice."

"Thank you, Doctor," Phillip acknowledged. "Believe me, I am deeply grateful to you and. . . ."

The old surgeon waved his thanks aside. "Having said

that, I'll confess that *I* am prejudiced in view of this evening's mishap. And, as I told you earlier, I don't much like the cut of your Mr. Quinn. You would be well advised to watch him, Commander Hazard."

"I'm watching him like a hawk, don't worry."

Phillip made to refill his guest's glass but again Angus Fraser shook his head. "No, thank you very much—I must away back to my patient now. Come with me, if you'd care to, although I expect the laddie will be sleeping." He rose. "It's a pity, all things considered, that Captain Crawford refused to let you have Mr. Laidlaw. But still, looking on the bright side of the coin, you will have Anthony Cochrane and your brother to back you up from now on . . . not to mention Mr. Grey and Mr. O'Hara who, unlike Captain Crawford, can be counted among your most devoted admirers. And, of course, the most partisan of them all—Able-Seaman Patrick O'Leary, for whose return to duty I can take some small credit."

"A very great deal of credit, my friend," Phillip amended. "I never imagined that O'Leary would walk again."

"He'll not be fit for more than light duty for some while yet," Angus Fraser warned. "However, being O'Leary and having contrived the posting he wanted, I don't doubt he'll make himself useful in any niche you're able to find for him. Failing all else, he'd make not too bad a Surgeon's Mate, believe it or not; he's been virtually acting as one in my sick bay." He laughed. "But keep an eye on your whisky—it's O'Leary's cure-all."

Phillip joined in his laughter. Together they made their way aft to the cabin which had been turned into a makeshift sick bay for little Lightfoot. The injured boy lay on his cot, swathed in bandages, a leg and an arm encased in splints and the former raised by means of ropes and a pulley fastened to the bulk head. He was, as Surgeon Fraser had said he would be, asleep, the sickly-sweet smell of laudanum on his breath, but he stirred and then, as if sensing Phillip's presence through the mists of unconsciousness, opened his eyes.

"Sir . . ." his voice was a croaking whisper but Phillip heard it and bent over the cot. "If you please, sir——"

"Yes, Mr. Lightfoot?" he said gently. "Is there something you want to tell me?" It would solve all his problems if Lightfoot were to admit that Quinn had mastheaded him, he thought. Even the threat of such a punishment would be sufficient for him to place his First Lieutenant under arrest and sail without him, pending an inquiry and possibly a court martial; but his hopes were dashed and he felt a little ashamed of having cherished them when the boy answered painfully, "Yes, sir, I . . . I have to admit that I did take the First Lieutenant's cigars. But it was . . . it was meant as a bit of a lark, sir. I didn't intend to steal them, sir, truly I didn't."

"I believe you, Mr. Lightfoot," Phillip assured him. He wanted to ask about the punishment but the small, pale face was lit by a relieved smile, the bright eyes closed and, an instant later, the boy had lapsed back into his drugged sleep. From the shadows behind the cot a voice said, "He'll sleep easy now, sorr, don't worry." Not entirely to his surprise, he recognized Able-Seaman O'Leary's cheerful, gap-tooth grin as the man moved into the beam of the hanging lantern above his head.

"Welcome aboard, O'Leary," he responded and held out his hand. "I'm extremely glad to have you."

"Aye, aye, sorr." O'Leary wrung his proffered hand vigorously. "And wasn't that what I was tellin' Captain Crawford and him doubting me word? Sure I knew you'd be needin' me. 'Tis loike old times, is it not, sorr?" He turned, still grinning happily, to Surgeon Fraser. "Beggin' your pardon, Doctor, but if you're lookin' for that young fella-me-lad that calls himself a Surgeon's Mate, he's not here. I took the liberty of sending him to his hammock, for to tell yez the God's truth, sorr, he was useless and only upsettin' himself, pukin all over the place at the soight o' a drop of blood. But if you're wantin' to get your head down yourself, sorr, you can leave the little fella to me, so you can, for I know well enough what to do for him."

"Thank you, O'Leary," the surgeon acknowledged

gravely. "I may well take you up on that offer before the night is out. In any case, we need detain the Captain no longer." There was an amused glint in his eyes as they met Phillip's. "An apt pupil, O'Leary, isn't he? Tell me—how does that leg of yours feel, now you've walked on it?"

"It feels very comfortable, thanks, Doctor. And . . . thank you for everything. Believe me, I am sincerely grateful. No . . ." as the old surgeon started to speak, "I mean it and I shan't forget. Well . . . I trust that, with O'Leary's assistance, you will pass a reasonably undisturbed night. If there is anything you need, you only have to ask. Good night, Doctor."

Phillip left them and made his way to the gun-room* where, as he had expected, he found Anthony Cochrane and his brother Graham. In the presence of the other occupants of the mess, they both greeted him formally but with evident pleasure and accepted his invitation to join him in his cabin for a nightcap.

"I'm sorry to have kept you waiting for so long," he apologized. "But I've been occupied with Surgeon Fraser since I returned from the flagship. You know of the accident to our cadet, of course . . . well, I've just been to visit him and he seems to have a better than even chance of pulling through, I am thankful to say."

Both officers expressed restrained relief at this news but, when they reached the privacy of Phillip's cabin, Graham said gravely, "We witnessed the boy's fall, Phillip. We had just come aboard when he hit the deck. God knows how he survived it, poor little devil! Have you found out what really happened and what he was doing aloft by himself on such a night? He——"

"No." Phillip flashed him a warning glance. "Not yet, but you may rest assured that I intend to get to the bottom of it. Sit down, both of you." He waved a hospitable hand. "A drink, Mr. Cochrane?"

"Thank you, sir." The red-haired young Cochrane was

_____
*In a frigate, officers of wardroom rank messed in the gunroom.

beaming his delight as he went on, "I'm gratified that you should have asked for me, Commander Hazard, and more pleased than I can possibly say to be serving once more under your command." He raised the glass Phillip gave him. "To your very good health, sir!"

"And to yours, Mr. Cochrane. Whisky for you, Graham, or a glass of Jack Lyons' excellent madeira?"

"Maderia, if you please, Phillip." Graham Hazard took the chair beside Cochrane's and he, too, was smiling. "I echo Mr. Cochrane's sentiments—it's good to be with you again."

His brother had aged, Phillip thought, studying him covertly as he poured the wine and conscious of a pang as he glimpsed the calloused seaman's hand into which he placed the glass he had just filled. Had it not been for that one fatal lapse eleven years previously, when the *Comet* had run aground at the mouth of the River Plate— due, in the opinion of a naval court martial, to Graham's negligence—he might now have attained post-rank and be in command of a ship of his own. His had been a promising career; he had been commissioned as a Lieutenant at twenty and, with the "interest" upon which an Admiral's son could always count, Graham might have gone a long way in the Service.

Instead he had wandered the world, serving before the mast in Indiamen and convict ships and finally as second mate of an Australian emigrant ship, cut off by their proud old father, his name never spoken in the Admiral's presence and his letters—when he wrote—burned unread, on the old Admiral's stern instructions. It hurt to think of what this elder brother of his must have endured since rejoining the Royal Navy at the first threat of war, as an able-seaman . . . and it hurt still more to recall the late Captain North's treatment of him, when chance had sent him to the *Trojan*, as one of a draft for the Black Sea Fleet nearly a year ago. Phillip gritted his teeth, remembering how North had had him flogged for no better reason than because he suspected Graham's relationship to

70

his First Lieutenant . . . a relationship they had both attempted to deny.

Months later when, as one of the survivors of the ill-fated *Tiger*, Graham had been released by the Governor of Odessa in an exchange of prisoners-of-war and wounded, Captain North's vindictive persecution had continued. Yet his brother had never weakened in his resolve to salvage what he could of his wrecked career and, above all, Phillip reflected with admiration, he hadn't allowed himself to become embittered, as many others in his position might have done. Indeed, he had displayed Christian charity of the highest degree when his persecutor had been stricken with the dreaded cholera, although it had been to no avail. Since Henry North's death—which had occurred on the eve of the attack on Sebastopol's harbor defenses by the Allied Fleets in October—Graham had been Second-Master of the *Trojan* and had acquitted himself well.

Now, on his transfer to the *Huntress* with the acting rank of Master, he had regained—in fact, if not yet in name—the status he had once enjoyed as a Lieutenant in Her Majesty's Navy. Admittedly a Master had, until quite recently, been a warrant and not a commissioned officer, but he held wardroom rank, was a watchkeeper and responsible for the navigation of the ship and—a curious anomaly, in this case—his rate of pay exceeded that of even a senior Lieutenant. Officially, of course, as First Lieutenant, Ambrose Quinn was his superior but . . . Phillip smiled, without amusement. If Quinn had even a modicum of sense, he would not try conclusions with the *Huntress*'s newly appointed Master, unless he were deliberately looking for trouble—and he probably wasn't. He. . . .

As Anthony Cochrane had done, Graham Hazard raised his glass. "To the *Huntress*," he offered quietly. "And to her Captain! My sincere congratulations, Phillip, on being given your own command. Judging by what I have seen of the ship, it's one a good many of your seniors will envy. The Old Man will be very proud of you. You've written to tell him, of course?"

"Yes," Phillip assured him. "I've written. But there has been no time for him to reply. My letter went from Varna and we've had no mail from home since November."

"The mail from England has just arrived, sir," Cochrane volunteered. "Ours was delivered this afternoon. You'll no doubt receive yours tomorrow morning."

"It is to be hoped that we'll receive it early, then." Phillip glanced from one to the other of them. "We're under orders to leave this anchorage tomorrow morning."

Both his guests regarded him enquiringly. "For Bulgaria?" Graham suggested, without enthusiasm. "To convoy more Turks to Eupatoria?"

Phillip shook his head. "No, heaven be praised—for Odessa. My orders are confidential but. . : ." He went into brief details concerning the nature of the vigil which the *Huntress* was to keep off the rocky, inhospitable enemy coast, telling them as much as he could. To Graham, later, he would and, indeed, must tell more, for on him would largely depend the success of the mission that Admiral Lyons had entrusted to him, if—in the Admiral's own words—"circumstances should permit its accomplishment without undue risk to the ship or her company."

His brother had spent the best part of five months as a Russian prisoner-of-war, mainly in Odessa; he had picked up a useful knowledge of the language or a working knowledge, at all events, and he knew the town well, since the *Tiger*'s seamen had been allowed almost complete freedom during their captivity. Whereas he himself had been confined to bed by his wound and had seen little more of Odessa than the four walls of the room placed at his disposal by the Governor, Baron Osten-Sacken, Graham—in common with the rest of his unwounded shipmates—had taken full advantage of their jailers' laxity and the unexpectedly generous hospitality lavished on them by the townsfolk. And . . . Phillip frowned, remembering. His brother's story had, somehow, become known to the Governor and, in the firm conviction that he would not refuse, Graham had been sent, with a number of the *Tiger*'s midshipmen, to the Imperial Naval

72

Academy, there to be examined in seamanship and subsequently offered command of a Russian frigate in the Baltic.

In the past, Phillip was aware, the Russian Navy had welcomed expatriate British officers to its service, many of whom—like the German soldiers of fortune in the Imperial Army—had risen to high rank, their loyalty to their adopted country unquestioned. To Baron Osten-Sacken therefore, as to the Naval Staff in St. Petersburg, the offer would not have seemed dishonorable in the circumstances, but, eternally to his credit, Graham had refused it. He had elected to return to Odessa and the British Fleet although, perhaps, even he might have reconsidered his decision had he been able to anticipate Captain North's reaction to it.

Indeed, but for North's death, Graham might well have found himself facing a court martial on charges of. . . . How had North framed them? *Having treasonable dealings with the enemy in time of war*—yes, that was the substance of the accusation he had made and such a charge would have been hard enough, in all conscience, to disprove. Had not the *Tiger*'s seamen met with stunned disbelief when they had described the receptions held in their honor by the citizens of Odessa and the lack of restriction placed on their movements, once the port medical authorities had given them a clean bill of health?

His own account of the consideration he had been shown by the Governor and the excellent medical attention he had received had, Phillip reminded himself, caused more than a few sceptically raised eyebrows . . . and small wonder since at Balaclava and on the Heights of Inkerman the war had been bitterly waged. During the great storm, a month ago, ship-wrecked seamen had been shot by Cossack marksmen as they struggled, half-drowned, to reach the shore. On the blood-soaked battlefields, as in the trenches facing Sebastopol, Russian soldiers —and the Cossacks in particular—had committed acts of savage atrocity on those who fell into their hands. They gave no quarter to the wounded and, deaf to pity, apparently expected none for themselves as, dying, they attempted to kill any who sought to succor them.

Odessa's attitude to its prisoners-of-war in May and June had stemmed, almost certainly, from the Governor, who was a humane and civilized autocrat. But he was now in the field himself, commanding Prince Menshikoff's reserves, and therefore that attitude—like the whole character of the war—had probably changed. Fear, hatred and mistrust were the inevitable outcome of any war, as he had learned by experience, Phillip reflected wryly. Chivalry and even respect for a gallant foe gave place to primitive brutality and indifference to suffering when men were killing and being killed; and when the only choice lay between taking the life of an enemy or losing your own, you did not pause to think, as a rule.

But if war revealed what was worst in human nature it also, on many occasions, brought out the noblest and best. *"Greater love hath no man than this, that a man lay down his life for his friends."* He had seen examples of that love too. Phillip felt a lump rise in his throat. He thought fleetingly of the girl who had come to him in his delirium in that small room in the Governor's palace at Odessa and then sternly banished the memory of her gentle kindness from his mind. In view of the Admiral's confidential instructions to him, it would be madness to remember Mademoiselle Sophie now. And it would be equally unwise to let his thoughts dwell on the Prince Narishkin, her husband and technically an enemy, who had died so valiantly in the battle for Balaclava and who now lay buried with the dead of the 93rd, against whose "thin red line tipped with steel" he had led the Russian cavalry charge.

He glanced again at his brother and uncannily, as if he had spoken his thoughts aloud, Graham observed flatly, "I have some exceedingly pleasant memories of my sojourn in Odessa—as you have also, no doubt, and with reason. Although perhaps even here, among friends, it's best not to say so."

"Perhaps," Phillip agreed. "I confess that I was think-

74

ing along those lines too. But we're at war and we've been given our orders, so. . . ." He shrugged. "Some more wine, Mr. Cochrane?"

"No, thank you, sir." Cochrane rose. "You'll want to talk to your brother, I feel sure so, unless there is anything else you wish to say to me, I'll ask your permission to retire."

"There's nothing that won't keep till morning," Phillip assured him. "I'll see you then . . . and Mr. Grey also, if you'll be good enough to pass the word to him." He accompanied Cochrane to the door of his cabin and then returned to his seat facing his brother. They spoke of Service matters and of Graham's application to have his commission restored and then, at some length, of the *Huntress*, going into technical details of her design and potential with professional enthusiasm. This absorbing subject at last exhausted, Graham said unexpectedly, "I received a letter from the Old Man, Phillip—the second in eleven years! Needless to tell you, he continues to applaud my 'patriotic and self-sacrificing decision' to re-enlist in the Royal Navy and he's even invited me, like the Prodigal Son, to return to the bosom of the family when this war comes to an end . . . if it ever does."

"Have you replied?" Phillip asked, careful to keep his voice expressionless.

Graham spread his big, scarred hands in a resigned gesture. "Not as yet. The letter only came in today's mail. I shall answer it, of course but . . . well, it remains to be seen whether or not I can accept his invitation."

"He would not have issued it unless he really wanted to see you again—and wanted it very much."

"Wouldn't he? Dear God, it's taken him long enough then!" The rigid control Graham usually kept over his emotions had relaxed a little and his tone was harsh with bitterness. "Eleven long years, Phillip, during every one of which I've felt his disapproval and his contempt reaching out to me, however great the distance between us! Eleven years without a word and without allowing me to utter a word in my own defense. It's a long time, you know."

"All the same, you will wound him very deeply if you reject his overture, now that he's made it," Phillip pointed out. "He has aged almost out of recognition and he's very frail. Oh, I haven't forgotten what he used to be like . . . that icy, unbending, quarter-deck manner, the way he could freeze you with a look . . . the stories he used to tell of the Service in *his* day and his own exploits, which you knew you could never match. And yet he always expected you to match them because you had a name to live up to; he never ceased to remind me of *that*! There have been times when, I confess, I've wished my name were anything but Hazard."

"You too?" Graham sounded surprised. "Why, for heaven's sake? You were always the apple of the Old Man's eye, Phillip."

"If that was the case, he never let me know it."

"No, that was his way, of course. But he'll have to change his tune now, so far as you're concerned. You've done well, Phillip my lad—you've lived up to the name, even by his standards." Graham's smile was warm. "You've got your own command which, I'd be prepared to wager, was the goal he set for you."

"Yes," Phillip confirmed, smiling too. "It was and, at the time, it seemed as impossible a goal as any of the others he wanted me to achieve." He recalled his last talk with his father and his smile abruptly faded. The Admiral had insisted on accompanying him to Paddington Station, despite a feverish cold and he remembered wondering, as he watched the old man drive off in the cab they had shared, whether he would ever see him again. He had looked ill and pinched and very small, seated alone behind the clopping horse. "If you could see him now," he told his brother, "you would be shocked by the change in him, believe me. He's nearly seventy and he hasn't worn well. Graham, he's a sick, proud and rather pathetic old man, still adhering to outworn values and living in the past, because the present has no meaning for him. Do you

76

remember, when we were boys, we used to imagine he was about seven foot tall? And how scared we both were of him?"

Graham nodded, his mouth tight. "I do indeed."

"He's a lot shorter than I am," Phillip said. "And there's no reason to be scared of him now—only to pity him. Besides, there's Mother and the girls . . . they'll want to see you, to welcome you back. Mother kept in touch with you, didn't she? She went on writing, in defiance of the Old Man's orders."

"Yes, indeed she did, bless her! But how did you know that she wrote to me? I thought she kept it a secret from the entire family."

Phillip clapped an affectionate hand on his brother's shoulder. "She told me just before I left home. I think she guessed what you were planning to do and hoped we might run into each other out here—as, in fact, we did, rather sooner than she had anticipated."

The talked nostalgically of family matters, closer to one another in spirit than they had been for years and, when Graham prepared to take his leave, Phillip had extracted the promise that he would not refuse their father's invitation. This, however, was the most he would concede.

"If Their Lordships restore my commission, I might see the whole question in a different light although, between ourselves, Phillip, I don't really imagine they will. I'll write to the Old Man before we sail, since you're so insistent about it, but without committing myself to a definite yea or nay. Will that satisfy you? I'm afraid I cannot find it in my heart to feel sorry for him—I wish I could." He smiled briefly. "Before bidding you good night, may I echo our Mr. Cochrane's sentiments? I'm grateful to you for having obtained my transfer from the *Trojan* and more pleased than I can say to be serving under your command. I owe you a great deal, Phillip my dear fellow—not least my promotion and much else that I fear I'll never be able to repay. But——"

"I need you," Phillip assured him. "If I'm to make anything of this ship's company, I really do need you and Cochrane and the two mids very badly, you can take my word for it. I wish I could have had Duncan Laidlaw too, for a number of reasons, but apparently Captain Crawford couldn't spare him."

"Captain Crawford *could* have let you have him, if he'd a mind to," Graham said dryly. He paused, a hand on the door of the cabin and his dark brows meeting in a frown. "Just one more small matter, before I leave you. It concerns your First Lieutenant, Phillip. I take it he's the reason for your having asked for Laidlaw?"

Phillip inclined his head. "In strict confidence, yes, he is. But I'd prefer not to say any more—you'll be working with him and can form your own opinion. One thing in his favor is that he's a very fine seaman. Like yourself, he was an officer in the merchant service. You met him, didn't you, when you came aboard?"

"Let's say I caught a glimpse of him through a heavy fall of snow, at a time when he was too preoccupied with that unfortunate cadet to concern himself with any newly appointed junior officers." Graham spoke cynically but there was a hint of anxiety in his eyes as he looked across at his younger brother. "I thought there was something vaguely familiar about him, though I could be mistaken, of course. But he's come in from the merchant service, you say, so it's possible that I might have run across him. What's his name, Phillip?"

"Quinn," Phillip answered. "Ambrose Quinn."

"No." Graham shook his head, still frowning. "I can't recall the name. It was probably my imagination—and the snowstorm. Unless . . . tell me, was he ever in the Navy?"

"Yes, he was—he had ten years' lower deck service, I understand, joining as a boy and finishing up as a chief bo'sun's mate. I don't know which ships he served in, I haven't asked him, but he makes it pretty plain that he has no love for the Queen's Navee and least of all for its commissioned officers. . . ." Phillip broke off, wondering whether to tell his brother what Surgeon Fraser had said

78

on the subject of Quinn, but finally deciding against it. As he himself had mentioned, a few moments before, Graham would have to work with the First Lieutenant and—in fairness to Quinn—it was best to leave him to form his own opinion.

Graham did not question him further, merely repeated his headshake. "No, I still can't place him. No matter . . . at least we'll have one or two things in common. Good night, Phillip, I trust you'll sleep well. I'll have a course for Odessa charted whenever you're ready for it."

"Thanks—and good night to you, my dear fellow," Phillip acknowledged. "I'm hoping to get under way as soon as we've transferred Surgeon Fraser and young Lightfoot to the *Trojan*."

The following morning, however, just after the surgeon's departure with his patient and the three officers who had been replaced, the *Huntress*'s orders were changed. Instead of proceeding to her station off Odessa, she was instructed to weigh at once and set course for Baltchik Bay, in Bulgaria, there to report to Captain Wilmot of the *Sphinx*, for the purpose of transporting more Turkish troops to Eupatoria.

Phillip received his new orders with oddly conflicting emotions, of which the strongest—to his own surprise—was relief. He did not enjoy transport duty but, in this bitter winter weather, a patrol off the enemy coast had very little of advantage to offer, and any activity was preferable to remaining at the Fleet anchorage indefinitely. Coal stocks in Bulgaria were relatively plentiful, which meant that he could use his engines in transit whereas, on patrol, he would have few opportunities to replenish the *Huntress*'s bunkers. In addition there were, of course, Graham's feelings and his own concerning the ethics of their proposed mission which, when he paused finally to analyse them, were the main cause of his relief.

"Thank you, Mr. Quinn," he responded cheerfully enough, when the First Lieutenant reported steam up and the ship ready to proceed to sea. "Weigh and proceed under engines, if you please. We are ordered to Baltchik Bay to pick up more Turkish troops."

"Aye, aye, sir." Quinn's stentorian voice bellowed his orders and, in obedience to the pipe, the duty watch assembled at their stations. In a fresh flurry of snow, the *Huntress* slipped from her moorings and headed out into the grey waste of water which separated her from her destination.

3

For the next four weeks the *Huntress* continued to plough her way across the Black Sea, carrying Turkish troops of Omar Pasha's Army of the Danube to Eupatoria. There were in the region of forty thousand men—veterans of the successful defence of Silestria—with their guns and horses, all waiting to be transferred to the Crimea. With few steam-transports available there was little pause for those ships engaged in the mammoth task and no rest for the weary seamen who manned them.

The weather was appalling but, no matter what conditions they met on the two-hundred mile passage, no sooner were their passengers disembarked than the ships were ordered to return to pick up more, sometimes from Baltchik, at others from Varna. The French, engaged in convoying their own reinforcements from Marseilles, could spare only two steam frigates to assist their British allies and the Porte possessed few transports which were not under sail so that, inevitably, the major burden was borne by the British Fleet.

Phillip, although he still chafed at the ill-effects of over-crowding on the good order of his ship, was pleased by the manner in which her crew were, at last, starting to shake down. The influence of his four reliable and experienced *Trojan* officers was, he knew, to a great extent responsible for the improvement in morale and efficiency at all levels; and this influence was, perhaps, most noticeable in the effect it had upon his First Lieutenant.

Ambrose Quinn appeared unusually subdued and willing to give at least a fair trial to the methods Phillip advocated for the enforcement of discipline. He made no open admission of his willingness and continued to express contempt for the unseamanlike errors of the untutored "plowboys and counter-hoppers"—as he persisted in calling them—who formed the bulk of the *Huntress*'s crew. But he ceased to drive them in his usual relentless fashion and the men responded gratefully. They were no less in awe of him than they had been previously and they still feared the lash of his tongue, but this, Phillip was well aware, was necessary if the results he wanted were to be achieved.

There were few opportunities, when the over-laden ship was fighting her way through winter gales, to exercise her crew aloft or at their guns. Returning empty, however, as she now frequently did, after discharging her human cargo on Eupatoria's small, congested wharf, any break in the weather was utilized to good purpose. Towards the end of the bleakest January most of them had ever known, the *Huntress*'s topmen were sending up and crossing yards, setting, reefing or taking in sail, their times for these exercises—if they broke no records—showing sufficient improvement to gladden the heart of their commander, as he watched and logged them.

The guns' crews, under the patient supervision of Joseph O'Leary, now rated Chief Gunner's Mate, loaded and ran out the twelve thirty-two pounders on the main deck and maneuvered the slide-carriages of the two formidable upperdeck sixty-eights in endless rehearsal, both in daylight and in darkness. Side competed against side, gun against gun and each crew, from gunlayer to powder-boy, worked until they came near to dropping from exhaustion, as drill followed drill. They were still a long way from the standard of perfection O'Leary demanded but here, too, a steady improvement was the reward for their efforts and Midshipman Robin Grey—recently promoted Acting-Mate and Gunnery Officer—began to show as much enthusiasm for marksmanship as he had hitherto reserved for the sending and receiving of signals.

His role of protective mentor to the occupants of the

midshipmen's berth was also proving effective, Phillip observed with relief. Lieutenant Quinn left his charges severely alone, although he maintained a keen and critical eye on their behavior when off duty and had been heard, on more than one occasion, to offer the opinion that an older hand than Grey would have been a better choice. That the young gentlemen themselves did not share his opinion became increasingly apparent in the smartness they displayed, the manner in which they applied themselves to their duties and—most significant of all, perhaps—by the respect they accorded the seventeen-year-old Grey.

In other departments there was a gradual, if less noticeable, raising of standards and throughout the ship a growing spirit of comradeship, as the *Huntress*'s people started to take a pride in her and to become aware of that indefinable sense of belonging together, which is the hallmark of a good ship's company. There were still a few weak links—the Third Lieutenant, Luke Williamson, a rather characterless individual, whose previous service had been as a Mate in the Coastguard; the warrant Gunner, Mr. Vicars, too elderly and slothful to give O'Leary the benefit of his long experience and the Paymaster, Mr. Haynes, who was also elderly and lacking in efficiency —the two latter, Phillip suspected, his First Lieutenant's men, rather than his own. And, of course, there was Ambrose Quinn himself who, although outwardly co-operative, still remained an unknown quantity, whose loyalty could never wholly be relied upon.

In general, Phillip was satisfied, but he waited eagerly for news of the arrival of more troopships from England and from Malta—promised for early in February—which would release the *Huntress* and her sister ships-of-war from their present arduous and unrewarding duties. There were rumors, as yet unconfirmed, that a Sardinian army of upwards of fifteen thousand men was about to join the Allies, and that transport would have to be provided for them, from the Mediterranean, again probably by the British Black Sea Fleet.

But the Fleet itself was being augmented by the arrival of more steamers from England. The *Royal Albert*, a new steam-screw three-decker of 121 guns, to which Admiral Lyons would transfer his flag as soon as repairs to her damaged rudder had been effected, and the *Hannibal*, 91, had already arrived, Phillip learned. The *St. Jean d'Acre*, 101, under his old and much revered commander, Captain Keppel, and Lord Clarence Paget's *Princess Royal*, 91, were expected at the end of the month, in addition to several newly built and commissioned steam-screw frigates and sloops, of the *Huntress* and *Arrow* classes, specially requested by the Admiral. All were carrying reinforcements of troops and Marines for the British Expeditionary Force on the Upland facing Sebastopol and hopes of an early and successful spring assault on the city were given fresh impetus, as were those of a naval expedition to the Sea of Azoff.

Even among the hard-pressed naval officers at Eupatoria, Phillip noticed, this information was received with general approval and a lifting of tension. Captain Hastings, of the 31-gun steam-screw frigate *Curaçoa*, the senior commander and, as such, responsible for the whole complex organization of the port, greeted him with a tired but optimistic smile, when he called to report his arrival with a further contingent of Turks from Bulgaria.

"You've heard the news, I take it?" the Captain said, motioning him to a seat. "And also, no doubt, that Omar Pasha paid us a visit a couple of weeks ago and, having expressed his approval of this place as a base for the Ottoman army, went on to Balaclava in the *Inflexible* to confer with Lord Raglan and Marshal Canrobert?" When Phillip nodded assent, he went on, still smiling, "As a result, we may look forward to the Pasha's assuming the entire responsibility for Eupatoria's defense in the foreseeable future, praise be to heaven! *And* to commanders like yourself, Hazard, who have performed what is little short of a miracle in ferrying his army across at this season of the year. I'm aware that none of you greatly relish your task and that I've had to drive you all harder

84

than I care to think about but . . . the end is in sight. And for you there is to be a short respite, you'll be pleased to hear."

"A respite, sir?" Phillip echoed, surprised. "I haven't asked for one."

"I know that. All the same. . . ." Captain Hastings searched among the mountain of papers on his table, finally bringing to light the package he wanted. "The *Banshee* brought orders for you to join Captain Broke in the *Gladiator* off the port of Odessa, where he is to deliver notification of the resumption of the blockade of the Black Sea ports, under a flag of truce. The Admiral anticipated that you might be at sea when his instructions reached me or that I might be unable to spare your ship from the service in which she is engaged . . . so he left the matter to my discretion. As it happens, I can spare the *Huntress* for the short time required. I've just been sent two steam transports by Captain Christie, each with accommodation for nine hundred to a thousand Turks, and I also hope to have the *Medway*, when she has discharged the British troops she is carrying at Balaclava. Therefore"—he eyed Phillip curiously—"I shall exercise my discretion in your favor, Commander Hazard—since I understand the Admiral considers it important—and permit you to proceed at once to join Captain Broke's squadron, which consists of the *Wrangler* and the French steam frigate *Mogador*, in addition to the *Gladiator*. I am to hand you these sealed orders and to tell you to carry them out, provided that you can do so without undue risk, either to your ship or of breaking the truce by which Captain Broke will be bound. Is that clear to you?"

"Yes, sir," Phillip responded, conscious of a quickening of his pulses as he recalled his interview with the Admiral, now almost a month ago. "It's quite clear."

"Well, it isn't to me," Captain Hastings complained. "But so long as you know what is expected of you, no doubt that will suffice. Captain Broke's squadron sailed from the Fleet anchorage last night, so you had better get under way at once." He issued brief details of the time and

85

place of the rendezvous with the *Gladiator* and held out his hand. "I'll bid you *au revoir* and good luck, Commander Hazard. And I shall expect you to report back to me here when you are free to do so."

"Aye, aye, sir." Phillip pocketed his orders and shook the extended hand. "Thank you, sir." He was thoughtful when, a few minutes later, he took his place in the stern-sheets of his gig and Midshipman O'Hara's crew rowed smartly back to the roadstead, where the *Huntress* lay at anchor between the *Valorous* and the *Viper*, in whose company she had left Baltchik the previous day. All three ships had steam up, ready for departure and he knew a moment's concern, as he assessed the depleted state of his coal bunkers. Coaling was usually done at Varna or Baltchik and he had taken on all his ship could carry while embarking his passengers, but they had had a rough crossing, with head winds throughout. A prolonged stay off Odessa would reduce his stock to danger level but . . . Phillip sighed. His orders were to get under way at once and they allowed him little enough time to make his rendezvous with Captain Broke's squadron, so that he was left with no alternative.

"Weigh and proceed to sea under engines, if you please, Mr. Quinn, as soon as the gig is inboard," he told the First Lieutenant and, seeing his brother Graham on the quarterdeck, called him over. "We are ordered to Odessa. I'll join you in the chart-room in ten minutes, if you would be good enough to plot a course. . . ." He saw a look of puzzled surprise on Ambrose Quinn's face but offered no explanation and, after a perceptible hesitation, the First Lieutenant gave him a dutiful, "Aye, aye, sir," and turned to pass on his orders to the Boatswain's Mate of the Watch. The pipe sounded as the gig was deftly swung inboard and secured. Phillip smiled quietly to himself and went below to change and study his sealed orders.

His brother was in the chart-room when he entered it, ten minutes later, clad in watch-coat and seaboots.

"Ah, there you are, Phillip. . . ." Graham turned, dividers in hand and his charts spread out on the narrow table in front of him. As Master, he was entitled to one of the main deck cabins opening off the gun-room, but long established custom decreed that, at sea, he should sleep in the chart-room, in a cot slung at its after end, so as to be instantly on call whenever a change of course was ordered or the ship's position had to be checked. He made to rise from his stool, but Phillip gestured to him to remain seated, coming to lean over his shoulder in order to study the chart.

They discussed the rendezvous with Captain Broke's squadron and agreed a course and speed calculated to bring the *Huntress* in sight of the other three frigates within the specified area. Having despatched a midshipman with the necessary instructions to the Officer of the Watch, Graham went to lie on his cot, vacating his stool to his brother. "Phillip," he said soberly, "am I right in supposing that the confidential mission with which we were entrusted before we left the Fleet anchorage is now on the cards?"

Phillip inclined his head. "Yes," he confirmed. "The Admiral is anxious to obtain up-to-date and accurate information as to the present state of affairs in Odessa. As I understand it, his main reason for requiring this information is because a second naval bombardment of the place is being urged upon him by General Canrobert, as the opening of a proposed offensive by the Allied Fleets in the spring."

Graham frowned. "And we are to spy out the land for this purpose?"

"No, for quite another purpose," Phillip told him. "Our Admiral and Admiral Bruat are convinced that such a bombardment would prove a costly waste of time and effort—if not of lives—since both are of the opinion that Odessa is now contributing little to the war. Little, that is to say, that cannot be contained by our blockade of the port and the Gulf of Perekop. In their considered view, supplies are reaching Sebastopol, together with substantial reinforcements, from Taganrog and the Don River, across the Sea of Azoff and from Arabat. Indeed, Admiral Lyons believes that the entire Russian army in the Crimea is now being supplied by these routes and in perfect safety. The Straits of Kertch—the only means of entry into the Sea of Azoff—are well guarded by strong forts and land batteries, and also by a line of sunken ships similar to those with which they've kept us out of Sebastopol Harbor. Let's see . . . you have charts of the area, haven't you?"

"Yes, I have." Graham got up to search among his neatly stored maps and charts. With the one he had requested spread out between them, Phillip went into careful detail, refreshing his own memory of the plan Jack Lyons had outlined to him as he did so.

"Both Admirals are firmly of the belief that, if Sebastopol is ever to be taken, it is against Kertch that the spring offensive must be directed," he explained. "And at once, as soon as the ice clears from the Straits and when the enemy aren't expecting an attack. Jack Lyons has, in fact, already drawn up plans for a steam squadron, consisting of light-draught frigates and gunboats, to enter the Sea of Azoff for the purpose of cutting the enemy's supply routes here and here and here. . . ." His finger indicated the lines of communication running across the shallow inland sea to its Crimean shore. "He has even devised a scheme to clear the barrier of sunken vessels across the Straits by means of submarine explosions. Divers, trained in the use of such explosives, are on their way out here from England, he told me."

"Good Lord!" Graham pursed his lips in a silent whistle. "So it is as far advanced as that!"

"It is," Phillip agreed. "And with Their Lordships' full approval and, as might be expected, also Lord Raglan's. He, too, is apparently as convinced as our Admiral that Sebastopol will never fall, so long as it continues to be supplied and reinforced. But General Canrobert is, I gather, opposed to the plan, chiefly—or so the Admiral hinted—because it could not be mounted as a purely naval operation. *He* would be required to furnish six or seven thousand French troops and he is exceedingly loath to withdraw any from the siege, even for a limited time. Lord Raglan could, at most, furnish a couple of thousand . . . and troops would, of course, be essential to the success of such an operation. Towns and forts would have to be taken and occupied, guns removed and munitions and stores destroyed, starting with Kertch and probably Kaffa. And so, you see——"

"Yes, I do see," Graham put in. "General Canrobert is advocating Odessa as the objective—instead of Kertch and the Sea of Azoff—because to bombard Odessa would be a purely Fleet action, involving none of his ground troops. Is that it, Phillip?"

"It would seem so. The matter was discussed at the Admiral's dinner-table when I was there—in confidence, of course—and Canrobert's objections weren't stated quite so plainly but. . . ." Phillip shrugged. "One was left with the impression that his were the *only* objections and that somehow they would have to be overcome if the Azoff operation is to be a practical possibility."

"Then an up-to-date and accurate report on the present state of affairs in Odessa, of which you spoke just now, might help to overcome his objections," Graham suggested shrewdly. "If, of course, it bore out the Admiral's contention that Odessa is no longer a supply base for the enemy in the Crimea and, in particular, for Sebastopol?"

"Yes . . . as I understand the situation." Phillip folded the chart and restored it to its box.

"That should not be hard to prove," his brother said thoughtfully. "When the Allied armies failed to take Sebastopol, which they could so easily have done after their victory at the Alma, Prince Menshikoff had committed all his reserves and was in desperate need of reinforcements. The only troops available were at Odessa and, as you know, Baron Osten-Sacken sent all he had, overland across the Isthmus of Perekop—a long and exhausting march—and he himself went in command of them. When I left Odessa, less than three months ago, he hadn't returned and the town's only defenders by that time were its garrison of pensioners and men who were unfit to march to Simpheropol or Bakshi-Serai . . . and, of course, the gunners manning the harbor batteries. I scarcely imagine that this situation can have changed. Travel in Russia is difficult at the best of times; in winter it is virtually impossible. But if General Canrobert requires proof, then I suppose we shall have to provide it. That's our mission, isn't it?"

Phillip nodded and Graham laid a hand on his arm. "Have you decided how we are to accomplish it?"

"I gave the matter a certain amount of thought after leaving the Admiral but when our orders were changed, well"—Phillip made a wry grimace—"that was the end of it. I must confess that I hadn't visualized our joining company with a squadron, least of all one bound by a flag of truce. But no doubt there's a reason for that—the presence of a French frigate, possibly, to vouch for ours, should Canrobert ever question our report." He explained the squadron's purpose and went on, "When he has delivered his notification of the re-establishment of the blockade, I imagine that Captain Broke will withdraw to await a formal reply from the neutral consuls, lying off in sight of the port. I've performed a similar service before, in the *Trojan*. Usually one sends a boat, which is met by another from the port after a certain amount of delay. The truce is punctiliously observed, both by the Russians and ourselves and——"

"And no one from our boat is permitted to set foot ashore?" Graham asked.

"No one, as a rule. They remain in the boat, sometimes for hours."

"But I take it that, if we are to furnish the Admiral with an accurate report, we shall have to go ashore and into the town, shan't we? And I also take it"—Graham smiled —"that you and I will form the shore party. Is that what you have in mind, Phillip?"

"Yes, it is, if you're willing." Phillip looked up to meet his brother's gaze and did not need to wait for his assent. "You are fairly familiar with the town and have sufficient knowledge of the language to understand what's being

90

said . . . and, I trust, to enable you to get us out of trouble, should we be challenged."

"I hope so. It's not an easy language and I'm not really very good at speaking it."

"Well, a few hours in the town should suffice, if we keep our eyes and ears open. Certainly those few hours will tell us more than days of observation from the deck of a ship," Phillip said. He was suddenly conscious of a feeling of excitement at the prospect of smuggling himself ashore in Odessa and, once again, his thoughts strayed unbidden to Mademoiselle Sophie. It was extremely unlikely that he would catch even a glimpse of her, of course, but he would walk through streets in which she had walked —or along which she had been driven—past buildings on which her gaze had rested and see again the scenes, the people and the places that were familiar to her. Remembering what Andrei Narishkin had told him, he wondered whether her child had yet been born and, if it had, whether it was, in fact, the son he had wanted so much. A son would be the heir to all that his father had owned: his proud title, the great, rambling, stone-built palace which lay hidden behind a high wall on the outskirts of the town. . . . Phillip bit back a sigh.

He would probably never know about the child, he told himself sternly, and, however many hours he spent in Odessa, the Princess Narishkina would not be aware of his presence there. Even if, by some miracle, he were to catch sight of her—in the distance, perhaps, or over the heads of a crowd of passers-by—he would have to remain silent, unable to speak her name or to call out to her, lest he draw unwelcome attention to himself. His brief elation faded as Graham, poring now over the chart of Odessa and its adjacent coastline, endeavored to choose a landing-place for them, near enough to the town for them to reach it on foot and far enough away for the arrival of their boat to pass unnoticed.

"There's fog about," he said, rolling up the chart at last. "Remember how thick it was, when the *Tiger* went aground? I never thought I'd welcome another fog like

91

that but it would certainly assist us to slip ashore without being seen." He hesitated. "Tell me, Phillip, is Captain Broke to be informed of our mission?"

Phillip got to his feet, stretching his cramped limbs wearily. "I presume that he'll have been informed but I shan't know until I've seen him." He stifled a yawn. "I fancy we've done as much planning as we can at this stage, don't you?"

"Yes, I think so," his brother agreed, rising also. "Just one small matter, before you go—concerning the First Lieutenant."

Phillip's brows lifted in a surprised curve. "Oh . . . what about the First Lieutenant, Graham?"

"How much do you intend him to know of the nature of our mission?"

"Well . . ." Phillip considered the question, frowning now. "I had not given it much thought," he admitted finally. "But the simple fact, I suppose, that you and I are to be set ashore and that we shall spend some hours on a reconnaissance of the port of Odessa. He'll be in command of the ship in my absence, so obviously he will have to be told what we are doing. No more, though . . . none of the whys and wherefores. In any case, my orders are confidential and I'm not at liberty to disclose them to anyone, apart from yourself, of course. I shall tell Quinn when and where to send a boat to pick us up, as soon as that point is decided . . . but until I've had a word with Captain Broke, I shall say nothing."

Graham nodded his approval but offered no comment. Phillip bade him good night and, leaving the chartroom, went to pace the quarter-deck for another hour, deep in thought. It was a cold, overcast night, with little wind and a damp, misty smell in the air and he wondered when, at last, he went to his own quarters, whether Graham's forecast of fog would prove to be correct. In a way, it would help them but, remembering the *Tiger*'s fate, he found himself hoping that the following day would dawn bright and clear.

His hopes were realized and the rendezvous with Captain Broke's squadron was made in watery sunlight during the early afternoon of 18th January. But within less than an hour of sighting the three ships, a thick mist descended to envelop them, and all three, in obedience to a signal from the squat, paddle-wheel corvette *Gladiator*, prudently dropped anchor. Phillip, with matching prudence, brought the *Huntress* to within hailing distance of the squadron and himself came-to on the *Gladiator*'s port quarter. In response to her commander's invitation, he went on board at once, being met at the entry port by both Captain Broke and Lieutenant Risk, commander of the steam-screw gun vessel *Wrangler*, whose gig secured to the *Gladiator*'s starboard chains a few minutes before his own.

"We will ask the Frenchman to join us in a little while," Captain Broke said. "But first, I think, we had better have a brief, all-British council of war to decide how best we can assist you to carry out your mission, Commander Hazard . . . without endangering the success of that with which we ourselves are charged." He waved a hospitable hand, inviting his guests to be seated, his steward offering wine and cigars.

The council of war, which he conducted with breezy good humor, began at once. It was agreed that the squadron should approach Odessa at first light, with the *Huntress* in company and the *Gladiator* in the van, under a flag of truce. When this had been acknowledged, a boat, commanded by Lieutenant Risk, would be rowed to within sight of the Imperial Mole, there to await the arrival of the Russian boat sent to meet it, to whose commander the blockade notice would be formally delivered. The squadron would then anchor just out of range of the shore batteries until such time as a reply to the notice was received.

"If this infernal fog persists," Captain Broke remarked, "it's to be hoped that the gunners on shore will see my flag of truce before opening fire on me! You were present at the bombardment of this place last April, weren't you, Commander Hazard? Tell me . . . what sort of marksmen are they in Odessa? As good as those fellows at Kimburn?"

"We found them too accurate for comfort, sir," Phillip told him. "But we gave as good as we got."

"Then it will behove us to be careful," his host said, laughing ruefully. "I had my foretopmast shot away at Kimburn. And my gunners are out of practice . . . indeed, there are times when I question whether I'm in command of a ship-of-war or a horse-transport! However, to return to our problem. This, to my mind, is the somewhat delicate one of how far I can support you in the carrying out of *your* orders, without infringing the truce by which I am bound. To be honest, Hazard, I should prefer to know as little as possible concerning your movements—officially, that's to say. But, speaking off the—er—record now, I presume that you'll make your own arrangements for getting ashore?"

"Yes, I will," Phillip assured him. "My gig will set us ashore and return to take us off."

"Excellent!" Captain Broke approved. "Dick Risk was afraid you might want to go ashore with him. But you say 'us'. . . . You won't be alone, then?"

"No, sir, I'm taking my Master, who was a prisoner-of-war in Odessa for nearly five months. . . ." Phillip gave a quick explanation and again the *Gladiator*'s Captain nodded his approval.

"A capital idea to take him along with you, Hazard . . . and if he can speak some Russian that should make your task easier. Not that it's going to be easy, I fear—I confess I don't envy you, my dear fellow, 'pon my soul I don't. Eh, Risk? What a pair of names yours are, come to think of it . . . Hazard and Risk! Hardly augurs well for this affair, does it? However, one cannot question one's orders, one simply has to carry them out . . . and I gather the Admiral has a strong reason for sending you to Odessa, Commander Hazard. For how long do you anticipate staying there—still off the record, of course?"

"I'm not sure," Phillip admitted. "So much will depend

94

on circumstances I cannot foresee. A day ought to allow us all the time we need."

"And if it doesn't?" Broke demanded bluntly.

Phillip's smile was apologetic. "Then we shall have to stay longer, I'm afraid, sir. I've tried to make my plans flexible so far as timing goes. If the fog lifts, we'll have to make our landing before first light but, if it persists, we may be delayed. We have chosen a spot that seems suitable, a small, sheltered cove a mile or so to the west of the town. . . ." He launched into a brief explanation, to which both his fellow commanders listened with interest and, in the case of the solemn-faced Risk, a certain amount of apprehension. Phillip was unable to decide whether his anxiety stemmed from concern for himself and Graham or because the *Wrangler*'s commander feared that he was being made party to an infringement of the truce, to the letter of which his conscience demanded that he should adhere. But he offered no open objection, taking his cue from Captain Broke, whose earlier qualms on this score appeared to have been allayed. Only when Phillip started to outline his plan for returning to the *Huntress* on the completion of his mission did Risk venture a question.

"When do you intend to order your boat to pick you up, sir?" he asked diffidently. "If you're unable to tie yourself to a hard and fast time?"

Phillip turned to face him. "Well, I think it likely that we shall have to wait at least until dark to attempt to make our way back to our landing-place, Mr. Risk. We can't bank on the fog, can we? So I propose to order my gig to lie off the entrance to the cove two hours after darkness falls and to wait for ten to fifteen minutes. If we are unable to rendezvous with him then, I'll instruct my boat commander to pull back to the ship and return to the cove an hour before daybreak . . . but again, only to wait for about fifteen minutes, just in case they're seen. Should we fail to make the second rendezvous, the third will have to be the following evening, obviously and——"

"And should you fail to join the boat then, sir?" Richard Risk persisted.

Phillip shrugged. "In that event, Mr. Risk," he said dryly, "I fear it will mean that we have fallen into the enemy's hands, so that it would serve no good purpose to send the boat back a fourth time. As I said, a day should suffice for us to make our reconnaissance . . . two days and a night would more than suffice, but, by allowing myself that much latitude, I am trying to anticipate any unforeseen contingencies which might delay us."

"A wise precaution, Commander Hazard," Captain Broke observed. "And, if I may, I should like to suggest one or two others, on my own behalf, to ensure that my squadron does not officially break the truce. For a start ——" He hesitated, meeting Phillip's gaze unhappily.

Guessing what he was about to say, Phillip put in quietly, "Of course, sir, in the—I venture to hope unlikely —event of our being taken by the enemy, you would be compelled to deny any knowledge of our existence."

Captain Broke smiled his relief. "I should," he agreed. "I'm glad you understand that, Commander Hazard. You've taken a weight off my mind. The other suggestions I should like to make are that you approach the port well astern of us tomorrow morning—no doubt you could feign trouble with your engines—and that you come to anchor at a distance from my squadron, so that my flag of truce—at any rate technically—does not cover you. Is that agreeable?"

"Certainly, sir," Phillip assented readily. Lieutenant Risk gave him a worried glance but said nothing.

"Thank you," Captain Broke acknowledged. He held up his glass. "I drink to the success of your mission and to your safe return, my friend. Between ourselves, I shan't know a moment's peace until I'm informed that you have returned safely to your ship but. . . ." He sighed heavily, glancing from one to the other of his guests. "I think we've settled all we can, don't you?" Both officers murmured their assent, although Risk still looked unhappy, and he rose to his feet. "Good—then we'd better invite the Captain of His Imperial Majesty's *frégate de battaille Mogador* to repair on board or he may take offense. He's a charming fellow but a trifle touchy. You'll stay and partake of a meal with us, won't you, Hazard?"

Phillip hesitated. "Well, it's most kind of you, sir, but I have a number of matters to attend to and——"

"Nonsense, my dear fellow!" Captain Broke interrupted forcefully. "Do you good to forget about tomorrow for a couple of hours. Besides, I have a shoulder of lamb for just such an occasion as this and my cooks are busy with it now. A pity to waste it, don't you agree?"

It was a pleasant evening, rounded off by an unusually good meal and the French Captain—belying Sir George Broke's suggestion that he was touchy—proved a congenial and entertaining guest, in whose light-hearted company even Lieutenant Risk thrust his cares behind him and began to relax. Phillip enjoyed himself but made his excuses soon after the meal had been cleared away, anxious to get back to his own ship in order to put the final touches to his preparations for the following morning, which—if everything went according to plan—would require him to be early astir.

And, he reminded himself, as his gig pulled away from the *Gladiator*'s bulky paddle-box, one of his first tasks would be to talk to Quinn. He had to make sure that the First Lieutenant fully understood his instructions and that he left no loophole by means of which these might be misinterpreted. Ambrose Quinn would be in command of the *Huntress* during the time that he and Graham were ashore and on his shoulders would rest full responsibility for the prompt appearance of the gig at the correct time and place . . . and for its recall, if this were necessary. As it might be, he knew. The chances of either Graham or himself arousing suspicion or being challenged by a vigilant sentry were fairly remote but they existed and had therefore to be taken into account, if only because of the delay they might cause.

He could, of course, put Anthony Cochrane in command of the gig, thus dividing the responsibility but . . .

Phillip's mouth tightened, as the ghostly outline of his ship loomed up through the darkness, her riding and deck lamps all but obscured by the mist. Conditions tomorrow night might well be as bad as they were now, he thought ruefully, and the search for two men, hidden in a tiny cove, as difficult as hunting for the proverbial needle in a haystack, in which case, Cochrane's experience—and his proven loyalty—would be invaluable. Nevertheless, responsibility for organizing the rescue was properly Quinn's and, in fairness to the man, he had to be allowed to take it. To place him in only nominal command would be to undermine his authority as First Lieutenant and this, Phillip decided, recalling how Captain North had behaved in a similar fashion to himself, this he could not do to Ambrose Quinn.

From the deck above them, a boy's piping voice hailed the approaching boat and Midshipman O'Hara answered crisply, "Aye, aye—*Huntress*!" The side-party was assembled when Phillip swung himself aboard and he saw, a trifle to his surprise, that the First Lieutenant was also standing by the entry port waiting to receive him, fingers touching the brim of his cap.

"Good evening, Mr. Quinn," he said, acknowledging the salute, which was a courtesy that, on occasion, his second-in-command found ingenious excuses for omitting. "I should like a word with you in my cabin, if you please."

"Aye, aye, sir," Ambrose Quinn responded. "I've been waiting for a word with you, too, sir, as it happens."

His tone implied mild reproach for his commander's lengthy absence but Phillip ignored this, offering neither explanation nor apology. He led the way to his own quarters in studied silence, sensing, from his companion's expression, that whatever news Quinn had to give him was not good.

"Well, Mr. Quinn?" he questioned curtly, as soon as they were alone. "What is it?"

"It's Mr. Cochrane . . . I regret to tell you that he's been taken ill, Commander Hazard—seriously ill, in my opinion."

"Oh . . . when did this happen?" If Cochrane was, in fact, seriously ill, one decision had been made for him, Phillip reflected wryly.

"About two hours ago," Quinn answered. "I relieved him of the deck and noticed that he wasn't looking himself, so I advised him to retire to his cabin and sent the Assistant-Surgeon to him at once." He described Anthony Cochrane's symptoms, his voice carefully devoid of expression. "The Surgeon has given him some medication but I understand that this has not helped Mr. Cochrane a great deal."

It would be surprising if it had, Phillip thought, in view of the Assistant-Surgeon's youth and inexperience. Poor lad, he did his best but he had barely completed his first year's training as a doctor and anything out of the ordinary run of medical emergencies left him helpless and perplexed.

"You'll go and see him, sir?" Quinn suggested.

"Yes, of course, in a few minutes. But first I have some instructions for you for tomorrow, Mr. Quinn. They're important and will require your full attention, because I shall be going ashore, with the Master, and you will be in command of this ship in my absence." Phillip saw his First Lieutenant's jaw drop in stunned astonishment but he recovered himself quickly and listened in attentive silence to all that his commander had to say.

"You mean," he asked uncertainly, when Phillip had done, "you mean that you intend to—to go ashore at Odessa tomorrow morning, Commander Hazard, and to remain there all day?"

Phillip inclined his head. "Those are my orders, Mr. Quinn, and I am not permitted to explain them to you. But, as I told you, the Master will accompany me and, as I have also told you, I shall require my gig to pick us up two hours after nightfall, at the point I have indicated . . . the same place at which we shall be set ashore. If we should fail to rendezvous with him then, the boat commander is to return for us one hour before daybreak. That's all quite clear to you, isn't it?"

Ambrose Quinn continued to stare at him as if unable to believe the evidence of his own ears, but he managed a puzzled assent. "Your instructions are clear enough," he conceded. "And, of course, I shall carry them out to the best of my ability, Commander Hazard, but. . . ." He broke off, shaking his head. "I'm wondering why you . . . well, frankly, I confess I find all this very confusing. You say that Captain Broke's squadron will be under a flag of truce, charged with delivery of a note to the port authorities?"

"Yes, that is correct."

"Is the Captain aware of your intention to go ashore, sir?"

"Officially he is not, Mr. Quinn—and officially the *Huntress* will not form part of the squadron under his command." Phillip spoke with quiet emphasis, repeating the directions for the *Huntress* to anchor at a distance from the other ships of the squadron, as Captain Broke had requested. "You will not communicate with Captain Broke's squadron by signal or by boat during my absence," he added. "And there can, of course, be no signals to me and I shall make none whilst I am ashore. You——"

"None, sir?" Quinn put in, brows knit. "Not even in an emergency? I understand what action you wish me to take should the gig, after three attempts, fail to rendezvous with you but I——"

"In that case," Phillip interrupted impatiently, "the gig must return to the ship at once. You may arrange a recall signal, if you wish—a single blast on the steam siren, rather than a flare, perhaps, which might attract too much attention."

"Very well, sir. But"—the First Lieutenant was still frowning—"I should like to mention one possibility you may have overlooked. Suppose, for any reason, that you wanted to warn the gig not to close the shore, to . . . well, to avoid its being seen or because there was a risk of its being fired on by a Cossack patrol or even taken by the enemy? Would it not be advisable to arrange a signal to cover such an eventuality?"

He was right, Phillip realized. He *had* overlooked this particular possibility and Quinn's suggestion was a sensible one. Yet how could he and Graham make any kind of signal from the cove? A flare would be seen, from inland as well as to seaward, even if the fog did not lift, and he was reluctant to carry one on his person or ask his brother to do so. For one thing, it would be a cumbersome burden and, for another, if they were stopped and searched, any signalling apparatus found in their possession would not be easy to explain. The same objections might apply to a lantern although they could, of course, take one ashore with them and conceal it somewhere near their landing-place, for use in the kind of emergency his second-in-command visualized. He turned to Quinn, about to tell him that they would take a lantern but, before he could speak, the First Lieutenant's frown lifted.

"A fire, sir—quite a small one, of brushwood and flotsam—might serve your purpose, I fancy. If you did *not* wish the gig to enter the cove or her crew to come ashore, you could warn them by lighting a small fire, couldn't you?"

"Thank you, Mr. Quinn—an excellent suggestion," Phillip agreed. "That is what we will do." He took out his pocket watch, uneasily aware that time was slipping by. He must visit Cochrane and he wanted to talk to his brother before he turned in. . . . he glanced at Quinn. "Is there anything else?"

Ambrose Quinn hesitated, looking down at his boots and avoiding his commander's gaze, as if in momentary indecision but finally he glanced up, his heavily jowled face a deeper shade of red than it normally was. "There is one thing more, sir," he answered, with unexpected diffidence. "I have a request to make."

"A request?" Phillip prompted, endeavouring to conceal his impatience. "And what is it, pray?"

The First Lieutenant drew himself up, an odd expression in his dark eyes which somehow defied analysis. "I'd be very much obliged if you would log the orders you've just given me, Commander Hazard . . . in full, if you please."

Phillip stared at him uncomprehendingly. "You're asking me to log my orders—why, for heaven's sake? Surely you understand them?"

"I understand them perfectly, sir, but . . . your instructions are somewhat unusual, aren't they? I mean, sir, I have to think of my own position and you are placing a heavy responsibility upon me. Not to put too fine a point on it, I *could* find myself in a situation when— in strict accordance with your orders—I had to abandon you and the Master of this ship in enemy territory. That is so, isn't it, sir?"

It was, Phillip was forced to concede and, as he stood facing his second-in-command, he was suddenly conscious of an icy stab of fear. He had never completely trusted Ambrose Quinn, never been certain of his loyalty, and all his instinctive misgivings concerning the man came flooding back into his mind. He recalled what Surgeon Fraser had told him about the court of inquiry into Commander Willoughby's death and the strangely contradictory evidence Quinn had given and his still unresolved doubts returned to plague him afresh. There was also the accident to little Cadet Lightfoot. . . . Phillip's mouth compressed. If he acceded to this request and logged his orders, he would be putting a weapon into Quinn's hands by means of which his First Lieutenant could destroy him with impunity, if he had a mind to . . . and there was no way of knowing what was in his mind. His expression betrayed nothing save, perhaps, for a flicker of uneasiness in his eyes but . . . young Lieutenant Risk had also been uneasy, Phillip reminded himself, when he had outlined his plan of action. In the circumstances, Quinn's request was not an unreasonable one and, rack his brains as he might, he could think of no excuse for refusing it.

If only Anthony Cochrane had not gone sick at this most inopportune of moments! There was Grey, of course, and also O'Hara but both were too young and too junior . . . for their own sakes, he could not confide his doubts to either of them, he knew, and Graham would be with him

102

on shore. Which left only Cochrane, if he were well enough and. . . .

"Commander Hazard"—Quinn's deep, grating voice broke unpleasantly into his thoughts—"shall I bring the log to you now, sir?"

"You may leave it here," Phillip told him curtly. "I'll attend to the matter after I have paid a visit to Mr. Cochrane. And I shall want to see the Assistant-Surgeon also—perhaps you'd be good enough to pass the word for him to report to me. Thank you, Mr. Quinn—that's all. Carry on, please."

"Aye, aye, sir." The First Lieutenant smiled, apparently satisfied. He went to the door of the cabin and held it open, standing aside to allow Phillip to precede him and then, as if suddenly changing his mind, he added in a conversational tone, "I understand, sir, that you and the Master were both prisoners-of-war in Odessa some months ago. You were taken with the *Tiger*, weren't you?"

The question, casually voiced, was so completely unexpected that Phillip halted in his tracks, smothering an exclamation. "Yes," he confirmed, after a barely perceptible pause. "We were, Mr. Quinn. Why do you ask? I scarcely think it is any concern of yours." He spoke with brusque impatience, anxious to be on his way but Ambrose Quinn was not to be put off.

"No, perhaps not, Commander Hazard," he said. "But I was curious, you see." The sentry on duty outside the cabin came smartly to attention and Quinn went on with studied insolence, making no attempt to lower his voice, "Is it true that your brother—the Master—was offered command of a Russian frigate, if he took service with the enemy? I heard a rumor to that effect and, as I say, I was curious . . . although I did not imagine there could be any truth in the rumor."

Phillip could feel the blood draining from his cheeks. In God's name, he asked himself bitterly, how had Ambrose Quinn got wind of that story? Not, surely not from Graham himself? From Cochrane . . . no, it could not have been from Anthony Cochrane who, except on

103

duty, hardly exchanged a word with him. And the two midshipmen had known nothing about the affair, so that he could not have learned of it from them. From whom, then? A cold anger filled him but somehow he managed to control himself and reply, with icy dignity, "I fear that you will have to contain your curiosity, Mr. Quinn—or at any rate confine it strictly to your own concerns. Carry on, if you please."

The First Lieutenant seemed about to question his dismissal but the appearance of the Assistant-Surgeon caused him, to Phillip's relief, to change his mind. With a stiff, "Aye, aye, sir," he stepped out into the narrow alleyway and the young Assistant-Surgeon, in a state of some agitation, brushed past him.

"Sir," the young man requested urgently, addressing Phillip, "may I have a word with you?" He was clutching a heavy medical tome to his thin chest, holding it open with a visibly trembling hand and, fearing he might drop it, Phillip took it from him before leading the way into his cabin.

Then, closing the door behind him, he thrust the boy into a chair. "Now, Mr. Brown," he invited quietly. "Tell me what's the matter."

Poor young Brown swallowed hard. He said, making a commendable effort to speak calmly, "It's Lieutenant Cochrane, sir—I . . . I've looked up his symptoms in my medical books, sir, and they're all here"—he gestured to the heavy book that Phillip was still holding—"I've marked the page, sir, and I—I'm very much afraid that he has the cholera." He swallowed again, frank terror in his eyes as they met those of his commander. "If you'd read that passage, sir, the one I've marked, you—you'll see I'm right."

"I don't need to read it, Mr. Brown," Phillip told him wryly. "I've seen a great many cases of cholera. Tell me —how many have you seen?"

"I. . . ." Brown blinked at him. "None, sir. But——"

"I was on my way to visit Mr. Cochrane when you reported to me. We'll go and see him together, I think, when you have calmed yourself. Here. . . . Phillip poured a measure of whisky into a glass and placed it between the young surgeon's trembling fingers. "Drink that, lad."

"Thank you, sir." Brown drained the glass at a gulp and some of the color started to return to his pale, bespectacled face. "I'm sorry, sir. I lost my head a bit. I thought at first that Mr. Cochrane had eaten something that had disagreed with him but then when I started to consult my books, I . . ." he shuddered. "I wasn't sure."

"You will probably find that your first diagnosis was correct," Phillip told him gently. "We'll go and make sure, shall we . . . if you're ready, Mr. Brown?"

"I'm ready, sir." The boy scrambled to his feet, flushed and shamefaced but again making a brave effort to pull himself together.

Phillip led the way aft without haste, at pains to present the outward appearance of calm.

There were still some cases of cholera among the troops and the Naval Brigade on shore, he was aware, but since the onset of winter the Fleet had been relatively free of the disease. It was, of course, possible that the infection might have been brought on board the *Huntress* by one or more of her passengers, although no cases had, to his knowledge, been reported of late among the Turkish troops. True, Varna—with its surrounding marshes—had been a notorious source of infection the previous year, when the British and French armies had been quartered there, and they had picked up the last contingent of Turks from Varna but. . . . He stifled a sigh. Please God young Brown had yielded to unnecessary panic, he prayed silently, as he pushed open the door of Cochrane's cabin and, lowering his head, stepped inside.

Anthony Cochrane, a trifle wan of face but otherwise more or less his normal self, looked up at him from the cot and Phillip saw, to his relief, that O'Leary was in attendance on the invalid, grinning his usual cheerful, gap-toothed grin which was, in itself, reassurance. Catching sight of the Assistant-Surgeon at his commander's back, the big Irishman, with a murmured "Beggin' your pardon, sorr," advanced on the pink-cheeked youth, who sought vainly to efface himself.

"Och, now, but you surely were not troubling the Captain with your crazy notions, were yez? And after me tellin' ye that Mr. Cochrane would be as roight as rain in a day or so? I'd loike to take the back o' me hand to you, so I would! You———"

"That will do, O'Leary," Phillip warned. "Mr. Brown is doing the best he can."

"Aye, aye, sorr," O'Leary acknowledged reluctantly. Then his grin returned. "So help me, I'll make a doctor of him yet, sorr, but he takes a powerful lot o' teaching."

Phillip's mouth twitched. "I believe you, O'Leary." He dismissed both Brown and his would-be mentor and turned to Anthony Cochrane. "How are you feeling?"

"I'm a lot better, sir. It was the brisket I had for dinner . . . it must have been tainted. But I'll be fit for duty tomorrow, if you need me, honestly, sir." The young watch-keeper struggled to sit up but, a restraining hand on his shoulder, Phillip shook his head. "You stay where you are, Mr. Cochrane—at least until the more reliable of your medical advisers pronounces you fit! I'll manage without you tomorrow."

Indeed, he would have to, he thought regretfully when, after exchanging a few pleasantries, he left Cochrane to sleep and, rather wearily, made for the gun-room in search of his brother. Poor Cochrane's bout of sickness had left him as weak as a kitten; whatever he said, he was obviously in no state to return to duty and, least of all, to undertake the arduous duty of boat commander within the next twenty-four hours. It was unfortunate but there seemed little he could do . . . except trust Ambrose Quinn. In the light of his second-in-command's parting remark, he felt less inclined to trust the man than ever before, but he had been left with no alternative—or none that his tired brain could think of just then.

Reaching the door of the gun-room, Phillip paused, going over once again in his mind what Quinn had said—and implied—concerning his brother. It might, perhaps, be best if he did not repeat any of it to Graham, at any rate not until tomorrow night . . . by which time, God willing, they would have accomplished their mission. The First Lieutenant had got his facts right—whoever he had obtained them from—and, even if the implication he had drawn from these was a distortion of the truth, Graham could neither deny nor disprove the underlying accusation, however damaging this might be to himself.

Phillip closed his eyes, conscious that his head was aching and that he had been a long time without sleep, for he had been on deck before dawn. He sighed and put out a hand to support himself against the bulkhead, feeling suddenly as weak as Anthony Cochrane had looked a few minutes ago. How long would it be, he wondered dully, before Quinn contrived to ferret out the story of his own brief association with the Russian Grand Duchess—a niece of the Tsar—to whom, prior to the declaration of war, the *Trojan* had given passage from England and whom he, in all innocence, had known as Mademoiselle Sophie? And how long would it take his second-in-command to guess that Mademoiselle Sophie was now, in all probability, in Odessa?

He sighed and then, rubbing the sleep from his eyes, pushed open the door into the gun-room. From inside, the sound of voices abruptly ceased and, as Phillip entered, the three occupants of the mess—Ambrose Quinn, Mr. Haynes, the corpulent, white-haired Purser, and Luke Williamson, the youthful Third Lieutenant—all rose, with varying degrees of slowness, to their feet. Graham was not with them and Quinn said quickly, anticipating his question, "If you're looking for the Master, sir, he took over Mr. Cochrane's watch and——"

Phillip cut him short. "Relieve the deck, if you please, Mr. Williamson," he ordered. "And request the Master to report to me in my cabin."

"Aye, aye, sir." Lieutenant Williamson, his thin, pink face oddly flushed, obeyed him with alacrity, evidently anxious to make his escape. For some reason he looked guilty, as if the unexpected arrival of his commander had surprised him in the commission of some act of which he was ashamed, but Ambrose Quinn appeared, by contrast, smugly pleased with himself. He exchanged a smile with the Purser and offered smoothly, "I have placed the ship's log in your cabin, Commander Hazard, as you requested. I trust you will find all quite in order, sir."

"Thank you, Mr. Quinn," Phillip returned. "I trust I shall. Pray resume your seats, gentlemen."

They did so, both smiling, and he left them, again aware of an instinctive uneasiness sounding, like an alarm bell, in his brain. . . .

4

THE fog cleared during the night and at five bells of the Middle Watch, Phillip was informed that the *Gladiator* had signalled the squadron, ordering them to set course for Odessa and proceed under engines. Well before dawn, all four ships came-to outside the port and dropped anchor, the *Huntress* almost a mile astern and to starboard of her consorts, her deck-lamps and riding-lights extinguished.

There was no wind and the air was damp and chill. Probably, Phillip thought, the mist would again close in —there was a smell of frost in the air and both moon and stars had been obscured for several hours. But, aware that he could not count on a return of the fog, he decided to go ashore at once. Turning to Graham, he said softly, "We might as well be on our way and get this over with, don't you think?"

His brother drew his boat-cloak about him and nodded. "Yes, I'm ready, if you are. It's going to be a long pull, so there's not much point in delaying." His face looked white in the dimness and a trifle pinched, as if he were feeling the cold, but he made no other comment and Phillip, peering at him uncertainly, resisted the impulse to inquire whether he was all right. Even if he felt unwell, Graham would, he knew, refuse to admit it.

"Call away my gig, if you please, Mr. Quinn," he instructed the First Lieutenant, who was on watch. "You've seen to it that Mr. O'Hara is supplied with a compass, I trust?"

"Yes, sir. Everything you asked for is in the gig, including a signal lamp, and the men are armed with cutlasses, as you instructed."

"Thank you, Mr. Quinn," Phillip acknowledged. They descended to the entry port accompanied, somewhat officiously, by the First Lieutenant, who put on a fine show of efficiency, barking orders at Midshipman O'Hara and his boat's crew, who received them wooden-faced and in silence. There was, of course, no side-party but, as Phillip stepped into the boat, Quinn stood, cap in hand, his round, red face unexpectedly grave as he wished him God-speed.

"Give way together, lads!" O'Hara ordered, in a hoarse whisper, as the bowman released his boat-hook and scrambled nimbly back to his place. There was a fairly strong current running against them but the men pulled with a will and the line of darker shadow, which was the enemy shore, came perceptibly nearer. As they rowed, Phillip checked the compass bearing by the light of a shaded lamp and then let its shutter fall. As his eyes became accustomed to the darkness, he was able to make out more of the rocky coast they were approaching and it was he who recognized the entrance to the cove they had chosen for their landing place and called out a low-voiced warning to O'Hara.

They ran in with infinite caution, the men pulling a few strokes and then resting on their oars but there was no sound save that made by the oars in their well-oiled rowlocks and the lapping of the changing tide against the stout timbers of the gig's quarter. The cove—in reality a narrow inlet from the sea—curved slightly in a northeasterly direction. It was bounded on its eastern side by high, almost perpendicular cliffs, which were a feature of the rugged coastline, but Graham had said that this cove dipped sharply from the foreshore from which, after a relatively easy climb of sixty or seventy feet, access to the coast road could be gained by crossing a mile or so of flat marshland.

It was to be hoped that his memory was not at fault, Phillip thought. In wintery conditions, the marshland ought to be frozen over with hard-packed snow and therefore possible to cross on foot although, since it would offer little or no cover, he wanted if possible to get to the road before full daylight. Once on the road itself, two men, muffled like local peasants against the cold, would not be likely to excite much interest . . . there were isolated farms in the neighborhood, whose owners presumably made periodic visits to the town, in order to market their produce. If he and his brother could pass as two such men, on their way to market, probably no one would spare them a second glance, except that . . . his cold fingers touched the smoothly woven wool of his boat-cloak. It effectively hid the uniform he was wearing beneath it but no peasant farmer would have owned a garment of such quality, he well knew, so that it would behoove them to do all they could to avoid submitting to close inspection . . . at all events, until they reached the town.

The gig grounded gently on the foreshore and two of the seamen lowered themselves gingerly into the icy water to drag her bows clear of a rock, which O'Hara's sharp eyes had spotted just in time.

"Right, Mr. O'Hara. . . ." Phillip laid a hand on the boy's shoulder. "You know your orders."

"Yes, sir." Midshipman O'Hara's voice was steady and controlled as he repeated his instructions but he fingered the dirk at his side and added eagerly, "Sir, may I not wait until I know you're safely ashore and that you've met with no resistance?"

Phillip looked up into the now gradually lightening sky and gave him a firm "No, you may not." Graham, he saw, was already wading through ankle-deep water to the beach and he got to his feet. "You'll hear shots, if we do meet with any resistance," he told the midshipman. "But it's unlikely . . . even the Cossacks don't enjoy patrolling at night in this weather. And it's of vital importance that your boat is not seen . . . so be off with you, lad. It will take you all your time to get back to the ship before dawn."

"Aye, aye, sir," O'Hara acknowledged reluctantly. "If

111

you say so, sir. Er . . . good luck, sir. We'll be back for you two hours after nightfall."

"Thank you, Mr. O'Hara. Don't forget to watch out for my signal. If you see a light in the cove———"

"I'm not to enter . . . aye, aye, sir."

"In no circumstances, Mr. O'Hara," Phillip warned him sternly. "And whether or not you hear shots . . . your men, remember, are only armed with cutlasses." He swung one leg over the gunwale and the stroke-oak grasped his arm to steady him. Despite the darkness, there was no mistaking the gap-toothed grin on the face so close to his own and he swore softly. "The devil take it, O'Leary! Since when did a Gunner's Mate become a member of my gig's crew?"

" 'Twas not until this morning, sorr," O'Leary returned, with a dry chuckle. "I'm a volunteer, as ye might say." His strong right arm guided his commander into the water. "Sure, I only came along to wish yez the luck o' the Oirish, sorr . . . but if ye'd consider taking me with yez, then you've only to say the word, for I———"

"No," Phillip said. "But thanks, O'Leary."

The boat put off and he waded ashore to join Graham, feeling curiously warmed by the encounter with O'Leary. He ought to disrate him for what he had done, of course, but. . . . He smiled to himself in the chill darkness and then, abruptly recalling his surroundings, halted to stand beside his brother, listening intently.

"I think we've got the place to ourselves," Graham told him. "Shall we press on?"

They did so, scaling the low cliff with little trouble in spite of the fact that it was crumbling in places but, having reached the top, they had to scramble over a number of massive boulders perched precariously along its edge before finally gaining higher and smoother ground. The marsh was, as they had anticipated, a frozen wilderness but at least it was level and, with the coming of dawn, they made better progress, no longer stumbling over unseen obstacles and able, now, to glimpse the huddled rooftops of the town of Odessa, which lay ahead of them to the north-east. They stepped on to the road—little more, in fact, than a rutted cart-track—some fifty minutes after leaving the cove, and concealed the signal lantern they had brought with them on its verge, a stunted clump of brush-wood as a landmark.

The sun rose over a desolate vista of low-lying, deserted countryside, all evidence of cultivation buried beneath a carpet of frozen snow and the nearest human habitation a cluster of peasants' huts which, like the fields about them, appeared quite devoid of life.

"They must hibernate in winter," Graham remarked. "Although probably there's little else they can do; the ground's too hard to till, I should imagine." He paused, looking about him and then pointed ahead to where the road they were following rose steeply, curving towards the bay round which the town was built. "We should be able to sight the squadron from up there, Phillip—unless the fog descends on us again. And I rather think it may."

His forecast proved to be an accurate one. By the time they breasted the slope, the sun had vanished behind a swirling succession of damp grey clouds and, as they looked down from their vantage point at the four anchored warships, the fog closed in, all but obscuring them from view.

"The *Gladiator* will have to stand-in to the port, if she's to make herself seen," Phillip said and, almost as if his words had carried across the intervening distance to her captain, the corvette weighed anchor. As they peered into the patchy mist, straining their eyes to follow her progress, she came slowly about and, her paddle-wheels churning, fired a gun to seaward. This was answered, after a considerable delay, by the boom of a single cannon from a battery situated—as nearly as Phillip could judge—in the coastal fort with which, during the naval attack on Odessa the previous April, the 50-gun frigate *Arethusa*, under sail, had so brilliantly tried conclusions.

"She's going in now," Graham observed, pointing. The *Gladiator*, still maneuvering very slowly, altered course and with the flag of truce streaming out behind her for

113

all on shore to see, she stood-in to the bay, dropping anchor once more when she was clear of the fog.

"It will probably take her all morning to get her boat away," Phillip said, frowning. "But I don't think we'd better chance that, all the same, do you? Obviously our best opportunity to inspect the gun batteries on the Mole will be when a crowd collects to watch the exchange of notes—as one almost certainly will. So perhaps we should be on hand, ready to join it, just in case the preliminaries are more speedily disposed of than they usually are."

His brother nodded in agreement but excused himself with a muttered excuse, and walked quickly over to the cover of some nearby bushes, from behind which Phillip was alarmed to hear him coughing and retching violently. He returned, however, a few minutes later, very pale and tight-lipped but insisting that he was fully recovered.

"It must have been some of that tainted beef Cochrane complained of," he said ruefully. "I had it too, alas!"

"It laid Cochrane exceedingly low," Phillip told him. "I think it might be as well if we waited here for a while, Graham, to make sure you've got over it. We've made pretty good time and——"

"No, no, there's no need for that. I feel a lot better now," Graham returned and added dryly, "Damn it, Phillip, my digestion is in a different class from Anthony Cochrane's. I've eaten lower-deck fare for years—my stomach is cast-iron. Come on, let us be on our way before the crowd becomes too numerous to permit our making a proper inspection of those batteries." Shoulders hunched, he started towards the road, but, concerned by his pallor, Phillip gripped his arm to detain him.

"No, wait. We can afford to give ourselves a ten-minute breather. In any case, I want to see what the *Gladiator* is up to. She's had no acknowledgement from the port yet and she appears to be waiting for one."

"You are in command," Graham said, a trifle stiffly, and then flashed him a brief smile as he relaxed, full length, on the ground. "Perhaps you're right, after all—my legs do feel somewhat unsteady."

Phillip returned the smile and passed him the small flask of brandy he had always kept topped up and carried with him since the battle at the Alma River. "Take some of this . . . it should help." He squatted down at his brother's side and asked, thinking to distract him, "Did you know that O'Leary was in the gig's crew this morning?"

"Oh, yes, I knew." Graham took a few sips of the brandy and, replacing its silver screw-top, returned the flask with a nod of thanks. "You told the First Lieutenant to volunteer a crew, didn't you? Well, about half the ship's company volunteered for the honor and it was finally decided—by O'Hara, I fancy—that they should draws lots for it. Poor O'Leary was unlucky—he drew a blank. It cost him his grog ration for a fortnight, I was told, to secure someone else's place! And young Grey also contrived to get himself into your crew but I didn't hear what *he* had to pay for the privilege. Possibly his payment will not be exacted until after his return to the ship, when our Mr. Quinn learns the reason for his absence . . . if, indeed, he does. He certainly won't hear it from any member of the gig's crew and I doubt if anyone else will volunteer the information." His tone was dry but he added, with sudden warmth, "You've worked a miracle with the whole ship's company, Phillip, in a remarkably short time. Their morale and their pride in the ship are both sky high."

This unexpected tribute—the more valuable because it came from his elder brother—took Phillip by surprise and he reddened. "I'm gratified that you should think so, but I haven't done it alone, you know. Indeed, I couldn't have done anything without the help I've had from you and the other *Trojan* officers . . . not to mention O'Leary."

"With or without our help, you've done it in spite of Quinn," Graham told him. "By any standards, that makes it a considerable achievement, believe me."

"Then," Phillip suggested, "you've formed your own judgment of Quinn?"

"Most certainly I have. It can be summed up in a nutshell: if the *Huntress* were my ship, I'd do all in my power

115

to replace her present First Lieutenant. Need I put it more plainly? I can, if you wish."

Phillip shook his head. "No, you needn't. And I intend to replace him but unfortunately it's easier said than done. He's a first-rate seaman and he's committed no crime of which I could accuse him."

"No, he's careful, I grant you, but he's a sadistic bully and he has no conscience. I would not trust him—to use an inelegant expression from the lower deck—further than I could spit, Phillip, and if you'll take my advice, you won't either. He pays you lip-service now, because he has to but. . . ." Graham sat up. "I feel in splendid heart now, thanks to your brandy and this interesting discussion, so shall we push on? The fog is becoming denser, I think."

Phillip rose at once. The ships anchored below them had not taken any further action that he could see, but the fog, as his brother had remarked, appeared to be closing in and was increasing in density. His gaze lingered for a moment on his own ship and then he followed Graham back to the road. They quickened their pace as it started to descend, walking in silence, each busy with his own thoughts.

The surface of the road improved as they neared the outskirts of the town and soon they were walking between rows of stone-built houses, seen dimly through the mist, which here was much thicker than it had been on the higher ground from whence they had come. But the fog —annoying as it must be to Captain Broke—was becoming their ally, Phillip thought, lending them anonymity. The few people they passed, all hurrying in the same direction as themselves, spared them scarcely a glance. They were talking agitatedly amongst themselves and Graham said, his own voice a whisper, "They've seen the ships and are afraid that the town is to be attacked again. Half of them don't seem to have understood that the *Gladiator* is flying a flag of truce—poor souls, they are scared out of their wits!"

Remembering the aftermath of that first bombardment, which had left the dockyard and the Imperial Mole ablaze and the lower part of the town a blackened, smoke-filled inferno, Phillip could understand the townsfolk's agitation. They wanted no repetition of the terror they had endured last April and clearly would flee their homes, rather than face anything of the kind a second time. Nearer to the center of the town, however, the panic largely subsided, as better informed citizens were met with and the news spread that the enemy warships wished only to parley with their officials. Despite the initial fear of attack, there were few soldiers in evidence until they reached the harbor, when they encountered a party in artillerymen's green uniforms—about thirty strong and few of them in their first youth—marching in somewhat slovenly fashion in the direction of the stone steps which led to the Imperial Mole.

"Garrison troops," Graham observed. "Mostly pensioners, by the look of them . . . and with no great enthusiasm for their task. Shall we follow them down?"

Phillip nodded assent. The harbor at Odessa lay at the foot of the cliffs on the south-east side of the town. It was an artificial one, he recalled, formed by four long stone piers, which projected into the sea and divided the harbor itself into two basins, known respectively as the Quarantine Basin and the Imperial Harbor. Each pier was guarded by a stone parapet, split with embrasures for cannon on the seaward side, but the port's main defenses were a citadel built on the cliff-top to the west and a series of gun batteries extending from the Quarantine Mole to the quay of the Port de Pratique, on the eastern side. Of these, the two immediately below the steps they were now descending had, Phillip remembered, caused the most trouble during the attack by Admiral Lyons' steam frigate squadron the previous spring. Each battery consisted of eight heavy caliber guns, well sited and massively protected by the cliffs into which they were built, and they had been bravely fought. Eventually, however, they had been silenced when the *Terrible* had hit and exploded the principal magazine by which they were supplied, and a squadron of rocket-boats, led by Commander

Dixon of the *Agamemnon*, had entered the Imperial Harbour with instructions to destroy the dock and shipbuilding yards and the main arsenal at the rear of the Mole.

The success of the rocket attack had exceeded even the Admiral's expectations and Phillip found himself wondering, as he and Graham approached the landward end of the first pier, whether the enemy had managed to repair the appalling damage which had been wrought that day. It seemed probable that they would have made an attempt to do so and he decided that he would find out, if he could, to what extent their repairs had progressed . . . although, perhaps, this was not essential. With the Allied Fleets in almost complete control of the Black Sea, the shipwrights of Odessa could only keep such vessels as they had contrived to build on the stocks, since none could put to sea without running the risk of capture. Even river craft were not entirely safe, if they were sighted by a patrolling British frigate. The *Trojan* had cut out and captured several small sailing vessels in this area the previous year and, with the blockade of the Black Sea ports now re-established, it was doubtful whether many of them would dare to run the gauntlet. At all events, not those under the Russian flag and even neutral ships, if they were carrying the grain which was Odessa's chief export, were liable to be stopped and searched, so that. . . .

"Hold hard," Graham warned softly. "There's a guardhouse, with a sentry on duty."

Phillip followed the direction of his brother's gaze and saw that the sentry—like the artillerymen who had just marched past his box—was an elderly man, clad in a tattered uniform. He was leaning on his musket, taking little interest in what was going on around him and, when two civilians, heavily muffled in fur-trimmed overcoats and wearing Boyar caps, drew level with him, the old soldier made no attempt to challenge them. A little knot of women had, it was true, collected to the rear of the guardhouse in a shrilly chattering group, evidently with the intention of watching whatever spectacle might present itself from there, but. . . . Phillip did not slacken his stride. In their

118

naval caps and boat-cloaks—and in the fog—he and Graham would probably pass as Russian naval officers, he reasoned, and, so long as they approached him with an air of authority, it was unlikely that the rheumy-eyed old soldier would dare to question their right of access to the Imperial Mole. At any rate, it was worth trying; they could, if necessary, beat a hasty retreat into the fog. He whispered his intention to Graham, who nodded in agreement.

The bluff succeeded, the sentry even rousing himself sufficiently to ground arms as they reached him and, at a deliberately measured pace, Phillip led the way on to the Mole. The fog was now so thick, at this lower level, that he could see only a few yards in front of him, so, once out of what he judged to be the sentry's range of vision, he halted to allow Graham to catch up with him. His brother was again looking very white, he noticed with concern, but shook his head impatiently to the suggestion that he might be feeling ill.

"Don't worry, I shall be all right. What have you in mind, now that we are here?"

"Well, if you're sure that you are up to it, I thought we might take this opportunity to look over their defenses. I doubt if we shall be given a chance like this again—and the fog is a godsend."

"Then let us waste no time," Graham advised. "We shall cover more ground if we separate, don't you agree? I'll double back and try to check the lower gun battery and meet you back here in what . . . fifteen minutes—twenty?"

"Fifteen," Phillip decided. "It should not take any longer but we'll allow another five for emergencies."

It was, indeed, a heaven-sent opportunity, he thought, but after a scant ten minutes spent groping his way about in the gloom, he had seen all that he needed to see. With a sense almost of shock, he realized that the harbor was virtually defenseless. The gun batteries on the Imperial Mole, which had so stoutly resisted the steam squadron's attack just over eight months ago, were non-existent. The

119

embrasures were manned but only by riflemen, the majority of these of the age and caliber of the sentry they had bluffed and the remainder mere boys, who handled their heavy muskets awkwardly, as if untrained in their use. The cannon had been removed, with the exception of four ancient brass pieces, beside which the gunners lounged in anything but a warlike state of readiness—although, he observed, all four guns were loaded and trained to seaward.

Graham, when they met again well within the stipulated time, had a similar story to tell.

"Both batteries at the foot of the cliffs appear to be armed," he said in a low voice. "I did not risk making too close an inspection, because they had a guard posted. The gunners were seamen, incidentally, but I would hardly class them as able-bodied. And for the rest. . . ." He shrugged. "The arsenal is a burnt-out shell, just as our rocket attack left it, and I only saw a couple of ammunition wagons that weren't empty." He supplied a few more details and added, a thoughtful frown creasing his brow, "Phillip, I think they must have sent everything they had in the way of troops and guns to Simpheropol during the summer, when the road to Perekop was passable. In fact, the coastal forts must now be virtually their only defense. If General Canrobert is serious in his desire to take this place, I honestly believe it could be done, without much trouble, by the four ships of our squadron now lying out in the bay. No wonder the people were so alarmed when they first sighted us—they probably imagined that this was our intention!"

Phillip felt inclined to agree with his brother's assessment, judging by what they had so far seen, but there was, he knew, always the danger of jumping to a premature conclusion and, when Graham asked if he had seen sufficient for their purpose, he shook his head. "No, not yet. We shall have to go into the town, of course, before we leave. First, though, I should like to take a closer look at what shipping is in the basin and try to find out if the batteries at the Port de Pratique and at Dohinafta are still in existence, if that is possible. And it may well be possible, under cover of the general excitement when the *Gladiator* sends her boat in. We can gain access to the inner harbor easily enough—there are steps down to it at intervals all along the Mole—and there's bound to be a dinghy or a boat of some kind that we can lay our hands on." He consulted his pocket watch. "It's only ten-thirty, so we have plenty of time. How do you feel?"

"All right," Graham assured him. "Lead on. The *Gladiator*'s emissaries cannot be much longer, can they?"

They strode on to within sight of the seaward end of the Imperial Mole and positioned themselves as inconspicuously as they could, on the edge of the small crowd which had gathered there. The majority of these were in uniform, either naval or military, the collars of their cloaks or of their heavy, ankle-length greatcoats drawn up to protect their faces against the cold as they peered anxiously into the fog to seaward. Amongst a group of harbor officials, Phillip recognized the Commandant of the Port in earnest conversation with two of its uniformed health inspectors and, recalling a previous occasion when two of these gentlemen had protested wrathfully because their quarantine regulations were being ignored, he permitted himself a wry smile. As always, it seemed, a strict quarantine must be imposed on all visitors to Odessa, war or no war, and he wondered what Lieutenant Risk would make of it, if the Harbormaster yielded to the pleas of the two with whom he was now arguing and. . . . His thoughts were interrupted by the crack of a musket shot, coming from somewhere fairly close at hand.

Graham whispered, mouth close to his ear, "The boat from the *Gladiator*, Phillip. I fancy it's coming in now. That was a blank, wasn't it, fired to seaward?"

They both listened intently. A few minutes later, heralded by the splash of oars cutting through the water and the creak of rowlocks, the *Gladiator's* pinnace emerged from the mist, followed by a second boat, each with a flag of truce prominently displayed. As the crew of the pinnace backed their oars, Phillip saw that she was carrying the

Gladiator's First Lieutenant, in addition to a midshipman, and that there was an officer from the *Mogador* in the sternsheets of the second boat.

"Messieurs . . ." the French officer, a speaking trumpet to his lips, announced the purpose of their visit and requested that a boat from the port be sent out to them, in order that they might deliver the communication they had brought which, he explained, was addressed to the neutral consuls resident in the town.

After a lengthy consultation with the Harbormaster, one of the port officials replied, also in French and with impeccable courtesy, promising that a boat would be manned and sent out to them as soon as possible. His reply ended with the plea that no one should attempt to set foot on shore, which would contravene the quarantine regulations and, hearing this, Phillip again found himself smiling. Then, recalling the reason for his own presence on the Imperial Mole, his smile faded and he nudged his brother.

"Now," he breathed softly, "while they are all occupied with the boat. The steps are on your right."

"I'll follow you," Graham answered, in an oddly strained voice. They had covered barely a dozen yards when he halted, gripping Phillip's shoulder. "Oh, dear heaven! I . . . I'm sorry, Phillip, I don't think I . . . can go on." His face was contorted with pain but, by the exercise of an agonizing effort of will, he controlled himself. "I . . . I'll try. If you could give me your arm——" Leaning heavily on Phillip's arm, he managed to gain the head of the flight of stone steps which was their objective but once there—out of sight, if not yet out of hearing of the officials on the Mole—he sank to his knees. "Go on . . . alone," he urged thickly. "I'll stay here . . . until you've made your——" he broke off, writhing helplessly in the grip of a fresh spasm of pain, his lips drawn back and teeth tightly clamped together in a valiant attempt to still the cry that rose to his throat.

"You will be safer at the foot of these steps," Phillip told him, endeavoring to hide his anxiety when at last

122

the spasm lessened in intensity and Graham raised a tortured, chalk-white face to his in mute apology. "Here" —he took the small flask from his pocket, unscrewed its top and, ignoring his brother's protests, held it to his lips. "Take a few sips, if you can."

Graham did so and then pushed the flask away. "Thanks, I . . . Oh, God, I'm sorry. It came on me without warning and I . . . for pity's sake, Phillip, leave me, won't you? This miserable attack will pass off and when it does, I can make my own way back to the cove. You'll be caught if you stay with me and——"

"No, we'll stick together." Phillip replaced the flask in his pocket. "I tell you, it's not safe for you to stay here; you'll be seen, if the fog lifts. Come on, put your arm round my neck and ease yourself down, one step at a time. Don't worry, I'll take your weight. But have a care . . . the steps are like glass and if either of us slips, we're done for."

Testing each step with his foot, he slowly assisted his brother to lower himself to the bottom of the flight of stone steps, fearing that at any moment they might be heard. By the time they had reached the sanctuary of the narrow slab of stone to which the steps led, he was sweating freely despite the dank chill of the water lapping about it . . . but at least it offered them a temporary refuge.

The fog hid them from anyone standing above them on the Mole and, to his infinite relief, he saw that there was a small, two-oared dinghy moored to an iron ring within arm's length of where they were crouching. He had counted on finding a boat of some sort fairly near at hand but this was nearer than he had dared to hope and of a size that he could manage single-handed and, as he drew the tiny craft towards him, he breathed a silent prayer of thankfulness. The boat gave them a better than even chance, he thought, pausing for a moment in order to look about him and get his bearings. In it they could cross the inner harbor and either return to the town by a different and safer route than the one they had taken to the Imperial Mole or . . . he studied his brother's face apprehensively. Or, if Graham's condition made this advisable, they could take refuge aboard one of the many small vessels lying in the basin, and wait there until the sick man recovered sufficiently to be able to reach their rendezvous at the cove on foot.

"Graham. . . ." The dinghy secured, Phillip leaned closer, an arm about his brother's waist. "One last effort, old man, if you can make it."

"All right, Phillip." Ashen-faced but grimly determined, Graham struggled to his feet and, with Phillip's help, managed to get into the dinghy, where he collapsed with a low moan on the bottomboards. He had lapsed into semi-consciousness long before Phillip had taken his place on the thwart beside him, his big body limp and helpless as a child's and his eyes closed.

Phillip took off his cloak and covered him with it, his anxiety suddenly acute. There was, he decided as he slipped the dinghy's painter and cautiously pushed off from the Mole, only one alternative left to him now. Somewhere, among the fog-enshrouded ships moored in the basin, he must find one in which, for the next few hours, his brother would be safe. Safe and, above all, warm and dry; protected from the deadly chill of the fog and the icy water lying in the bottom of the dinghy for, in spite of the additional cloak, Graham had started to shiver violently, he saw, and his face was blue with cold.

For an instant, such was his concern for his brother, that he was tempted to abandon their mission and, instead of pulling further into the harbor, to put about and endeavor to row out to the *Gladiator.* But, almost as soon as this wild idea entered his head, he decided against it. For one thing, this small, leaking boat was unseaworthy and might founder in the open bay; for another, he knew that their chances of passing the seaward extremity of the Mole unobserved would be extremely slim. The fog might lift without warning or a vigilant gunner, hearing the splash of oars, might open fire on them . . . and he dared not attempt to make contact with the *Gladiator*'s pinnace, even in his extremity, since to do so would be to violate the truce and, perhaps, draw the enemy's fire on the pinnace or even cause it to be seized.

Phillip glanced quickly over his shoulder and then bent to his oars, pulling in the direction of the first line of anchored ships. He *had* no choice but to get his brother aboard one of them, he told himself resignedly, and that soon, before Graham's condition deteriorated still further. But he must take care not to select a vessel with a watchman on board—no easy task in the fog—and he could not afford to make a mistake, which must rule out the larger ships, many, if not all, of which might be expected to set a harbor watch.

In the end, he found what he was looking for by chance . . . a small brig, moored at some distance from the rest, into which he ran the dinghy's bows inadvertently and with a resounding thump. He waited, his heart pounding, for some response to the noise he had made, but there was none and, after pulling round the hull—still without eliciting any sign of life—he secured the dinghy to the brig's midship chains and, leaving Graham where he was, slipped silently on board. Satisfied, after a careful inspection, that she was deserted, he located a snug cabin on the lower deck, piled blankets on to the single berth this contained and then went back to get his brother out of the dinghy.

This proved almost the hardest part of his task, for Graham resisted all efforts to rouse him and had, eventually, to be half-dragged and half-lifted on to the brig's deck. Once there, however, Phillip was able to turn him on to his back and, staggering drunkenly under the unconscious man's weight, to carry him to his cabin.

5

FOR the next hour or more, Phillip worked desperately to
restore his brother to consciousness, stripping him of his
damp clothing, chafing his cold limbs and hunting for
more blankets with which to cover him, in the hope of
putting a stop to the fits of violent shivering by which he
was periodically convulsed.

The brig possessed a galley but the risk of lighting a fire
was, he decided, too great. In any case, there were no
provisions on board which might have made the risk
worth taking, apart from a keg of foul-smelling water
that—even if he had managed to boil it—would probably
have been undrinkable.

The blankets had been stored for a long time and had a
musty odor but at least they were dry and he had been
fortunate to find them, Phillip thought as, after a while,
the warmth began to return to his brother's body and the
ghastly shivering became less frequent. Finally it ceased
altogether, to his heartfelt relief, and he made another
search for provisions, which yielded some oilskin coats—
which he put aside for future use—but nothing edible.

When he returned to the cabin, Graham had dropped
into what seemed to him a deep sleep and he wondered,
as he stood looking down at the white, shuttered face on
the bunk, whether he dare leave him to sleep off the ill-
effects of his food-poisoning, in order that he himself
might complete their mission alone. There was, of course,
the language difficulty; without his brother to translate
for him, he might find himself in trouble, from which his
schoolboy French would not suffice to extricate him. Only

the better educated of Odessa's 70,000 inhabitants would be likely to speak or understand French and he hesitated to take any action which might delay his return to the brig without, at least, informing Graham of his whereabouts and intentions.

Finally, after a careful weighing up of the situation, he decided to compromise. The fog still shrouded the harbor and would enable him, if he were careful, to row across to investigate the battery at the Port de Pratique and get back to the brig before nightfall. He could, at the same time, plan their route to the cove and choose a point on the quay where they could go ashore without attracting any unwelcome attention and, in case Graham woke before he was able to rejoin him, he could leave a note for him, with a brief explanation.

This decision reached, Phillip lost no time in putting it into effect and luck was with him. He had completed the task he had set himself and was back on board the brig a good hour before dusk, to find that his brother was still sleeping, the note where he had left it, unread. And the sleep had done some good, judging by the sick man's improved color and the lack of tension in his face. Whether he would now be capable of tackling the exhausting journey to the cove on foot was, of course, another matter but . . . he leaned over and gently shook Graham's shoulder.

"Graham . . . wake up, old man. It's me, Phillip!"

Graham opened his eyes, to regard him dazedly at first and then, as memory stirred, with some anxiety. "For heaven's sake, where am I?"

Phillip told him and saw his expression change to one of shamed contrition. "Oh, my God! I've let you down badly, haven't I? I'm exceedingly sorry. I don't know what came over me. I . . . I must have gone out like a light, because I remember nothing after you dragged me down those steps on the Mole. Except that I was as sick as a dog and. . . ." He accepted the flask Phillip offered him and gulped down a few sips of the brandy it contained. As he handed back the flask, his fingers touched his brother's damp cloak. "Where have you been?"

"I had a look at the gun battery on the Port de Pratique and rowed round the basin but I could not see a great deal —the fog has lifted a little but it's still persisting. However, there's no doubt that extremely little has been done to repair the damage we caused during last year's bombardment. . . ." Phillip went into details and Graham said thoughtfully, "I recall hearing of an edict from the Tsar, which the Governor received after the bombardment. His Imperial Majesty, after praising the citizens of Odessa for their heroic defense, made *them* responsible for the full cost of restoration! I imagine that they may well feel that they have made their contribution to the war and, in view of what it has cost them, they now intend to stay out of it—if they can—by offering no threat or provocation which might lead to a second attack."

"If that is the case," Phillip returned dryly, "let us hope that General Canrobert will see their situation in the same light!"

"Let us, indeed, hope he does." Graham pulled himself into a sitting position and glanced round the tiny cabin. "You found me a very snug refuge! But I don't suppose that you want to stay here for much longer, do you?"

"That depends on you." Phillip eyed him searchingly. Anxious though he was to get his brother back to the *Huntress*, he knew that it would be madness to attempt to reach the cove until Graham had recovered his strength sufficiently to walk unaided. "We could delay our departure for a few hours," he pointed out. "The gig will come in for us a second time, an hour before daybreak, if we fail to make the first rendezvous. And we are safe enough here, I think, at any rate during the hours of darkness, so I'm quite prepared to wait. On the other hand, you'll be better off on board the *Huntress*—there's no food here and——"

"Food, my dear Phillip," Graham said and could not suppress a shudder of revulsion, "is the last thing I want, believe me. But I agree . . . the sooner we can get ourselves back aboard the ship, the better. I take it that you

128

have now seen enough of Odessa to enable you to make a full report to the Admiral?"

Phillip hesitated, his conscience pricking him. The day had not, alas, gone according to plan. He had, it was true, with his brother's help, made as close an inspection of the Imperial Harbor and its immediate defenses as, in the circumstances, anyone could ask of him. Nevertheless, his report would have to be based largely on conjecture, he realized. The fact that the only troops they had actually seen had been garrison troops, while it undoubtedly suggested that Odessa possessed no others, was not proof—it was supposition. He sighed, glancing uneasily at Graham. He had not entered the town itself, had not so much as glimpsed the main barracks where—if they were anywhere—troop reinforcements for Prince Menshikoff's army in the Crimea would be quartered, awaiting the clearing of the ice and snow from the Perekop road before they could be transferred.

And, he reminded himself, in the past, Odessa had been the principal depot for the export of the vast grain harvest of the whole of southern Russia and he had not, as yet, made any attempt to ascertain whether the city's granaries were full or empty. If he were to carry out to the letter the orders he had been given, he needed a few more hours . . . but hours of daylight, not of darkness. At night he would be able to see very little and might arouse suspicion if he were found in the vicinity of barracks or granaries at a time when few people were abroad, save those who were compelled to be—such as sentries or watchmen—for the nights were bitterly cold.

Again he looked across at Graham, brows furrowed as he took in the shadowed eyes and the pinched tightness about his face. The attack had taken a lot out of him; his brother was still far from well and, even if he managed to summon up sufficient strength to make the return journey to the cove before daybreak, this, Phillip decided, was the most that could be expected of him. If he himself remained in Odessa for another day, it would have to be alone. . . .

Graham said, misunderstanding the reason for his

hesitation, "Well, if the hour of our departure depends on me, I had better test my legs, don't you think?" He did not wait for Phillip's assent but, thrusting aside his covering of blankets, dragged himself unsteadily to his feet. "Oh, the devil take it! Phillip, I'm truly sorry—I'm as weak as a kitten, I'm afraid. But if you give me a hand, perhaps I. . . ." The cold of the small cabin struck him, almost with the force of a physical blow, and he started to shiver uncontrollably.

"That's enough," Phillip told him firmly and assisted him back into the bunk, once more piling the blankets over him. "We'll wait and endeavor to make the second rendezvous. Try to sleep . . . and I shall do the same."

Once more, he thought, a decision had been made for him and he was left with no alternative. And perhaps it was as well; he, too, was weary and the strain was begining to tell on him. A few hours' sleep might help to restore his reserves of energy and his mental alertness, both of which he would need in full measure, if Graham's condition did not improve. After a brief visit to the deck, to make certain that there were no fresh signs of activity, he took two more blankets from the brig's store and, rolling himself in them, lay down on the cabin floor. Years of training himself to sleep in any conditions, and for however long or short a time might be available, came now to his aid. He dropped off almost as soon as his body relaxed against the unyielding timbers of which the brig was constructed and, exactly four hours later, awakened, feeling rested and refreshed. Before waking Graham, he took another careful look round from the open deck. The fog had vanished and the night sky was bright with stars but, as before, the harbor appeared to be deserted—a forest of bare masts and spars, rising from the hulls of abandoned ships, aboard none of which could he make out any sign of life.

Satisfied, he went below to rouse his brother, taking with him the two rough, oilskin coats he had come across when searching for blankets. Graham sat up as soon as he entered the cabin and, although in the darkness it was

130

impossible to see his face, he asserted—in a voice that was noticeably stronger—that he had fully recovered. In proof of his assertion, he walked with perfect steadiness across the cabin and was able to clothe himself with very little assistance.

"I feel a new man, Phillip," he said jubilantly. "But it's not before time, is it? The few hours we've delayed have made all the difference, so far as I'm concerned. My legs feel as if they belong to me now, which is an enormous relief, believe me. All the same . . ." he sighed. "I let you down and——"

"Don't be an idiot!" Phillip put an arm affectionately about his shoulders, cutting short his attempted apology. "You could hardly help eating tainted meat, could you? The Purser's to blame for that, if anyone is . . . and he shall hear about it, I promise you. I might have eaten the stuff too, if it hadn't been for Captain Broke's invitation. Well . . ." he helped his brother to don the oilskin jacket. "This smells rather unpleasant, I'm afraid, but it will keep out the cold and make us look slightly less conspicuous. . . ." He put on his own and moved towards the deck hatchway. "If you're ready, it's time we set off."

The first part of their return journey was accomplished without incident. They landed on a deserted quay, left the dinghy moored there and found their way without difficulty to the coast road, scarcely meeting a soul and making better progress than Phillip had anticipated. Graham stood up well to the rough going, plodding stoically at his side through the ankle-deep filth of Odessa's noisome back streets and later bravely breasting the slope of the narrow, ice-bound cart track which led to the cove, only occasionally having to pause for breath or in order to accept a helping hand. From the summit of the hill, the sight of the riding-lights of the British squadron, lying peacefully at anchor in the bay, gave them fresh heart and they both tackled the downward slope at a swinging pace, grinning at each other when the rutted track caused either to slither on its icy surface.

They were within less than half a mile of their objective

131

when, as suddenly and unpredictably as it had struck him down on the Imperial Mole that morning, Graham suffered another attack of sickness and was compelled to lie writhing on the ground for fully fifteen minutes before the attack wore off. Uneasily aware that, although he had allowed ample time for their journey, the most gruelling part of this was yet to come, Phillip forced a few sips of brandy between his brother's clenched teeth and assisted him to his feet. He had virtually to carry him to the point at which—in order to cross the marshy wilderness that lay between them and their destination—they must leave the road. Breathless and spent, he set down his limp burden and went in search of the lantern, which he found untouched, where they had left it and, after checking his bearings by the now fading stars, he returned to Graham's side.

"Come on, old man," he urged. "We're almost home and dry now. Just one more effort . . . if you could lean on me and try to walk, we'll make that rendezvous with the gig. . . ." But Graham seemed scarcely to hear him and could only stagger a few paces, held upright by his arm as, once again, the ghastly, convulsive shivering seized his tormented limbs. He was dazed and barely conscious, just as he had been before and, cursing the Purser and his tainted meat with impotent fury, Phillip bent wearily to heave the sick man on to his back.

Thus burdened, he made desperately slow progress, constantly stumbling over obstacles hidden from him by the darkness and twice sprawling, full length, over large boulders with which, as he drew nearer to the cove, the marsh seemed to be strewn. And the way down to the rocky foreshore was, he reminded himself despairingly, a mass of loose boulders. If he were to get Graham to the shore, he would have to call on his gig's crew for help. His own strength was beginning to fail and he knew that to attempt to carry his brother any further unaided would be to risk injury to them both. Already the unconscious man had been flung, with bone-jarring violence, on to the hard ground when he had lost his footing a short while ago; to subject him to much more of this rough treatment might cost him a limb or even his life.

The breath rasping painfully in his chest, Phillip covered the last few yards to the edge of the rocks and there, as gently as he could, lowered Graham's limp body on to a level patch of frosty earth. He knelt beside him, spent and gasping, to recover his breath and, as he did so, heard the faint but unmistakable splash of oars. The gig, he thought with heartfelt relief, still some way out but right on time, and he jerked himself unsteadily to his feet. Before he called on any of his men to come to his assistance, he must be certain that he would not be jeopardizing their safety, must make sure that both the cove and the marsh-land behind it were deserted, and he hadn't much time—if O'Hara obeyed his orders—to do this and climb down to the foreshore. Calling on his last reserves of strength, he tottered over to a high rock, which he could just make out silhouetted against the lightening skyline and clawed his way to its summit. From this eminence, he strained his eyes into the darkness, forcing himself not to hurry and, finally satisfied that it was safe to do so, he descended slowly to the shore to meet the incoming boat.

It came in cautiously—even with what Phillip, tense with strain, considered over-caution—and he had been waiting for nearly ten minutes before it was near enough to hail. Cupping his hands about his mouth, he called out impatiently, "Boat ahoy—*Huntress*!" and his hail was greeted by a subdued cheer, sternly suppressed by the gig commander, whose voice he recognized as Ambrose Quinn's.

"You, Mr. Quinn?" he said, when the boat grounded, too tired to feel more than mild surprise. "And where is Mr. O'Hara?"

The First Lieutenant came splashing towards him.

"I'm sorry, sir, but I had to discipline Mr. O'Hara for insolence. He's on watch and watch and relieved of his other duties." He did not trouble to lower his voice, apparently indifferent to the fact that his criticism of O'Hara could be heard by his gig's crew. "In any case, Commander Hazard, I did not consider that a task like this ought to be entrusted to a midshipman, so I decided it was best to undertake it myself. I . . . er. . . ." He glanced about him, clearly puzzled. "Is the Master not with you, sir?"

"He has been taken ill—with food poisoning, I can only suppose, like Mr. Cochrane. I've had to leave him up there, in the rocks." Phillip waved a hand in the direction from whence he had come. "I shall need two men to carry him down—two good men, it will be an awkward climb. I'll guide them."

"Aye, aye, sir. Jackson . . . Williams, look lively, the Captain wants you." Quinn rapped out his orders and, as the two men he had chosen were wading ashore, Phillip asked curtly to whom he had entrusted command of the ship in his absence. "Why, to Mr. Cochrane, sir," the First Lieutenant answered promptly. "He is next in seniority to myself, so that naturally I——"

"He's recovered, then?"

"Well, no, not completely. I did not think he was fit to take command of the gig's landing party, that was why I came myself. But Mr. Cochrane assured me he was fit for light duty aboard the ship."

Phillip was relieved by this news. If Cochrane had got over the worst of his sickness, then Graham might do likewise and, perhaps, with equal rapidity, once he was back aboard the *Huntress* where he could be properly cared for. He glanced at the faces of the two men from the gig, recognizing both more by instinct than by sight in the semi-darkness. They were in his regular crew and so, he thought wryly, Lieutenant Quinn must have put a stop to poor young O'Hara's "volunteers", and O'Leary would have bartered his grog ration for nothing. But he made no comment, simply turned with a quiet, "Right, follow me, lads," and limped back to the rocks. Quinn, a trifle to his surprise, came with him, solicitously offering him an arm which, notwithstanding his dislike of the man, he was glad enough to accept, for his legs—and, indeed, his whole body—in Graham's words, no longer felt as if they belonged to him.

134

As they toiled up the steep foreshore, his second-in-command asked, with interest, how he had fared in Odessa and he answered evasively, too weary and short of breath to welcome questions, least of all from Quinn.

"Oh, well enough, I suppose. It was, of course, most unfortunate that Mr. Hazard was taken ill."

"Indeed yes . . . you were depending on his services as interpreter, weren't you? For how long did his indisposition last, sir? Was it of the same severity as Mr. Cochrane's?"

The ghastly, racking sickness that had attacked his brother could scarcely be described as an "indisposition," Phillip reflected, but he let it pass. "Oh, off and on from the time we went ashore. And I'm afraid he's in a pretty bad way now, so the sooner we. . . ." He stumbled and would have fallen but for Quinn's firm grip on his arm. "Thank you, Mr. Quinn," he acknowledged and forced himself to limp on. "I fear that I'm not much better."

"You are worn out, sir," the First Lieutenant suggested, his tone unexpectedly sympathetic. They climbed in silence for several minutes and then he said, lowering his voice, so that the men plodding at their heels could not hear, "You will pardon me for asking, Commander Hazard, but do you intend to remain ashore until nightfall or will you be returning to the ship with the Master?"

His inquiry, natural enough in the circumstances, took Phillip momentarily by surprise and he halted, frowning, undecided as how to answer it. He thought longingly of the hot meal that would be awaiting him aboard the *Huntress*, of a change into warm, dry clothing and of the sleep for which his weary body was crying out and then, urged on by Quinn's arm, he resumed his slow, upward climb without replying to the question. But Ambrose Quinn was not to be put off.

"You did not confide to me the exact nature of the orders you received, sir," he pointed out. "So that I don't know for what purpose you and the Master went ashore. But I take that you——"

Phillip cut him short. "No," he snapped. "I did not

explain my orders to you, Mr. Quinn. And I do not propose to explain them now, since they are confidential."

"I understand that, sir," Quinn assured him. "And in view of the secrecy with which you were set ashore and the risks involved—not only to our gig's crew but to the whole squadron—I also understand their importance. But presumably Mr. Hazard's indisposition made it impossible for you to complete your—er—your observations in the port? Obviously, with a sick man on your hands, you could not possibly do so . . . although I'm only guessing, of course, putting two and two together, as you might say. That's why I inquired as to your intentions. You see, sir, I realize you're all in and I wasn't sure whether you had decided to—well, to give up the attempt to carry out your orders." He hesitated, as if in embarrassment, and then added softly, "No one could blame you, if you did decide to give up, Commander Hazard. In the circumstances, it might be more prudent to do so, perhaps."

This suggestion, uttered in the same sympathetic tone as he had used earlier, nevertheless stung Phillip on the raw . . . as, he thought resentfully, no doubt Ambrose Quinn had known it would. It lacked subtlety and the implied criticism of him was there, as always, thinly disguised. He expelled his breath in a frustrated sigh.

Since leaving the brig, he had given the question of whether to go or stay no thought; his sole object had been to get Graham safely back to their rendezvous in the cove but—Quinn was right, he was forced to admit. His observations were not yet complete; his report to the Admiral would have to be based largely on supposition and, if he went back to the ship now—while there was still a chance that he could carry out the whole of his mission—he would be, as Quinn had put it, giving up the attempt to carry out his orders.

Quinn's opinion of him did not matter, of course, but to give Admiral Lyons an incomplete report, merely because he had suffered a slight setback and felt exhausted, was scarcely to enhance his own opinion of himself. The hours of daylight lay before him. He could see all that he needed to see quite easily during those hours and, even without Graham to interpret for him, the danger that he might arouse suspicion was comparatively slight. Had they not proved this, during their visit to the harbor? No one had questioned or paid them any attention—in fact, they had walked as freely about the town and the harbor as had the *Tiger*'s seamen, throughout their brief captivity. He had only to do as he had done the previous morning, Phillip told himself, in order to achieve his purpose, and the gig could come back here for him tonight. . . . He turned to Quinn.

"Has any reply yet been received to the note the *Gladiator* delivered to the port, do you know?"

Quinn shook his head. "No, sir, not yet." There was an odd gleam in his eyes as he looked up into Phillip's face. "Where did you leave your brother, sir?"

They had reached the top of the rocks, Phillip realized and he stood there for a moment or two in tired perplexity, peering about him and becoming aware, as he did so, of the first grey streaks of dawn in the sky.

"We haven't much time," Quinn reminded him unnecessarily. "If we're to get back to the ship before daylight."

"To the left," Phillip said thickly, getting his bearings at last. "A few yards below that high, misshapen rock, I think . . . no, further to your left, Jackson."

One of the seamen, following these directions, called back a low-voiced, "Aye, aye, sir—here he is!" and Phillip limped across to join him. Graham lay as he had left him, still apparently unconscious but he stirred uneasily when Able-Seaman Jackson bent over him, feeling for his heart.

"Well, sir?" Quinn prompted impatiently. "Shall we get him down to the gig? It'll be daylight soon and——"

"A moment, Mr. Quinn, if you please." Phillip dropped to one knee beside his brother and, at the sound of his voice, Graham roused himself and opened his eyes. "Phillip—is that you?" he asked dazedly.

Phillip laid a restraining hand on his shoulder.

"Yes, I'm here and so is the boat. Don't you fret, old man, we'll have you aboard the *Huntress* almost before you know it." He got to his feet to find Quinn at his side, regarding him expectantly and he said, before his second-in-command could question him again, "I shall remain ashore in accordance with my orders, Mr. Quinn. Take Mr. Hazard back with you to the ship at once and you may send the gig to pick me up, as we arranged, two hours after nightfall. Should I fail to rendezvous with it then, it should return once more, an hour before daybreak. I'll show a light, should there be danger."

"Aye, aye, sir," Quinn acknowledged, unable to hide his satisfaction. "I'm aware that you have good reason for your decision to remain here but I should be failing in my duty were I not to point out to you the risk you'll be running. You are exhausted and without food, sir, and——"

"I have my orders, Mr. Quinn," Phillip returned, careful to control his voice. "And I must carry them out."

"Yes, I know and I . . ." Quinn hesitated, watching his face in the dim light. "If you could see fit to acquaint me with the nature of your orders, Commander Hazard, then perhaps——"

"My orders are confidential, Mr. Quinn."

"I'm aware of that, sir, and of the fact that you received them from the Admiral himself," Quinn said, his tone faintly resentful. "But I presume you have been instructed to make—er—well, to make observations in the port of Odessa and carry back a report to the Admiral of what is going on there. Is that not so?"

"Your presumption is reasonably accurate," Phillip conceded.

"Well, sir,"—the First Lieutenant raised his voice and hearing this, both seamen turned instinctively to listen to what he had to say—"I am physically in a better state than you are and, if I may make so bold, sir, just as capable of using my eyes and ears. Let me stay, while you go back to the ship. I'd be only too willing to take your place, Commander Hazard."

What was the man driving at, Phillip wondered. "Do you speak Russian, Mr. Quinn?" he enquired, with a distinct edge to his voice. "And are you familiar with the port of Odessa?"

Quinn shook his head. "No, to my regret, sir. All the same, I——"

"Then I fear—to *my* regret—you cannot take my place." Was this the answer his second-in-command had expected, Phillip wondered and then, observing the relieved smile with which Quinn received his refusal, knew that it was. He wished he were not quite so tired, so that his dull wits could follow the tortuous working of Quinn's mind. But . . . the gesture had been made and the two men from the gig's crew would carry the tale of how it had been made and rejected back to their shipmates. He had no one but himself to blame if the tale grew in the telling, either. . . . He gave vent to a resigned sigh and motioned to the still gaping seamen to pick up his brother.

"Have a care with him, if you please, both of you. He's in a bad way and——" but Ambrose Quinn had not yet done.

"Commander Hazard," he put in quickly, intent, it seemed, on gilding the lily, "if you need a volunteer to replace your brother, you have only to say the word. I'm quite sure that any one of us would willingly offer his services and I——"

"Are *you* volunteering to remain on shore with me, Mr. Quinn?" Phillip asked and, despite the dim light, had the satisfaction of glimpsing what he could only suppose to be an expression of dismay on his First Lieutenant's face. But it swiftly vanished as Quinn answered smugly, "I did not imagine that you would wish us both to be absent from the ship for any length of time, sir. It may have slipped your mind that Mr. Cochrane is still indisposed but, if you are satisfied to leave him in command then, sir, of course I'll remain here with you. Or either of these men would, I am confident, be proud to do so—eh, lads?"

Both seamen, thus invited, nodded assent and the younger of the two, a strapping young Welshman, offered eagerly, "Take me, if you please, sir." His hand went

139

to his cutlass and he grinned. "I would dearly love a go at them Roosians, sir, truly I would."

Phillip clapped a hand on his shoulder, smiling. "Thank you, Williams, but no. That's not what I'm here for, unfortunately. Carry on, both of you, and get the Master down to the beach as quickly as you can." The men looked crestfallen but they went obediently about their task. If one of them had been O'Leary, Phillip thought, he might have been tempted but as it was. . . . He went to the cliff edge, to assist them to find the easiest route and, kneeling there, called out a warning to watch for loose rocks, which Williams acknowledged with a confident, "Aye, aye, sir." They disappeared from view, the sound of their descent, punctuated by the occasional clatter of falling stones, continuing to reach him as he crouched on the cliff top, all the energy suddenly draining from him.

He would wait to make sure they got down without mishap, he decided and, smothering a yawn, wondered whether he dare snatch half an hour's sleep before setting off on the long, cold walk back to Odessa. It might be a wise precaution if he did; he was reasonably safe here but, once in the town, he would have to keep his wits about him and certainly could not afford to rest for very long, if at all, while he was there. Ambrose Quinn, preparing to follow the two seamen, paused to set the lantern down beside him with a murmured, "In case you need this, sir," and then, evidently divining his intention, gestured to a cleft in the rock a few feet below them. "That's a snug spot, sir, if you were thinking of a cat-nap. Shall I lend you a hand to get down there?"

"No, no, I'll manage, thanks—you get under way." Phillip pointed to the now rapidly greying sky. "It will take you all your time to pull back to the ship before sunrise, Mr. Quinn, so don't delay on my account." He repeated his instructions for his next rendezvous with the gig and nodded, in brisk dismissal. But Quinn ignored the nod.

"You won't delay me, sir, and I've got to climb down

140

in any case. Better let me help you. It wouldn't do to break a leg now, would it? This way, sir."

His tone was insolently assured and Phillip, too tired to argue with him—or to wonder why—permitted his second-in-command to assist him to the spot he had indicated which, he realized, as he lowered himself into it, was indeed ideal for his purpose. Hidden from anyone standing on the cliff top by what appeared to be a slight overhang, it was dry and sheltered from the wind and, thankful to be able at last to relax, he drew his cloak about him and lay back, his head pillowed on his linked hands.

"Sleep well, Commander Hazard," Ambrose Quinn said softly and set off after the two seamen, his surefooted silence in marked contrast to their noisy, slithering descent. Phillip listened for the sound of his footsteps and then, determined not to allow himself to fall asleep until he was quite certain that the whole party had reached the foreshore safely, he sat up, staring down into the blackness below him.

He heard someone cough and then, from behind him, a sharp crack and the patter of tiny stones, followed by a low rumbling sound, as if rock were grating on rock. Instinctively sensing danger, he flung himself forward but a fraction of a second too late. A heavy object struck him on the side of the head with such force that he collapsed with a smothered groan, his last memory of a dreadful, searing pain, followed almost instantaneously by merciful oblivion. . . .

On the beach below, Able-Seaman Williams and his companion were joined by two more men from the waiting gig, who came splashing through the shallows to relieve them of their unconscious burden, when the sound of a heavy fall of rock caused all four men to look back apprehensively at the cliff face.

"That will be the First Lieutenant," Williams said. "Coming down after us, he was, at a rare pace . . . and it is all loose rock, that cliff is, believe me."

"Maybe he has broken his bleeding neck, then," an anonymous voice suggested, from the stern of the gig.

"No such luck, boyo," Williams told him glumly. "Here he is, coming now, the bastard . . . and he is running like a mountain goat!"

The coxswain reproved him half-heartedly and, as they lifted Graham into the boat and settled him carefully in the stern, he asked sharply, "Where is the Captain?"

"Oh, he is staying on shore. He——"

"Alone?" the coxswain snapped incredulously.

"Yes, alone. Oh, we were all volunteering to stop with him, of course . . . even the First Lieutenant—but he would have none of us. We are to take him off tonight, I believe and. . . ." Williams broke off, as Lieutenant Quinn came running across the foreshore towards them. He was breathing hard but swung himself into the gig with practised ease, bawling an order to the coxswain to put to sea at once.

"Look alive, there!" he admonished, as one of the men, who had been engaged in pushing the boat out of the shallows, lost his footing and had to be dragged bodily from the icy water, soaked to the skin and shivering. Quinn cursed him long and fluently for his carelessness but, for some reason, his admonition lacked its accustomed venom, and the seaman glared back at him in sullen surprise before picking up his oar. "Handsomely now," the First Lieutenant bade them. "We've to be back aboard the *Huntress* before daybreak, on the Commander's express instructions . . . so put your backs into it, my lads, or I'll mark 'em for you! This isn't a pleasure boat outing for Margate—that is the enemy coast astern of us, and don't you forget it!"

"We are not likely to forget it," Williams muttered rebelliously, out of the side of his mouth, to the man on the thwart next to him. "For haven't we just left the Captain there, all on his own? Aye and brought the Master back from there, half dead, into the bargain!"

Lieutenant Quinn affected not to hear him. He was smiling quietly to himself as, with belated solicitude, he bent to lift Graham Hazard into a more comfortable position at his side. The Captain's brother looked in very

142

poor shape, he thought, so that it seemed probable that neither he nor Lieutenant Cochrane would be fit to command the gig on its return journey to the cove at nightfall. . . .

6

PHILLIP recovered consciousness to feel the sun on his face, his first thought the guilty fear that he had overslept. He struggled into a sitting position, unable at first to establish his whereabouts, for the sky whirled about him, weaving kaleidoscopic patterns of light and shade before his startled eyes and he had to cling to the rock on which he lay in order to remain upright.

His head was throbbing painfully, his mouth parched and dry and his left arm appeared to have neither strength nor feeling in it. Gradually, however, by dint of closing his eyes for several minutes and then opening them again, he was able to make out that he was lying on a narrow ledge of rock some twenty feet below the summit of a cliff. Below him he could see a small cove, hemmed in by crumbling cliffs similar to the one on which he was so precariously perched. The cove was deserted, although there were what looked like footprints here and there on the few patches of sand the cove boasted . . . footprints which disappeared when they reached the tide-line, suggesting that whoever had made them had left the cove by boat.

But . . . his brow furrowed in perplexity. *What* boat? Whence had it come and where had it gone? And where, in the name of all that was wonderful, *was* the cove? Rack his brain as he would, he could not remember, could not recall ever having been here before. There were no familiar landmarks, nothing to offer him a clue and, after a while, he gave up the useless attempt to identify the cove and, turning with infinite difficulty, gave his attention to what lay above his head. He was lying in a cleft in the rock face, he saw, with nothing above him but the sky . . . a grey, somewhat forbidding sky, lit by a watery sun. And it was cold, bitterly cold. Instinctively he put out his right hand to draw the cloak he was wearing closer about him, in the hope of keeping out the cold. It was his boat-cloak, he realized, and he was in uniform but, in addition to the cloak, an unpleasantly smelling oilskin—a fisherman's oilskin, judging by its smell—was wrapped about him. He fingered it distastefully, noticing with some astonishment that both cloak and oilskin were stained with dried blood—heavily stained.

Had he, then, been hurt? Was this blood his own? Gingerly he felt along his forehead, up to the hair line and then swore softly as his questing fingers encountered a painful swelling just above his right ear, which extended to the back of his head. His hand, when he withdrew it, was wet with blood. So he *had* been injured, he told himself, and the blood was his own but . . . how and when? More important, perhaps, by what—or whom—and why? And where, in heaven's name, was he?

Phillip expelled his breath in a sigh of exasperation and attempted to get to his feet. It took four attempts and all the will power he possessed but finally he forced his cramped and feeble legs to obey him, only for his earlier attack of vertigo to return with greater severity than before. He had again to cling to the rock face until at last it ceased and he was able to clamber unsteadily to the top of the cliff. This change of situation, while it afforded him a more extensive view of his surroundings, was of little help to him in deciding where he was.

On all sides, a flat, marshy wilderness stretched in front of him, seeming more like a nightmare landscape than one which actually existed. As far as he could make out, the bleak plain had no end. All he could see was mile upon mile of frozen, featureless ground, with a few stunted bushes, on whose drooping branches earlier falls of snow had been caught and immobilized into ice. There were no tracks, no signs of human habitation and nothing moved, animal or human, within his range of vision.

A description of the Russian Steppes, which he had read as a boy, in a geography lesson, came suddenly, unbidden, into his mind and he stared about him, shocked, unable to believe that he could be in Russia. This was a dream, he told himself, a nightmare, as he had thought a few minutes ago . . . and yet the injury to his head was no dream and the blood, on cloak and hands, was real enough. He moved forward a pace or two and his foot kicked against a small metal object that, when he bent to examine it, proved to be a lantern . . . a signalling lantern, with a shutter, by means of which the light from its squat, slow-burning tallow candle could be shown or cut off, at will.

This, also, was real enough, Phillip's numbed brain registered and, convinced now that he was not dreaming, he sank down, still holding the signal lamp in his cold hands as if—absurdly—he could derive some warmth or comfort from his contact with it. Or, perhaps, some clue to unlock his memory of what had gone before. . . . He closed his eyes, making a great effort to think, to remember why and for what purpose he had come to this desolate place. The lantern had some purpose, obviously—tied in, perhaps, with his own—if only he could recall what either might have been.

Slowly, in odd, seemingly unrelated flashes, memory returned. He was in—or near—Odessa. Yes, that must be so, for the name of the town persisted, as if it had been burned into his brain. Odessa and . . . oh, God, of course, the *Tiger!* She had run aground in the fog—it was strange with what vivid clarity he was able to remember every detail of the illfated *Tiger's* end. He and his brother Graham were together—Graham had been his Assistant-Master—and he had brought a boat in, to try to take off some of her crew . . . but the boat had been hit and he had had to swim to the stranded frigate. He could see the cannon-flashes, smell the acrid smoke, as red-hot shot from the Russian guns on the cliff top struck her wooden deck,

146

setting it ablaze, whilst salvo after salvo of chain-shot wrought havoc with her masts and rigging until, the work of destruction almost complete, the gunners had loaded with grape and brought their field-pieces to bear on the men struggling for their lives in the water.

And then, he recalled, appearing with dramatic suddenness from the fog and smoke of battle, a rider on a splendid white Arab horse had come to the cliff edge, to direct the gunners to concentrate their fire on the single 32-pounder which still spat abortive defiance from the *Tiger*'s smouldering upper deck . . . Narishkin, Prince Andrei Narishkin, Colonel of the Chasseurs of Odessa and aide-de-camp to the Tsar. That name, too, was burned indelibly into his memory, Phillip thought, for had not Mademoiselle Sophie married the Prince Narishkin in the Cathedral at Odessa, a few weeks after the loss of the *Tiger*? He tensed and then felt his stiff, chilled body relax, as the memory he had secretly treasured for so long came, in its turn, to fill his mind, erasing that of the loss of the *Tiger* and of the wound he had sustained during the battle . . . a wound that had come near to costing him his life and, indeed, might have done so, had it not been for Mademoiselle Sophie.

He had not allowed himself to remember or to think of her for months but now, no longer conscious of his sternly imposed self-discipline or of any reason for it, he gave his thoughts free rein, pleased to find that—whatever else the blow on his head had caused him to forget—his recollections of the slender, dark-haired girl, whom he had known as Mademoiselle Sophie, were as fresh and clear as if their parting had been yesterday. Instead of . . . he shook his head in bewilderment and, as the agonized throbbing began again, wondered how long ago that parting had been. Weeks . . . months, perhaps? Yes, months ago, he was sure. And yet she was in Odessa and so, too, was he but he had not gone to her, had not tried to find her . . . although that might be the reason for his presence here.

It was possible, surely, that he had been on his way to Odessa to seek her out when something—or someone—

had struck him on the head, with the object of . . . what? Of preventing their meeting? But who could have wanted to prevent him seeing Mademoiselle Sophie? Who could have guessed that this was his purpose in landing here? There was the war, of course . . . fool that he was, he had forgotten that a state of war existed between his country and hers. But if he had been seen by a Cossack patrol, they would have shot him or taken him prisoner. No Cossack would have been content merely to strike him down and leave him where he had fallen. Who, then, could have done so? Prince Narishkin, perhaps? No, Narishkin was dead, killed at Balaclava. He had died of his wounds in the tent of one of the 93rd's women . . . and died gallantly, with his wife's name on his lips and . . . Phillip felt his throat tighten.

This memory was also very clear and he knew that he could not have imagined it. Narishkin had given him back the ring that had been Mademoiselle Sophie's gift to him when she had left the *Trojan* and. . . . he felt for it in his pocket, his fingers closing about the case in which he always carried it. The case snapped open and, as he had known it would be, the ring was there—a magnificent emerald, carved with the double-headed eagle crest of the Imperial Family of the Tsar, flashing in the pale winter sunlight as it lay in the palm of his hand. The ring was no dream, he told himself, and, replacing it carefully, let his throbbing head fall on to his outstretched hands, as he endeavored to decide what his next move should be, his thoughts again confused.

But, it was obvious, he could not stay here in the biting cold. He would have to find his way to Odessa and. . . . he dragged himself awkwardly to his feet, to stand at the cliff edge, looking about him. He would have to clean himself up, wipe the blood from his cloak and jacket, and fashion some sort of dressing for the wound on his head before he dared risk showing himself in Odessa. Very slowly and carefully, his limbs like leaden weights, Phillip made the descent to the cove. At the water's edge, he knelt and examined his head, as well as he could, using

148

his watch-case as a mirror. The time, he noticed, with some surprise, was seven-thirty—early enough to allow him ample time for his cleansing operations, so he set about them methodically.

The wound on his head—if its reflection in the silver watchcase was to be believed—was an ugly one, a jagged cut, extending from the top of his right ear almost to the nape of his neck. But, although he appeared to have lost quite a lot of blood, the wound itself was drying up now and, using his handkerchief dipped into the ice-cold water, he bathed it gingerly and, wincing with the sting of the salt as it penetrated the cut surface, rolled up the handkerchief as a dressing. This he secured in place, after one or two attempts, by means of a strip torn from one of his shirt-sleeves. His jacket and cloak were less easily dealt with, both being thickly caked with blood but, wrapping the foul-smelling oilskin about him to keep out the cold, he gave the collars of both garments a thorough soaking. The sun was not strong enough to dry them so, when the soaking had removed most of the bloodstains, he squeezed out as much of the water as he could and donned the jacket and cloak again immediately, shivering at the damp touch of the cloth on his skin. But he felt better by the time he had finished and the discovery of a half-filled flask of brandy in one of his jacket pockets raised his flagging spirits. He gulped down the entire contents thirstily and with little thought of the consequences and once again the sky whirled about him in crazy circles, so that he was compelled to delay his return to the cliff top until his head cleared.

Nevertheless, the effect of the brandy was exhilarating and the climb back, though still laborious, far less exhausting than the descent had been. Phillip was in an oddly reckless frame of mind when, reaching the ledge on which he had recovered consciousness, he glimpsed his cap, lying some yards to his left. It must have fallen from his head when the rock—or whatever it was—had struck him, he thought. If he could recover it, the cap would serve the useful and, perhaps, essential purpose of hiding the bandage on his head from curious eyes, so . . . he inched his way across to where the cap lay, caught and held by a cluster of bushes growing out from among the loose rocks on the cliff face. At first it eluded him but, after two or three abortive grabs, he succeeded in grasping his prize and, absurdly pleased by this achievement, he donned it triumphantly.

It was then that he noticed the ominously stained boulder, lodged just below where the cap had been and, his interest swiftly awakened, he levered himself down in order to examine it. This undoubtedly was the heavy object that had struck him, he decided . . . and it must have come—must have fallen—from the top of the cliff, for part of its surface was covered with lichen. Straining every muscle, for the boulder was unwieldy and heavier than he had anticipated, he managed to turn it partially over. There was no lichen growing on what he judged to be the underside, only some deep cracks and scratches of obviously recent origin, which suggested that it had struck against other rocks as it fell or . . . Phillip drew in his breath sharply. Or that it had been wrenched from whatever had originally held it in place. . . . He glanced upwards with narrowed eyes and then resumed his ascent, making again for the ledge on which he had lain.

He had been fantastically lucky, he reflected, in that the blow he had received had been a glancing one, on the side of the head. Had that boulder struck him squarely, it must have smashed his skull to pulp. . . . he shuddered and, once more, memory stirred. He recalled the sudden premonition of danger that had caused him to fling himself forward—he had heard some sound which, although he could not remember now what the sound had been, had set the alarm bells ringing in his head, and he had reacted to it instinctively. Reaching the ledge, he halted, peering from side to side uncertainly. There was a cleft in the rock, not a very deep one but large enough to take a man's body and, if he lay full length along it, deep enough to afford protection from wind and weather. *A snug spot for a cat-nap* . . . the words drummed at his ears. Someone had said them, he was certain but he could not remember who . . . he might even have said them himself, for all he knew.

He paused, trying vainly to remember and staring at the traces of lichen on the inside surface of the rocky hollow. Then, struck by a sudden idea, he hauled himself up to the summit of the cliff and dropped to one knee, looking down now into the cleft from above. It was possible, he supposed, measuring both with his eye, it was just possible that the boulder he had examined might at one time have been wedged or balanced across the upper end of the hollow—or that it had formed part of an outcrop, extending above the upper end. The cliff was irregular, crumbling in half a hundred places and, from where he knelt, he could see several similar eroded clefts and hollows. The one above the ledge might or might not have been the "snug spot" he had chosen for a cat-nap and . . . he sighed despondently. The boulder which had dealt him so savage a blow could have been dislodged accidentally; there was not a shred of evidence to suggest that anyone had deliberately hurled it down in his direction, with the intention of hitting him. Or, if there was any such evidence, he had not found it and ought not to waste any more time searching for it. If he were to seek out Mademoiselle Sophie—the Princess Narishkina—in Odessa, he must delay no longer.

Phillip rose, bracing himself. His head still ached and the momentary elation induced by the brandy had long since evaporated. His body felt numb with cold—as numb and useless as his brain, he thought gloomily—and he had no notion of which direction to take, no clear idea of why he should be going in search of Mademoiselle Sophie. Yet the sense of urgency when he thought of her persisted and it was this, rather than any reasoned motive, which sent him plodding across the desolate marsh in what he could only pray was the right direction. Proof that it was came only a few minutes later, to his surprised relief, when he heard the distant ringing of church bells and then glimpsed the tall spire of what he remembered was the

Orthodox Cathedral, rising above the domes and cupolas of Moslem mosques and temples and the red rooftops of stone-built dwelling houses. He set his face towards the Cathedral spire and plodded doggedly on, coming to a road about twenty mintues later, which he joined. This—deeply rutted and rough—led him uphill and, from the summit of the hill, he found himself looking down, with some bewilderment, at four British ships-of-war, lying at anchor in the bay.

Their presence gave him comfort but, although he stood watching them for nearly fifteen minutes, he saw nothing—apart from a white flag of truce, flying from the main of a paddle-wheel corvette—to account for their being where they were. The *Trojan* was not among them and he knew a moment's unreasoned disappointment, when he realized she was not. The *Trojan* was his ship and therefore, presumably, she had brought him here and must be somewhere in the offing . . . although, without his glass, he could not see her. Before leaving his vantage point, he spent several minutes in frowning contemplation of a steam-screw sloop, which was anchored at a considerable distance from the other three ships and which, for some reason, seemed familiar and held his interest for longer than the rest of the small squadron. But she was too far away from him to identify her with any certainty and, still puzzled by his failure to do so, Phillip returned to the road.

He met people in increasing numbers as he approached the center of the town but, busy with his own confused thoughts, he ignored them, striding so purposefully on his way that no one questioned him, although he attracted a good many curious glances. The unusual cut of his clothes, the fact that he looked ill and that a bandage protruded from beneath his cap made him an object of interest to several passers-by but he was not aware of this and, probably because he showed no fear and met their glances indifferently, even the most curious shrugged and let him pass. A wounded naval officer—and one who had been wounded in the head—could be permitted even the eccentricity of walking, instead of riding, through the muddy streets, his fine boots ankle-deep in slush and his bruised, deathly white cheeks unshaven.

Blind instinct was guiding him now. He was in an odd, dreamlike daze, barely conscious of where he was or of where his feet were taking him. He passed empty granaries and later a deserted barrack block without being aware of their significance or sparing either a second glance. The church bells continued to ring and it dawned on his bemused mind that today must be Sunday and that the people who thronged the streets were, like himself, on their way to the Cathedral—although, until that moment, he had not known that the Cathedral was his objective.

But Mademoiselle Sophie would be there, he told himself and, in his dazed state, did not doubt the truth of this assumption. Carriages were passing him occasionally and he turned to stare into each one, wondering if it were hers but unable to do more than catch a fleeting glimpse of the occupants through the steamy, mud-spattered windows.

It was sheer chance that brought him to within sight of the Cathedral steps when a splendid equipage, drawn by four matching bays and escorted by two outriders, came to a halt at their foot. He stood, jostled by the crowd, to watch a small, veiled figure in black, step from the vehicle and mount the steps very slowly, leaning on the arm of the older woman who accompanied her. Even from where he waited, Phillip recognized the somberly clad figure, despite the veil and the widow's weeds and knew, from the sudden clamorous beating of his heart, that his search was over. Mademoiselle Sophie—Her Imperial Highness the Princess Sophia Mikailovna Narishkina—was there, a few yards from him and he had only to walk towards her, only to call her name. . . .

He was on the point of doing so—had, in fact, taken a pace or two in the direction of the steps—when once again instinct warned him to take care. He could not accost her publicly in full view of the other churchgoers, flocking devoutly to their worship, but. . . . a long-drawn

153

sigh escaped him. He could, surely, enter the vast Cathedral with the crowd, unnoticed and cloaked by their anonymity, without risk either to Mademoiselle Sophie or himself, couldn't he? He came to a standstill close to the steps, keeping her in sight and, when a soberly dressed merchant and his wife approached at the head of a small procession of relatives and children, he followed them into the Cathedral. Once inside, he left the merchant's family to go their own way and, evading an usher who was directing new arrivals to seats on either side of the nave, he slipped quietly into the shadows of a side aisle and paused there, looking about him.

Beneath the domes of its golden cupolas, the interior of the Cathedral glowed with light. Walls and ceilings were covered with luminous frescoes and, before the altar at the opposite extremity of the nave, a gold iconostasis, encrusted with jewels, reflected the gleam of hundreds of flickering candles, bathing the mitred priest who stood before it in a flood of iridescence.

Mademoiselle Sophie and her companion were, he saw, after some anxious searching, being ceremoniously conducted to what appeared to be a private family pew, with ornately carved and gilded seats and a vaulted roof, at the far end of the aisle in which he had taken refuge. Heavy velvet curtains hung at the entrance to the pew which, if drawn, would hide its occupants from the rest of the congregation and Phillip's heart sank when he saw the usher's hand go out to pull the curtains across. He moved closer and, as if his silent prayer had reached her—as well as the God to whom it had been addressed—he saw Mademoiselle Sophie shake her head. The usher bowed and left the curtains undrawn. When he had made his dignified departure, Phillip inched his way into a seat from which, by dint of craning his neck, he could observe the interior of the pew and catch an occasional glimpse of both occupants, when they leaned forward or rose to their feet.

The service, rich in pageantry, made little impression on him. He scarcely heard the musical intonations of the

154

bearded, gold-robed priests or the responses of the packed congregation and, although he made a conscious effort to stand or kneel in unison with those about him, all his attention was concentrated on the tiny, heavily veiled figure in the pew in front of him. Mademoiselle Sophie kept the veil over her face, so that he could see little of it and her glance seldom strayed from the prayer book in her hands, save when she knelt in prayer and even then she covered her eyes with one hand, fingers spread out and head devoutly bent.

He guessed, from the slight clumsiness of her movements, that she was still carrying the child—the child of which Andrei Narishkin had spoken, with such joyous pride, as he lay dying in the 93rd's picket lines, after the Battle of Balaclava—but there was no other sign of this in the dignified erectness of her small body. Indeed, he thought, she looked very much as she had when he had seen her for the first time, alighting from Lord George Melgund's carriage at Paddington Station. She had worn a veil then and had been just as dignified. It had not been until she had removed her veil in the train and turned the gay warmth of her smile on him that he had realized how young and charming she was . . . and how beautiful.

He had also realized that, for him, she was and always would be unattainable but the realization had made no difference; from the moment of meeting her, he had had eyes for no other woman. Not even for Catriona Moray, to whom he owed his life. . . .

Phillip hunched forward in his seat, praying that Mademoiselle Sophie would look in his direction but this time his prayer went unanswered. It was not until the long service was drawing to a close that she turned her head, to give him so brief a glance that he wondered whether he had imagined it and decided, after a moment or two, that he had. He saw her sink to her knees and, realizing that the entire congregation was kneeling for the Benediction, belatedly followed their example. As he knelt there, he found himself re-living the strange little scene in his

155

sickroom at the Governor's Palace, when Mademoiselle Sophie had come to take her final leave of him, the day before her wedding.

Her words had come to him through a mist of pain, incomprehensible at the time she had uttered them, yet locked in his memory and now suddenly released, so that he heard them again, as he knelt watching her.

"Phillip, I do not know if you can understand or even whether you can hear me but I . . . tomorrow is my wedding day. Here, in the Cathedral, I am to be married and then I have to go away. I have no choice, you see. I have to go with my husband. First to St. Petersburg, where we shall present ourselves to Uncle Nikita for his blessing and then . . . then I do not know. We may go to Sebastopol, perhaps, or to Georgia . . . there is fighting everywhere."

The voice, charmingly accented and infinitely sad, was as clear as if she were seated beside him as she spoke and Phillip closed his eyes, willing her to go on.

"We shall not meet again, we cannot meen again," he heard her whisper. *"I know my duty . . . I must bid you farewell. But you will grow strong and well again, you will live . . . for my sake, you must live, Phillip. To know that you are living somewhere in the world will comfort me. I shall think of you and pray for you . . . for you and your valiant Trojan. And one day, when you are the Trojan's Captain, I shall know . . . because my heart will tell me. The heart does not forget, Phillip, however sad it is . . . and when peace comes, I shall see you with the eyes of the heart, as you set your course for England. May God be with you, now and always, my dear English sailor. . . ."*

Phillip's throat was tight, the palms of his hands clammy with perspiration. Then someone nudged him and a man's voice, close to his ear, muttered words he could not understand. He opened his eyes and saw that the service was over, the lights in the vast Cathedral dimmed, as attendants snuffed out some of the candles. He was the only one still on his knees and he rose stiffly as Made-

156

moiselle Sophie and her companion led, as before, by an obsequious usher, emerged from their pew. They would, he realized, pass right in front of him if he held his ground, and he did so, ignoring the usher's wand, which motioned him to stand aside. The man who had nudged him spoke to him again and, grasping him by the arm, pulled him back, obviously wanting him to leave the Cathedral. Phillip shook him off impatiently, heedless of the possible consequences, and waited, the blood pounding in his brain, as if a thousand tiny hammers were beating inside his head.

Mademoiselle Sophie's eyes, behind their concealing veil, rested for an instant on his face and then, without a flicker of recognition, she walked past him, leaning on the arm of her companion, her small, thickened body still erect, despite the burden of the child she carried. She did not look back, did not speak and Phillip watched her go, powerless to move, his stiff lips unable even to whisper her name. The shock was so great that it was as if a deluge of icy water had struck him full in the face and suddenly, as he stood there, the floodgates of his memory opened and Mademoiselle Sophie's failure to recognize or acknowledge him faded from his mind.

He remembered now what had brought him to Odessa, remembered his mission and the Admiral's confidential orders, remembered why he had stayed ashore, after sending his brother Graham back to the *Huntress*: it all came back to him vivid clarity. The ships he had seen in the bay were, of course, his own *Huntress,* with the *Gladiator,* the *Wrangler* and the French steam frigate *Mogador.* Under their flag of truce, they were awaiting a reply to a note the *Gladiator's* pinnace had delivered that morning . . . no, yesterday morning, to the port officials on the Imperial Mole. He and Graham had watched the delivery of the note, under cover of the fog which had shrouded everything, until Graham had been stricken down by a ghastly attack of the same sickness that had laid young Anthony Cochrane low. He had been compelled to send his brother back to the ship, with their mission uncompleted and . . . with returning memory came the awareness of danger and Phillip let out his breath in a gasp of horror, as he realized the plight he was in.

There was no fog in which to hide now, he thought grimly. He was standing alone in Odessa's Orthodox Cathedral, in British naval uniform, conspicuous by reason of the filthy state of his cloak and boots and the bandage about his head and, judging by the curious stares he was attracting from the departing worshippers as they shuffled past him, he was inviting question—if not arrest. Even the former would be a disaster; he spoke only a few words of Russian and would be quite unable to understand, much less answer, any questions that were put to him. He would inevitably be taken, if he remained here.

Forcing himself to do so without haste, he started to move towards the main door of the Cathedral and saw, out of the tail of his eye, that the bearded man who, a few minutes before, had attempted to hold him back, had now gone over to one of the ushers. He was whispering and gesticulating, pointing to where they had both stood and, after listening to what the fellow had to say, the usher went to confer with a superior, the bearded man at his heels. All three men came thrusting a way through the crowd after him and Phillip heard one of them call out but, with no idea of what they expected of him, he effected deafness and did not pause. If he could reach the main door before his pursuers caught up with him, he thought desperately, he might manage to make his escape. A dash down the steps, to mingle with and, if he were lucky, vanish into the crowd in the square below—that seemed his only hope. The crowd might, of course, react in a hostile manner to his appearance in their midst but he would have to chance that. So long as no one spoke to him expecting a reply, he could probably bluff his way through, his uniform affording him at least temporary protection, as it had done before.

He gained the head of the Cathedral steps and was about to make his dash for safety when a giant of a man,

158

in resplendent livery, moved swiftly to block his path. Doffing his furred cap, he bowed and offered Phillip a folded scrap of paper. The two ushers and the bearded man jerked to a standstill at the sight of this liveried messenger, clearly disconcerted by the fact that he had approached their quarry. One ventured a nervous question and the messenger shouted at him disdainfully, gesturing to the note he had just delivered, upon which both ushers shrugged and turned to retrace their steps into the Cathedral. The bearded man, after hesitating uncertainly, took to his heels and—as Phillip had planned to do, a moment or so before—vanished into the crowd thronging the square.

Greatly relieved by his disappearance, Phillip opened the note. It was written in English and was very brief, scribbled hurriedly in pencil on a sheet torn from a memo pad. *"This man is my servant and may be trusted,"* it informed him. *"He will guide you to where my carriage is waiting. Come quickly and speak to no one."* There was neither address nor signature but, in no doubt as to who had written it, Phillip's heart leapt. He was filled with so reckless a sense of elation that, forgetful of his recent narrow escape in the Cathedral, he went bounding down the steps ahead of his guide and had to wait for the giant to catch up with him.

The carriage, he realized, had moved away and the servant, a restraining hand on his arm, led him across the square and into a deserted side street where, to his joy, he saw the vehicle waiting, the coachman at the horses' heads. The door opened at his approach and Mademoiselle Sophie's voice bade him enter. He did so, a prey to conflicting emotions, at once eager and afraid now that the moment had come, and she gave him her hand, looking down at him as he kissed it with anxious, tear-filled eyes.

"Phillip . . . oh, Phillip, is it really you? I had not expected to see you ever again . . . and least of all here! Did you not realize the risk you ran in coming to the Cathedral, showing yourself openly as you did? And you are hurt . . ." her fingers gently touched the loosely

159

wound strip of cloth on his head. "Come . . ." she indicated the seat beside her. "I will take you to my house, so that your wound may be attended to and you may rest and eat. You look exhausted."

Phillip took the place she had indicated and the carriage slowly moved on. Her companion, seated opposite, eyed him curiously but did not speak and Mademoiselle Sophie answered his unspoken question reassuringly, "Do not fear—she is my maid and she does not understand English. You may speak quite freely in her presence." She drew back her veil, smiling at him a trifle hesitantly through her tears. "I . . . it is wonderful to see you again . . . so wonderful that I cannot really believe it. But, oh Phillip, you are in such danger, every minute you remain here, that it worries me, for your sake. Why did you come? Not—surely not—to see me?"

"I came to the Cathedral in the hope that you would be there," Phillip admitted truthfully. He felt suddenly as gauche and awkward as a schoolboy, uncomfortably aware that his whole body was trembling violently and misunderstanding the reason for this, Mademoiselle Sophie, with a little cry of pity, placed a heavy fur rug across his knees.

"You are cold . . . and you look so ill. It was a great shock to me, when I recognized you in the Cathedral. I was afraid, I did not know what to do . . . I had not dreamed that you were here, because I . . ." there was a catch in her voice. "The *Trojan,* it—she, I mean—is not with the other English ships. I looked with a telescope, when the fog cleared and they were anchored in the bay, but I did not see her there."

So she had looked for him, Phillip thought. She had looked for his ship, daring to hope, perhaps, as he had hoped that the impossible might happen, as . . . he sighed, bemused by the sheer, incredible wonder of their meeting. As it *had* happened, so miraculously that neither of them could yet believe it . . . unless, of course, it was a dream.

"No," he said, somehow finding his voice again. "No,

the *Trojan* is not here. I have my own ship now, the *Huntress* and——"

"And you are its—*her*—Captain?"

"Yes," he confirmed. "I'm in command of her."

Mademoiselle Sophie exclaimed in innocent delight at this news, her smile the lovely, radiant smile of a happy child, the memory of which he had carried in his heart for so long. He kept his gaze on her face, refusing to let his eyes stray to the small, swollen body with its mute evidence that she was no longer a child, refusing to accept —in this miraculous moment of meeting her again—that, for him, she was and must always remain unattainable.

"Oh, my dear English sailor, I am so pleased for you! And the hateful Captain North?"

"He is dead of the cholera."

"Oh?" she shrugged. "I cannot pretend to feel any sorrow for him, Phillip. But. . . ." She was grave again. "So much has happened since you were last here, so much that is cruel and tragic and wrong. But that is war, I suppose. And . . . the war goes on. We are enemies, Phillip."

"Yes," he conceded regretfully, thinking of her husband but, to his heartfelt relief, she did not mention Narish-kin's death. Instead, still gravely searching his face, she asked, "Phillip, *why* did you come? You are not fool-hardy or reckless. You are English, the Captain of an English ship, and the English are always well disciplined, obedient to their orders . . . that is why they fight so well. Tell me the truth, I beg you—you did not land here without orders, did you?"

Phillip shook his head. He owed her the truth, he knew —nothing less would suffice. "No, I did not. I had orders to come ashore. Will you permit me to tell you why I came?"

Her dark eyes reproached him. "You came to spy on us, I am afraid. And you believed that I would help you because once I . . ." she broke off, colour flaming in her cheeks, and then went on bitterly, "I will help you to return to your ship but that is all. I am betraying my

161

country by doing even that, Phillip. I should have let them take you in the Cathedral but I—I could not. They do not treat prisoners-of-war in Odessa as they did the last time you were here."

"I went to the Cathedral with no thought of asking for your help," Phillip assured her quietly. "I give you my word . . . all I wanted was to catch a glimpse of you, perhaps to speak to you. Please, Mademoiselle Sophie, will you not allow me to explain my purpose here and the reason for my orders?"

She smiled faintly at his use of the name by which she had been know aboard the *Trojan* and then bowed her head. "Very well—I am listening."

Without mention of the proposed expedition to the Sea of Azoff, Phillip told her of his mission and its underlying purpose, and of what he and Graham had so far accomplished. He dwelt briefly on his brother's illness and his own return to Odessa that morning, to enable him to confirm the conclusions they had drawn the previous day. Mademoiselle Sophie listened to what he had to say in pensive silence and, when he had done, she spread her hands in a sad little gesture.

"I think I understand, Phillip," she said. "Your mission is, in fact, one of mercy—of mercy, that is to say, for Odessa? It is the French who want to bombard us again, not your Admiral?"

"So I was informed, mademois—madame."

"Oh, Phillip, this poor town is not worth the expenditure of powder and shot! It is as you observed, when you and your brother were on the Mole . . . the last attack by your Fleet left half the town in ruins!" Her voice shook with the intensity of her feelings. "There are few men left here and little money for the repairs that should have been made, so nothing has been done. We have sent all we had —every soldier fit for fighting service, our guns, what was left of our grain and materials of war, everything—has been sent to the Crimea. In order that Sebastopol may be defended, Odessa has been left defenseless. Phillip, the only soldiers we have are old men or boys, our ships rot in the harbor basin, as you have seen for yourself; not even the fishing boats dare venture out. Our trade is at a standstill and we are even short of food. It has been a bad winter for us, the roads to the interior blocked by snow and the river by ice. When your naval blockade is resumed, it will be worse."

She caught her breath on a sob and Phillip did not doubt that she was telling him the stark, unhappy truth.

"I will show you, if you wish," Mademoiselle Sophie offered. "And if it will enable you to convince those who would bombard us again that we are not worth their trouble, I will show you everything you need to see. Do you require the proof of your own eyes?"

Her voice was flat now, devoid of feeling and, sick with pity, Phillip inclined his head. "It would assist me in making my report, certainly . . . although, I assure you, *I* do not require proof—nor, I believe, does the Admiral. But the French have to be convinced and——"

"Very well. You shall have your proof, Phillip. But"—again her eyes searched his face anxiously, pleading for reassurance—"I am trusting you, not only with my life—which is of small account to me now—but also, perhaps, with the lives of many of the citizens of this already sorely stricken town. I believe that you came here for the purpose of which you have told me but . . . it is possible that you did not. We are at war and . . . oh, Phillip, it is possible that your appearance will be followed by an attempt to—to invade us, for which I might be, if not wholly, in part responsible. Will you give me your word that I can trust you?"

Phillip flushed but he met her frightened gaze steadily. "I give you my word of honor, Your Highness, that what I have revealed to you of the purpose of my mission is true, to the best of my knowledge and belief. I am not a spy and I was not set ashore in order to initiate an attack on this town, but rather, as I understand my instructions, to prevent one. But"—he hesitated—"in all honesty, I cannot tell you that there will be no attack in the future, because I do not know—such decisions are made by the High Command. I do know, however, that my own Commander-in-Chief is opposed to the suggestion and that he sent me here in order that my observations might confirm information received from deserters and prisoners we have taken."

Mademoiselle Sophie considered his words and then solemnly laid her small, gloved hand on his. "I will trust you, Phillip." She spoke rapidly in Russian to her maid and the woman obediently leaned out of the carriage window to pass on her orders to the coachman. The heavy vehicle lurched to a standstill and the tall footman, who had been Phillip's escort from the Cathedral, jumped down from the box, to stand bareheaded in the open doorway, while his mistress gave him precise instructions as to the route they were to follow. His face was wooden and expressionless, as the maid's had been, neither showing surprise at the change of plan. They resumed their journey, the carriage jolting over the rutted road as the coachman skilfully brought his horses' heads round, and Mademoiselle Sophie motioned Phillip to take the seat her maid had occupied.

"You will be able to see better from there," she told him quietly. "It will not take long to provide you with your proof that we are defenseless, Phillip—an hour, perhaps. And then you must go, you must return to your ship . . . I dare not let you stay much longer. Will they send a boat for you?"

"Yes—two hours after nightfall. The boat will pick me up at a cove some five miles along the coast and——"

"Five miles? Then you will need a horse. And there will be time to have your wound attended to, for which I am glad." She smiled at him again and there was tenderness in her smile. Phillip felt a knife twist in his heart as he looked across at her.

"Thank you, Mademoiselle Soph—forgive me, Your Highness. I . . . I keep forgetting to address you as I must now, I——"

"And I prefer 'Mademoiselle Sophie' from you, my dear English sailor," she said softly. "It reminds me of happier times, although, alas, those times will never come again, for either of us, I fear. But now. . . ." She leaned forward in her seat. "We are approaching the Cavalry Barracks, where once the Chasseurs of Odessa were quartered under my husband's command. Look well, Phillip."

Unhappily, little relishing his task, Phillip obeyed her. By no stretch of the imagination had he expected to complete the final part of his mission from the safe refuge of a princely carriage-and-four, with a niece of the Tsar as his guide, but fate had ordained that he should and, he supposed, he was fortunate. The tour on which he was taken was a comprehensive one and it confirmed all that Mademoiselle Sophie had said concerning the stricken town. Odessa had been left in ruins by that first naval bombardment and was now, it was self-evident, sucked dry and abandoned, no longer capable of contributing anything to the prosecution of the war.

"You see?" Mademoiselle Sophie asked, her eyes filled with tears. "Have you seen enough now, Phillip, to convince even the French that this poor town offers no menace and would make a—a truly unworthy target for your Fleets?"

He bowed his head in pitying assent. "Yes, I have seen enough, more than enough, I——"

"Then rap, if you please, on the roof of the carriage. That will tell the coachman to drive us to my house."

Phillip did as she had asked. "Why do you stay here?" he ventured diffidently. "Surely you need not?"

"Why?" she echoed, sounding almost angry. "Because this is now my home and because it was my husband's wish that our child should be born here." Her momentary anger faded. "You . . . Phillip, you do not perhaps know that my husband died of his wounds at Balaclava?"

This was the question he had been dreading but, aware that he must answer it truthfully, Phillip braced himself.

"Yes, I know," he told her gently, his mind going back to the lamp-lit tent in the 93rd's lines, to which Catriona Moray and some of the Highlanders' women had carried the dying Narishkin, wrapping his broken body in a tartan plaid. "I was with him and we talked of you, madam—Mademoiselle Sophie. Of you and of the child . . . he was happy about the child, happy and proud."

"He wanted a son, Phillip," she whispered brokenly. "I pray that I may give him one—with all my heart I pray that I may give him one. He . . . how did he die?"

"Most gallantly, madame. And what could be done for him was done, I give you my word."

Mademoiselle Sophie's small, gloved hands were tightly clasped together, in a vain attempt to hide their trembling. "Phillip, how did you find him, when there were so many killed that day, so many on both sides? God Himself must have guided you, I. . . . Please tell me, please tell me all you can."

Phillip told her briefly, with scrupulous honesty, sparing her only the details of Andrei Narishkin's long agony and the fact that he had lain for so many hours on the field of battle before Catriona Moray had found him.

"Your name was constantly on his lips and at the end, he. . . . There was a girl, a young Highland girl—one of those who found and brought him in—who looked a little like you. She sat with him and he imagined that you were there, that you were caring for him. She played her part well and he was comforted."

"Oh, I am thankful." Her voice was choked with sobs but she controlled herself, bravely fighting back the tears. "I had wondered . . . about his death. I am glad that you were with him, you and that girl, glad and . . . grateful to you both, so truly grateful. Poor Andrei . . . he had not fully recovered from the wounds he received at the Alma." Remembering the empty sleeve and the dreadful, partially healed leg wound which, Catriona had told him, was already gangrenous, Phillip nodded, not trusting himself to speak. "He could have stayed here," Mademoiselle

Sophie went on, her hands, in the tightfitting black gloves, still moving restlessly. "But he would not. His regiment was with the Army of the Crimea. It was his duty, he said, to lead them when they went into battle. He could not walk but he could sit a horse and so, when the time came and I could not persuade him to wait until his wounds were healed, I—I went with him to Simpheropol and later to Backshi-Serai. He sent me back here when I—when we knew that I was with child. He would not permit me to stay with him."

So that had been her marriage, Phillip thought, the muscles of his throat tight . . . and he had envied Andrei Narishkin, God how he had envied him! And yet he had had so tragically little—a few short weeks and then the war had claimed him. He had fought at the Alma and returned from there, for another few weeks, with an arm amputated and one leg so badly injured that he could not walk and then, with everything to live for, he had thrown away his life in the shambles that had been Balaclava.

"Phillip. . . ." Mademoiselle Sophie's smile was tremulous but she managed to smile at him and he leaned forward, putting out a hand to separate her tightly-clasped fingers. They were cold, in spite of the gloves, and their trembling hurt him, as if her pain were his own. With his free hand, he took the ring she had given him from his pocket and, opening the case, held it out to her.

"Your husband returned this to me before he died. He said that the gift came from you both."

In the light from the mud-splashed carriage windows, the splendid stone gleamed dully and Mademoiselle Sophie looked down at it in startled recognition. "It is the one *I* gave you!"

"Yes, the same."

She sighed. "Our destinies and the destiny of this ring are strangely interwoven, aren't they, Phillip? And yet, when I was leaving the *Trojan* and asked you to accept it as a souvenir, I had no thought that it might take on such significance for us both . . . and for Andrei. I—I wanted

167

to make a small gift to you and I had nothing else of value with me. Nothing except this. It was my father's and . . . oh, Phillip, I am pleased that Andrei returned it to you, for . . . for many reasons, of which it is better not to speak, I think. Keep it, I beg you, as the . . . the souvenir I intended it to be. A souvenir by which to remember us both."

She laid it on his palm but Phillip shook his head. "I need no souvenir. I shall not forget you; I shall not forget either of you for as long as there is breath in my body. But if it has a destiny, will you permit me to make a gift of it now to your—your unborn child?"

Mademoiselle Sophie tried to answer him but could not. Finally, in tearful silence, she held out her hand to him and Phillip, after a moment's hesitation, took the ring from its case and slipped it carefully on to one of her small, cold fingers. For him, the action was strangely symbolic and, as she bent her head to look down at the intricately carved jewel now adorning her hand, the conviction that this was to be their farewell grew in his consciousness, until it became certainty. He had given her back the ring which had linked them together—given it of his own free will, without coercion—so that their destinies might no longer be interwoven. They would not meet again after he left for the cove this evening, he knew instinctively . . . yet could feel no regret. It had been enough that he had known and loved her, without hope and without fulfilment. This was the end of a road they had travelled together, the end, perhaps, of a dream for both of them and, since it could be no more than a dream, the only end.

As if she had intuitively guessed his thoughts, Mademoiselle Sophie raised her head, her eyes still bright with tears as they met his. She subjected him to a long and thoughtful scrutiny, her small, lovely face grave and unsmiling, yet oddly tender, and then whispered, as if it were a benediction, "The heart does not forget, Phillip, however sad it is . . . and my heart will not forget. May God be with you, now and always, my brave English sailor."

Phillip bore the hand he held to his lips and they sat facing each other—both wordless, because there were no words now to say—as the carriage entered the walled Narishkin estate and came clattering to a halt outside the heavy, iron-bound front door of the palace.

7.

PHILLIP left the ancient, stone-built palace of the Narish-kins at sunset, mounted on a horse from the palace stables and accompanied by the same giant footman, Boris, whom Mademoiselle Sophie had sent to guide him from the Cathedral, a few hours before.

"Boris is completely to be trusted," she had assured him. "He speaks no language save his own, alas—our peasants are not linguists—but I have instructed him to ride with you to your rendezvous and then, when you no longer require his services, to return here with both horses. It is unlikely that you will be stopped or questioned but, if you should be, Boris knows what he is to say. And should anyone molest you, he will defend you with his life."

As he trotted along the rutted coast road, with Boris a length behind him, Phillip found himself looking back on the hours he had spent as a guest in Andrei Narishkin's vast, opulent house with a sense almost of disbelief. He had been transfromed from a weary fugitive, in blood-stained clothes and with a battered head, into an honored guest, waited on by a small army of servants, who went about their business with silent efficiency. His wound had been cleansed and carefully bandaged; tea from a huge samovar had been served to him as he soaked his bruised and aching body in a tub of hot water, in which healing herbs had been infused to banish his stiffness.

When he was wrapped in a thick bathrobe and seated before a blazing log fire, a meal had been brought to him—course after course, accompanied by lavish offerings of wine and vodka—to which he had been too long without food to do full justice but had nevertheless enjoyed. Later the major-domo and a liveried manservant had assisted him to dress in a uniform they had contrived somehow to dry and renovate, so that it fitted him comfortably again, over fresh linen that was not his own but which fitted him as comfortably as the rest. His boatcloak had, however, defied their efforts and, in its place, the major-domo solemnly laid out a selection of fur-lined coats and cloaks, inviting him by signs to make his choice and seemingly blind to his repeated head-shakes until, eventually, finding it impossible to argue, he had chosen a garment most nearly resembling his own torn one. His fingers went out to touch the costly fur at his throat and he smiled wryly to himself, wondering what Ambrose Quinn would make of his reappearance in this borrowed and obviously Russian finery. His second-in-command would make something of it, no doubt—it would not be like him to miss such an opportunity for innuendo, if not open accusation—but . . . Quinn himself had some explaining to do, hadn't he?

Phillip sighed. His brain was clear now, his memory perfectly restored and, frowning, he cast his mind back to the scene on the cliff top that morning. True, he had been in a confused state this morning and might well have exaggerated the implications he had drawn from the position of the rock which had descended upon him with such force in the darkness. The infernal thing could have fallen accidentally, without Quinn's knowledge and without assistance from him or anyone else—the whole cliff face was a mass of loose, crumbling rock and piled-up boulders. On the other hand, the possibility that the rock fall had *not* been accidental could not entirely be dismissed. Quinn had known exactly where he had taken shelter and had, in fact, pointed out the cleft in the rock to him, suggesting it as a . . . what had he said? *A snug spot for a cat-nap* . . . yes, indeed he had, although it was somewhat out of character for him to concern himself with so trivial a matter as his commander's comfort.

Yet last night he had . . . Phillip involuntarily reined

171

in his horse, stifling an exclamation, and Boris drew level with him in swift alarm. He shook his head, smiling apologetically, and the man returned his smile and dropped back.

There was, perhaps, a way in which he could find out the truth, Phillip reflected, as his horse settled down once more to a steady trot. An inconclusive way but, for his own peace of mind, he had to know the trtuh, had to decide whether his injuries had been caused deliberately or accidentally last night. He might be unable to prove this, of course, but at least he himself would know and, in the future, would take good care never to relax his guard with Ambrose Quinn. It was curiously ironic, though, to reflect that he had been in less danger from his country's enemies today than—last night—he had been from his own second-in-command. *Had* been? No. . . . He stopped himself. *Might* have been; he had proved nothing against Quinn yet, even to himself. In fairness to the man, he must keep an open mind, until he was able to do so, must give him the benefit of the doubt, as—he shrugged—as he had given his First Lieutenant the benefit of the doubt when little Lightfoot had fallen from the rigging, and as the court of inquiry into the death of Commander Francis Willoughby had also elected to do, according to Surgeon Fraser. . . .

Phillip's mouth tightened and he dug his heels into his horse's sides, suddenly impatient, his mind made up. He would put his suspicions to the test, he decided, and either justify them or dismiss them completely from his thoughts. It would be simple enough to make the test, in all conscience. He had only to return to Quinn's "snug spot" on the cliff face and wait there . . . wait, to see who came to him. If Quinn came, he would know and all his doubts would be resolved, because Quinn would *not* come unless he expected to find him still lying there injured, as he had left him . . . or even dead.

He breathed a deep, troubled sigh, suddenly sick with revulsion at the thought of what he would have to do and reluctant, even now, to believe that his half-formed suspicions could be justified. Quinn was a British naval officer and. . . .

Boris touched his arm, pointing ahead of them to where, bathed in the crimson glow of the sinking sun, the British squadron lay at anchor. He nodded in acknowledgement and shook off his depression, resolutely thrusting the thought of Quinn to the back of his mind. Kneeing his horse to a canter, he breasted the rise ahead of his escort but, after a quick glance to satisfy himself that the ships had not changed position, he did not draw rein. All appeared to be well; the *Gladiator* was still flying her white flag of truce at the main and his own *Huntress* was continuing to keep her distance from the rest of the squadron. His mission was complete, thanks to Mademoiselle Sophie, so that the sooner he rejoined his ship and delivered his report the better. He turned in his saddle to wave to Boris and, when the Russian caught up with him, again put his horse to a canter.

They turned off the road, ten minutes later, and crossed the marshy wasteland in semi-darkness, slowing down to a cautious trot as the light faded. At the cliff top, Phillip dismounted and gave his reins to the big footman, indicating by signs that they had reached the end of their journey. But Boris did not immediately accept his dismissal; reaching into his saddle bag, he brought out a bottle of wine and provisions of some kind, wrapped in a linen napkin which, dismounting, he laid at Phillip's feet. Then he bowed and remounted and was swiftly lost to sight in the gathering darkness, the thud of his horses' hooves on the iron-hard ground continuing for a short while after the darkness had swallowed them up. When this sound had also faded and he knew that he was alone, Phillip made a careful reconnaissance of the cliff top and the shore of the cove. Satisfied that both were deserted, he located the cleft in the rock which Quinn had found for him and, having retrieved the lantern—still lying, up-ended, as he had left it—he took the thoughtfully provided food and wine and, lowering himself on to the ledge, settled down to await the arrival of the gig.

The boat came, commendably on time, heralded as before by the muted splash of oars and, as before, its approach was cautious, which suggested that Lieutenant Quinn was again in command. It was now so dark that Phillip could not see the gig from his hiding-place but the sounds of its coming were borne to him quite clearly across the water, and he heard its bows ground on the stony foreshore some ten minutes after entering the cove.

His pulses quickened, as he crouched in the darkness, waiting for men to splash ashore and for one man—or, perhaps, two—to scale the cliff in search of him. But, to his bewilderment, no one came and, after only four or at most five minutes, he heard Quinn bark the order to shove off. The realization that his gig was about to put back to the *Huntress* without him came as an unexpected shock, and almost decided him to abandon the trap he had baited. He was on his feet, hands cupped about his mouth preparatory to calling the boat back, when he thought better of it.

He had proved nothing, had neither allayed nor confirmed his suspicions and, he told himself wryly, he must do one or the other if he were ever to know peace of mind where Ambrose Quinn was concerned. The gig would, in any case, return to the cove an hour before daybreak, in obedience to his orders, and he could wait until then . . . another night in the open might not be pleasant but would do him no great harm. It was cold but he had food and wine, as well as the splendid fur-lined cloak with which Mademoiselle Sophie's major-domo had supplied him, and there was plenty of shelter. He could afford to bide his time and it would give him the opportunity to think and, perhaps, to decide, about Quinn.

He let his hands fall and resumed his seat, brows puckered as he endeavored to analyse the possible reasons for his First Lieutenant's behavior. Ambrose Quinn, he reflected, was nobody's fool, and he was not in the habit of taking risks. Obviously he would play for safety now if he had anything to hide. Yet he had acted rather oddly. He had made no search, even of the foreshore of the cove, and had permitted none of his gig's crew to set foot on land. Why? There had been no warning light, the cove had been silent and deserted but, although his orders allowed for a wait of ten to fifteen minutes, Quinn had barely waited for five minutes before putting out again—an action, surely, that required explanation, since the gig was in no apparent danger?

Phillip stared into the darkness, his eyes narrowed as he listened to the receding splash of oars and endeavored to decide whether his second-in-command's failure to make even a cursry search for him could be construed as the act of an innocent man or—he shifted uneasily, his back against the hard, unyielding surface of the rock—or as that of a man with attempted murder on his conscience—because this, in effect, was what it amounted to, wasn't it? He sighed. Well, supposing it was, supposing that Quinn had known, when he entered the cove this evening, that his commander was in all probability lying injured near the top of the cliff, what line of reasoning would have dictated his actions?

He lay back, pulling his cloak about him. He had most of the night to give to the solution of his problem, so he might as well make use of the time at his disposal, he told himself, and consider the question logically, from every angle. It was an ill wind, for at least it would serve to occupy his mind, keep his thoughts from straying to Mademoiselle Sophie, of whom he dared not let himself think. Not yet, not until the pain of their parting had dulled a little. He felt his throat muscles stiffen and forced himself to concentrate on Quinn. For a start, he would try to put himself in Quinn's place, he decided, and assess the situation through the eyes of his First Lieutenant.

Taking it then that he *had* been responsible for the dislodged rock—deliberately or even accidentally—would he have scaled the cliff this evening to look for his injured commander? Or would he have postponed the search, until there was a better than even chance that the unfortunate fellow had succumbed to his injuries? In Quinn's eyes, his commander's failure to meet the gig on the beach just now would suggest that the rock had found its target and that, as a result, he was dead or dying—but this was by no means certain. The missile could have struck him only a glancing blow—as had, in fact, been the case—from which he had recovered, partially or completely. This contingency could not be ruled out. In Quinn's place, Phillip thought grimly, he would *not* have ruled it out. He would have postponed the search—as Quinn had done—until, adhering strictly to his orders, the gig returned next morning to the cove, because. . . . he frowned, not liking the trend of his thoughts.

Quinn's brief call at the cove a few mintues ago would have confirmed the fact that his commander had been unable to make the first rendezvous. The reason for his having failed to do so remained still in doubt but there was a strong possibility that the injured man was lying on the cliff face, the "snug spot" in which he had sought refuge having now become his final resting-place. If he were not yet dead, a second night's exposure to the icy cold would almost certainly bring about his death: there was no disputing *that* supposition.

Despite the protection of his thick, fur-lined cloak, Phillip shivered. Dear heaven, it *was* cold now that the sun had gone, he thought, and began to regret his implusive decision to spend a second night in this desolate place. But he was here and it was too late for regrets. He sat up and, opening the bottle of wine which Mademoiselle Sophie had sent for him, poured a liberal draught of it down his throat. The wine, as he hoped it would, induced an illusion of warmth and well-being and, after a while, he forced himself to continue his analysis, still viewing the situation from Ambrose Quinn's angle, and still supposing the man guilty of a deliberate attempt on his life.

By putting off the search for him until morning, Quinn could allow for any eventuality because he had committed himself to nothing and time was on his side. If his commander survived two long, cold nights on the cliff face, he would be in no condition to make accusations or even to remember what had occurred in the interim. If he did not survive, then his body would be found by the landing-party and his death attributed to an unfortunate accident —or even to enemy action—for which, of course, no blame could be attached to Quinn. He could claim that he had carried out to the letter the instructions he had been given, while quite truthfully pleading ignorance of the reason why his commander should have gone ashore, in enemy-held territory and in flagrant branch of the flag of truce the squadron was flying.

Even if his commander's injuries were slight and he reappeared on the foreshore next morning, Quinn need only deny that he had seen or heard the rock fall or that he had been aware that his commander had been struck by it. He would have little to fear, so long as he stuck to his denial—as he had done quite successfully in Lightfoot's case, Phillip reminded himself glumly. No one could expect him to investigate an accident of which he had not been aware . . . and yet he *must* have been aware of what had happened. Damn it, he had been so close at hand, he could not have failed to hear that rock crashing down, whether or not the darkness had hidden it from his sight and even if it had been dislodged accidentally. But . . . he had returned to the gig, without waiting to ascertain that his commander had suffered no ill effects, he . . . Phillip swore softly. He took another gulp of the wine, suddenly experiencing a strong desire to drink himself into a stupor, in order to escape from the torment of his own thoughts and the conclusions he was beginning to draw from these. Then he capped the bottle and laid it down at his side. He hadn't yet done, he chided himself. In justice to Ambrose Quinn, he had now to go back over the same ground, assessing the whole series of events on the basis that his second-in-command was innocent of any attempt —deliberate or otherwise—to do him injury or to take his life.

For the next two hours, battling against an almost overwhelming longing for sleep, he compelled himself to review everything that had occurred on the cliff top the previous evening, from every possible angle and to the best of his recollection. At times he endeavored to defend Quinn, at others to condemn him, going carefully over what they had said to each other both privately and in the hearing of the two seamen, who had carried Graham down to the boat—the Welsh lad, Williams, and the one-time fisherman, Jackson. But, for all his efforts, he came no nearer to a solution of his problem. Whether Quinn had hurled that rock at him intentionally or whether the fall had been sheer chance, he could prove nothing, he decided wearily, and without proof—however strong his suspicions might be—his hands were tied and he would be compelled to give his First Lieutenant the benefit of whatever doubt existed.

At length, despairing of ever being able to find a satisfactory answer to any of the questions which plagued him, Phillip ate the food Boris had left with him and settled down to uneasy slumber, so numb with cold that he had twice to swing himself back to the summit of the cliff and there pace up and down, stamping his feet to restore his circulation. It was a clear, moonlit night and he could see quite a distance across the flat, marshy plain, although a low-lying, patchy mist, creeping slowly in from the sea, obscured his view of the entrance to the cove.

Well, that would be to the advantage of the gig, he reflected, and possibly to his own, when the time came for his second attempt to set a trap for Ambrose Quinn. He smothered a sigh and once again lowered his cramped body into the cleft in the rock, swallowing the last few mouthfuls of wine before lying down. This time, sleep came more easily and deeply but he wakened, after what seemed to him quite a short while, with the uneasy conviction that something was wrong. He lay there tensely, listening for whatever sound had awakened him and flexing his stiff limbs, in the hope that they would obey him, should he need to move swiftly. Then, without warning, two hands came out of the darkness above his head, one to grasp him by the shoulder, the other to close over his mouth to prevent him crying out.

Still bemused by sleep, his first thought was that Quinn

178

had come, for the purpose of finishing what he had started, and he struggled desperately to free himself. But the hands holding him down were immensely strong . . . yet, he realized, in bewilderment, their grasp was quite gentle. Whoever had found his hiding-place clearly had no desire to harm him and, as soon as he had ceased to fight against them, the hands relaxed their grip, permitting him to sit up. When he did so, still too numb with cold to rise to his feet without assistance, he found himself looking into the round, smiling face of Boris, Mademoiselle Sophie's giant footman. The man held a finger to his lips, to enjoin silence and then assisted Phillip to join him on the summit of the cliff. He was on foot, his horses nowhere to be seen, and he gestured urgently to the cove below them, muttering something unintelligible in his own language.

The mist still lay low over the water but above it, lying perhaps half a mile off the entrance, Phillip could just make out the riding-lights of a ship. As he stared at her, the moon came from behind a cloud and he recognized her, from her rigging and upperworks, as his own *Huntrees*. But what, in the name of all that was wonderful, he asked himself, was she doing here? Why had she shifted from her anchorage, to lie off the cove? As if in answer to his unvoiced question, Boris pointed, again saying something he could not understand, and Phillip bit back an exclamation of dismay as he saw a light flash from the *Huntress*'s upper deck. It was followed by a second and a third, in rapid and rhythmic succession—three short and then one long . . . *interrogative*. She was making a signal, evidently intended for himself which, after watching the light flashes for a few moments, he read as: *Are you there?*

He stared across the intervening stretch of water in angry disbelief. What strange game was Ambrose Quinn playing now, he asked himself. Had he not left specific instructions that the ship was to remain at her anchorage, astern of the rest of the squadron, and that on no account were signals of any kind to be made to him during the time he was ashore? All four ships of the squadron could be seen from the road and the coastal fort and, depleted

179

though the garrison of the town might be, it was unlikely that the fort, at least, would fail to post a night watch for as long as enemy ships lay in the offing. By shifting her anchorage, the *Huntress* must, sooner or later, draw the attention of the fort look-outs to this cove and it would certainly not be long before a cavalry patrol was sent to his hiding-place to investigate the reason for the signals, which—Phillip's mouth tightened—which, presumably, was Lieutenant Quinn's intention, although he was at a loss to understand why. But he wasted no time in trying to think of reasons; his brain, wide awake now, was racing, as he considered what he must do.

It could well be disastrous for Captain Broke's squadron, as well as for himself, if he were found here, in breach of the truce and . . . he caught his breath in agonized realization of how disastrous his arrest, in these circumstances, might prove for Mademoiselle Sophie. He had been seen leaving the Cathedral this morning, escorted by her footman in his distinctive livery and seen, also, probably, entering her coach so that, for her sake, he dare not stay here, dare not let himself be taken, still in the company of that same all-too-conspicuous servant. He turned to Boris, with the intention of sending him back to his mistress at once but the man gestured into the darkness behind him, indicating by signs that he had the horses tethered nearby. The loyal fellow must have waited, Phillip thought, having realized that the gig had left without him, presumably in obedience to Mademoiselle Sophia's orders, to make sure that he returned safely to his ship. And had not Mademoiselle Sophie said that, if need be, Boris would defend him with his life?

He hesitated in momentary indecision, reluctant to keep the footman with him and thus put his life at risk. But . . . it would take a cavalry patrol, riding hard, some twenty-five to thirty minutes to reach here from the town and, if he went with Boris now, they would have a good chance of eluding the patrol, so long as it was dark. He glanced skyward, frowning. It would not be dark for much more than an hour and a half, he calculated. In daylight, even on horseback, it would not be easy to escape pursuit and he could no longer seek sanctuary at the Narishkin palace, lest his presence there endanger Mademoiselle Sophie. At all costs he must avoid that and, if he kept Boris with him, he might be exposing her to considerable danger, he was unhappily aware. Besides, his mission was completed and there was his report to deliver to the Admiral. If he did not get back to the *Huntress* now, it might be days before he was able to do so and each day he remained ashore would add to the risk of capture, once the hunt for him was on. Broke's squadron could not stay at anchor off Odessa indefinitely, either. Once a reply to his note was delivered, Broke would have to put to sea, taking the *Huntress* with him.

The gig was due to pick him up very soon, unless . . . Phillip became aware of a swift, prickling sensation of alarm. Did the signal mean that the gig would *not* be sent for him, unless he replied to it? Oh, dear God, was that Quinn's game? Was that why his second-in-command had made the signal, why was he continuing to make it at regular intervals—to afford an excuse for not sending the gig to pick him up? Or was he using those flashing lights from the *Huntress*'s deck to direct an enemy search party to the cove, so as to ensure his capture, if he were alive or the discovery of his body, if he were not?

It was hard to believe, even of Quinn, but, Phillip had bitterly to admit, it was a possibility he could not discount. He wondered for how long the signals had been coming before Boris had wakened him. Not for long, probably, since he had not slept for more than ten or, perhaps, fifteen minutes. But even that might cut down the time he had estimated for a cavalry patrol to reach here from the town, reducing by nearly half the margin of safety he had allowed himself. Boris caught urgently at his arm, pointing to their rear and clearly anxious that he should mount his horse and make a run for it but he shook his head, his mind finally made up.

He would endeavor to get back to his ship, he decided, he *must* get back to her, whatever the risk. It was his duty, if what he had achieved in Odessa was of any value at all. He had already waited too long, thanks to his abortive attempt to set a trap for Quinn—an attempt which, he recognized regretfully now, had been a grave dereliction of duty, for which he had no excuse and could only reconcile with his conscience if he did rejoin his ship without further delay.

But how? If he called the gig in at once, ordered it to lie off the entrance to the cove—out of range of the muskets or carbines of any search party that might arrive on the scene—he would have a chance. A slim chance, admittedly, but he would have to take it. He could order the boat in, if it was safe to do so, or, if not, then . . . he shuddered at the prospect. If not, he would have to brave the icy water and swim out to the boat; there was no alternative.

Boris again tugged at his arm and Phillip repeated his headshake, trying to make the fellow understand that he was to make good his own escape and, whether or not he had made his meaning clear, the Russian released his arm and obediently vanished into the darkness. Relieved, Phillip bent down, feeling for the lantern he had hidden in the cleft of the cliff face when he had first taken shelter there. He must stop Quinn's signals, that was imperative, and send his order for the boat for, without a boat, he could not hope to reach the *Huntress*. A swim of a hundred yards or so might be possible—just possible—but it would, he knew, be suicidal to try to swim much further. He found the lantern and, with numb fingers, struggled to set it alight, succeeding in doing so after two abortive attempts. Then, shielding the light with his body, he crouched low beneath the overhanging cliff top and opened the signal shutter.

The naval code was a simple one, easy enough to remember but requiring time to send and Phillip knew that his time was running out. His message must be brief but explicit, for it could be sent only once and he found himself praying that Acting-Mate Grey was on the *Huntress*'s deck to read it. He sent *Stop*—three long flashes—

182

and to his heartfelt relief, the signals from the ship ceased at once. Perhaps Grey was on deck, he thought; the acknowledgement had been almost instantaneous. His fingers getting colder and more clumsy in his haste, he sent the rest of his message and thankfully closed the shutter but, in the act of extinguishing the signal lantern, changed his mind. Shuttered, it would be quite safe to take with him to the foreshore and should an enemy patrol appear before the gig entered the cove, he could use the lamp for its original purpose—to serve as a warning to the boat commander to back off, which—Phillip smiled wryly to himself . . . which had been Quinn's suggestion, he recalled and, ironically, had proved invaluable to him in this crisis.

He straightened up, still holding the lantern against his chest and, to his dismay, heard the pounding of horses' hooves coming towards him. His first instinctive impulse was to hurl himself down the cliff in the hope that he might gain the foreshore before he was seen or his descent could be heard, but then he realized that the hoofbeats were too few for a cavalry patrol and he stayed where he was, ready for instant flight should this prove necessary. There were only two horses approaching him, one riderless and he guessed that Boris, misunderstanding his attempt to communicate his instructions by signs, had returned, bringing both horses with him. How, in heaven's name, he asked himself, was he to persuade the faithful giant to seek safety and leave him to his fate, when the man so obstinately refused to accept his dismissal? Boris was trying very hard to tell him something but he had no idea what it was until, climbing up beside him, he saw lights flickering on the curving coast road, as nearly as he could judge about two miles away. If this were the patrol, then he might just have time to call his gig into the cove to pick him up before the cavalrymen crossed the marsh, Phillip calculated, but it was going to be a close-run thing and he had somehow to induce Boris to abandon him.

He gestured to the cove, going through the motions of rowing and then pointing in the direction of the *Huntress* and, at last, saw comprehension dawn on the Russian's round, moon face. He fumbled in his pockets, searching for some reward to give him but all he could find were his pocket watch and compass. The watch had been a gift from his father and, on this account, he was loathe to part with it but Boris deserved some recognition for his tenacious loyalty and, after only a momentary hesitation, he unclipped the chain and thrust the silver timepiece into the footman's hand. Then, realizing that when he waded —or swam—out to meet the incoming boat, he might have to leave his borrowed cloak on the foreshore, he quickly divested himself of the garment and handed this, too, to Boris.

"Narishkin!" he said aloud and pointed in the general direction of Odessa. "Sophia Mikailovna Narishkina . . ." adding, in halting Russian, "Go . . . go quickly! *Je te donne congé . . . laisses-moi partir!*" He had no idea whether he had the right words or whether Boris had understood his schoolboy French but his gifts had the desired effect. The man pocketed the watch and draped the cloak about his massive shoulders, a pleased smile lighting his face as he did so. Still mindful of his duty, however, he pointed to the cove, the gesture almost pleading and only when Phillip nodded acquiescence did he take his leave. A hand raised in parting salute, he set spurs to his horse and was off at full gallop across the desolate marshland, the led horse pounding after him.

Phillip waited no longer. Slithering and sliding like a drunken man, he flung himself down the cliff face, careless of how much noise he made or how many loose rocks he sent cascading down ahead of him. He gained the beach, bruised and breathless but somehow, miraculously, still clutching the signal lamp and limped painfully across to the water's edge. He was below the level of the sea mist now, he realized, and was thankful, since the mist— though patchy—meant that neither he nor the gig would present an easy target to any marksman firing down at them from the top of the cliff. It would also mean that the gig's commander might experience some difficulty in reading his signal but, if he kept his eyes on the shore, he ought to be able to make out the glow from the signal lamp and, so long as this was intermittent, there should be no likelihood of his mistaking it for the warning to lie off the entrance to the cove. Unless Quinn were in command of the gig. . . . in the act of raising the lantern shutter to make sure that the candle was still alight, Phillip let it fall back into place, the brief elation he had felt on gaining the beach fading abruptly.

With his First Lieutenant in command, his signals might be ignored or deliberately misread, he thought. But *would* Quinn be in command? He would not risk his neck, if he could help it, being Quinn and, if he had good reason to believe that the gig's crew might be met—or even be taken—by the enemy, surely he would be more likely to send O'Hara or Cochrane, perhaps, in his place? Sweet heaven, of course he would! Quinn hadn't merely good reason, he had every reason under the sun to believe that, by this time, a Russian patrol would be on its way to the cove! Hadn't he done all he possibly could to draw the attention of the fort's look-outs to the cove, with his infernal, unauthorized flashing light signals and his shift of anchorage? What he hoped to gain by his efforts was beyond comprehension . . . unless he intended to recall the gig before it could enter the cove or wanted to justify his failure to send it at all. In either case, he had gone to an extraordinary amount of trouble to achieve very little and laid himself open to a charge of disobeying his orders, which wasn't like Quinn. It wasn't like him at all . . . unless he *wanted* the gig's crew to be taken, together with the person, if living, or the dead body of his Captain. Could that be the explanation of his recent maneuvers?

If it was, then surely . . . Phillip swore, aloud and bitterly. Fool that he was, he reproached himself, not to have seen what Quinn's game was until this moment! He had thought it a strange game but he hadn't understood, hadn't guessed for what stakes the man was playing or to what lengths he was prepared to go to ensure the safety of his own skin.

His hands clenched impotently at his sides. He had answers to the questions which had plagued him for so long, answers in which he found it well nigh impossible to believe, but they fitted the facts. Not even Quinn would have gone as far as he had tonight unless he had attempted murder on his conscience—attempted murder or worse —and, in consequence, feared for his skin. Although, Phillip realized, it was of small use to him now to know, with growing certainty, that the rock fall the previous evening had been deliberately contrived to kill or maim him . . . because Ambrose Quinn would see to it that he did not return to the *Huntress*. A whole boat's crew would, if necessary, be sacrificed to prevent his doing so and to enable Quinn to go through the motions of rescuing him . . . motions that were not intended to succeed. He shivered, the cold biting into his very bones now that he lacked the protection of his cloak.

The proof would come within the next five minutes, he thought wretchedly. If his deductions were correct, Quinn would send the volunteer crew with the gig this time— a crew that included Grey, O'Hara and O'Leary; and, very probably, Williams and Jackson, the two seamen who had been on shore when that thrice-damned rock had fallen and who, no doubt, had heard it fall. There would be a risk that either or both might have wondered why the First Lieutenant had failed to hear it and why he had taken no action and so, like the rest, they would be sent with the gig . . . Graham, too, perhaps, if he had recovered sufficiently. As Russian prisoners-of-war their recollections would not harm Quinn, and if he were to lose a boat's crew, he would obviously select one that he could afford to do without. Phillip gave vent to a tense and troubled sigh.

For God's sake, he asked himself, was he going out of his mind? Or was this—as he had thought it must be, when he had first recovered consciousness on that precarious ledge of rock—was this a nightmare, an ugly dream from which he would waken? He found himself praying that it might be a dream, unwilling even now to believe that any man, least of all an officer of Her Majesty's Navy, could be capable of such callous and even treasonable behavior as that which he was being forced to attribute to Ambrose Quinn.

Yet the facts did fit. They were as logical as, waking or dreaming, his deductions were. With the gig's crew taken, as well as himself, Quinn would be left in command of the *Huntress* for the second time, with a clean sheet and an effectively purged ship's company. He might, with reason, expect to be confirmed in command when he brought the ship back to the Fleet anchorage and made his report, the accuracy of which could not be contested and in which, obviously, he himself would figure with credit. Not too much credit, perhaps, but he would appear to have done all he could to rescue his late commander from a situation into which that officer's own impetuosity had precipitated him . . . just as he had done all he could to save his other unfortunate commander, Francis Willoughby, from the death he had so tragically brought upon himself.

And, if there should be a court of inquiry, Quinn would be exonerated, possibly even commended, because . . . clearly across the intervening stretch of water came the splash of oars and Phillip stiffened. The gig was approaching and would wait at the entrance to the cove until he ordered it in. His frozen fingers felt for the key of the signal lamp he was holding but, before depressing it, he turned, listening intently for the arrival of the cavalry patrol on the cliff top. He could see little for the mist but . . . was it his imagination or was that the pounding of hooves that he heard? He stood immobile, straining both ears and eyes, and heard the sound again, unmistakably —the patrol was advancing across the marsh, steadily at a trot. He could make out the thud of iron-shod hooves, the jingle of bridles and a slithering sound, as one of the horses stumbled. Quinn's timing, he reflected cynically, could scarcely have been better.

He opened the shutter of his lantern to allow a steady beam of light to shine from it and raised the lantern high

187

above his head. Small though the glow it emitted, the gig's commander ought to see it. He glanced back in the direction of the cliff, realizing, with a flash of wry amusement, that he need not have worried about his warning to the gig's commander to back off. The cavalry patrol carried several flaming torches with them—the lights, of course, that he had glimpsed on the coast road—and these were shining through the mist, a much clearer and more menacing injunction than his own could possibly have been and one the gig's commander could not ignore . . . unless his name was O'Hara. Heaven grant that it was Cochrane . . . Phillip let his lamp fall. Moving a few paces to his right, he kicked off his boots and started to unbutton his jacket, only to think better of it. While he clothing might impede his movements a little when he tried to swim, he would need its protection against the cold. It would be a swim of close on a hundred and fifty yards, and. . . . he tensed, as a subdued hail carried across the water to him.

"Beach ahoy! Captain sir—enemy patrol to your rear! I can see your light. May I come in, sir?"

It was O'Hara's voice, distorted by the speaking trumpet but shrill with suppressed excitement and Phillip's heart sank. Quinn, as expected, had chosen his boat commander well, for O'Hara, despite his size, had all the courage in the world and he would come in, orders or no orders, if he thought his Captain was in danger. Conscious that his sole remaining chance to save the gig's crew and himself lay in convincing O'Hara that he was in control of the situation, Phillip cupped his hands about his mouth and yelled at the pitch of his lungs that the boat was to hold station and come no closer.

"I'm coming out to you, Mr. O'Hara. Prepare to return to the ship immediately. On no account enter this cove. That is an order, you understand."

Aware that his voice would have been heard by the patrol, he did not wait for O'Hara's acknowledgement but, taking a deep breath, ran as far as he could to his right and flung himself into the water. Despite the fact that he

188

was fully clothed, the icy chill took his breath away and he floundered helplessly, waist deep, before he reached deeper water and was able at last to head in the right direction. His arms and legs felt like lead but he contrived to swim a few strokes and, after that, it was easier.

He had always been a strong swimmer and he was making good progress until a ragged volley came from the cliff top and, like a crowd of angry hornets, a hail of musket balls spattered the water ahead of him, forcing him to change direction. The Russians were firing blindly into the mist and, with little idea of the position of their target, their aim was poor, but they kept up their fire, stray shots more than once striking uncomfortably close. Phillip was tiring rapidly in the intense cold and, when cramp seized him, he knew that it was all over. He had covered less than half the distance to the waiting boat and now he could barely keep his head above water.

His gamble had failed but there was no help for it, he could not go on, could not drive his frozen body or his leaden limbs to swim one more stroke. All he could hope to do now, he told himself, was to save the gig's crew from any attempt at useless heroics on the part of their young commander. Quinn should not have their lives, please God he should not! Even if he took the *Huntress*, he would have to take her with these men—whom he had selected as expendable—and perhaps, one day, one of them might remember enough to draw the conclusions *he* had drawn and Nemesis would seek out Ambrose Quinn and destroy him as, in justice, he deserved . . . if there was any justice.

Phillip gritted his teeth and, summoning the last reserves of his strength, he ordered O'Hara to return to the ship. His voice was a harsh croak, coming from somewhere deep in his straining chest but he knew it had carried to the boat when someone—not O'Hara—acknowledged the order with an obedient, "Aye, aye, sir!" Sick with relief, he recognized the voice as Grey's but was too far gone to wonder what had happened to O'Hara until, using the speaking trumpet this time, Grey called out to him again.

"I'll obey your order, sir, but keep going—keep going for just a little longer, if you can. Two of our lads are coming to your aid. You'll make it, sir, if you hang on!"

Two men, two more swimmers in this terrible, freezing sea . . . and one of them probably O'Hara! Phillip tried to warn them, tried to tell them to go back to the boat while they still could but his voice was now only a faint, half-strangled whisper in his throat and he knew that they could not hear him. He did his best to keep going, as Grey had urged, but an overwhelming lethargy was starting to take possession of his body and invade his senses, so that it no longer seemed of the slightest concern to him whether he sank or remained afloat. Indeed, he thought weakly, if he drowned, he might well disappear without trace and then no accusations of truce-breaking could be levelled at Captain Broke.

From the beach, he could dimly hear the clamor of raised voices, as men shouted unintelligible words to each other but this did not worry him and a fresh fusillade of musket shots, screaming overhead, left him unmoved. He felt himself sinking and did not struggle, even when the sea closed over his head. His body rose sluggishly to the surface and he let it drift where it would, suddenly seeing Mademoiselle Sophie's small, sweet face. like a vision from heaven, floating above and ahead of him and moving in the direction of the beach and the clamorous voices. He felt himself drifting after his vision and realized dimly that the tide must have changed but he had neither the will nor the strength to resist its pull, although it was taking him away from the boat and the men whom Grey had said were swimming to his aid.

When hands seized him roughly by the shoulders, he did not question whose they were and did not struggle against them and he only knew that he had been taken prisoner by the enemy when he found himself lying on his back on the stony foreshore of the cove. A number of shadowy figures in long greatcoats were grouped about him, talking in a tongue he did not understand, one of whom aimed a kick at him with a spurred boot. Although the kick connected with his ribs, Phillip was silent, conscious of no pain and no resentment. His refusal to cry out appeared to annoy the soldier, who struck him again, this time with the butt of his carbine on the side of the head and, though he did not feel the blow, Phillip was relieved when another man—evidently an officer—intervened, curtly barking out an order, which he emphasized by thrusting his assailant aside. The soldier who had struck him sullenly took off his greatcoat and, kneeling at Phillip's side, covered him with it, his reward for this compulsory act of self-sacrifice a blow across the shoulders from his officer's saber.

The greatcoat did not noticeably add to his comfort but the fact that he had been given it nevertheless raised Phillip's flagging hopes that his captors did not intend to let him die and he rallied a little, managing to turn over on to his side so that he could look out across the cove. There was no sign of the gig and the shooting had ceased. Young Grey, then, must have kept his word and returned to the *Huntress*—but there were men in the water, some of them waist-deep, making a great commotion and shouting at one another and, even as he watched, he saw two of them bend to pick up something which, seemingly, had come floating in on the tide. Their cries of triumph suggested that, whatever it was, their prize must have been the object for which they had been searching and Phillip stared in dismay as, almost with one accord, they all splashed back through the shallows, bearing what could only be a body between them. A small body in dark clothing . . . O'Hara's body, it had to be, he knew, and he prayed despairingly that the boy might have survived his ordeal in the icy water of the cove and the musket balls that had rained down upon it as he swam.

The cavalrymen dumped their burden unceremoniously beside him and, making a great effort to overcome his lethargy, Phillip rolled over and succeeded in putting out a hand to touch O'Hara's face. But there was no feeling in his fingers and, to his distress, the boy did not respond either to his touch or to his croaking whisper and, ex-

191

hausted by the effort he had made, he fell back, gasping for breath. His brain was clear enough, if a trifle slow, but his body seemed to be virtually paralyzed and he wondered for how much longer he could last before, like O'Hara, he lapsed into unconsciousness. Unconsciousness or—again he looked apprehensively into the midshipman's face—or death. The face was a white blur in the dim light and he could detect no sign of life in it at all, no flicker of movement, nothing to give him hope that his prayer might have been heard and answered. He let his heavy eyelids fall and went on praying.

A fresh commotion among the Russian cavalrymen roused him—he had no idea how much later—and he opened his eyes to see that they had lit a fire. The brushwood and flotsam they had collected was damp and relctant, at first, to burn, but after a while the fire took hold and the damp wood blazed away, the soldiers clustering round it to warm themselves and dry their saturated uniforms. Two of them, evidently on instructions from their commander, came to him and stripped him of his own wet garments, which they carried off to dry at the bonfire, wrapping him meantime in a horse blanket, in addition to the greatcoat. The same two men performed a like service for O'Hara and Phillip again attempted to speak to him. The boy did not answer but at least, he thought, must still have retained a spark of life or their captors would not have troubled to strip him.

The heat of the fire began gradually to restore some feeling to his numbed body, but, with the return of sensation, came pain so excruciating that Phillip was hard put to it not to scream his agony aloud. He fought against it for some time and then lapsed into a semi-conscious state, from which he finally emerged to find himself lying full length on what he supposed was a horse-drawn cart. It was broad daylight and O'Hara was lying beside him wrapped, as he himself still was, in a horse blanket. The cart was unsprung and, though lined with straw, its jolting jarred every aching bone in his body so that, once again, he had to exert all the self-control of which he was

192

capable to stop himself crying out. But, apparently also roused by the jolting, he felt O'Hara stir and, to his joy, saw him open his eyes a few minutes later. He groped for the boy's hand and this time felt an answering pressure, as his fingers closed about it.

"Sir . . . sir, you're alive!"

The voice was faint and coming from what seemed a long way away but Phillip heard it thankfully. "Yes," he managed, from between stiff and swollen lips. "And you too, Mr. O'Hara, heaven be praised!"

To his consternation, the boy started to apologize in a choked whisper, for having failed to reach him. "It was . . . the tide, sir. It . . . turned and there was such a strong current running, I—I couldn't get near you and then I got cramp. I'm sorry, sir, truly I am, I——"

Phillip cut short the apology, conscious of a lump in his throat that he could not swallow. "You did your best, lad . . . and better than most grown men could have done. I commend your courage; needless to say, I've never doubted it. But you ought never to have tried to reach me. You should have stayed with your boat and taken her back to the ship, as I ordered you to. I had good reason for giving you that order, believe me."

"But, sir," O'Hara protested, sounding much stronger now, "I *am* your gig's midshipman and it was my duty to bear a hand when you needed one. Anyway, that was how I looked at it, sir, at the time. I couldn't just leave you to drown. And I knew Mr. Grey would carry out your order and take the gig back for me. I only let him volunteer on the understanding that it was *my* command and that he wouldn't interfere, whatever happened and whatever I decided to do. I made him give me his word on that, before we left the ship . . . so it was my fault, sir, not his, and I'm sorry."

This boy apologizing, Phillip thought, for an act of selfless heroism few lads of his age would have attempted! He wanted to tell him so but knew that, in the interests of discipline, he could not. Although, he promised himself, if he ever got back to the British Fleet, O'Hara

193

should be given an official commendation . . . and the commendation would make no mention of the order he had ignored.

"Very well, Mr. O'Hara." His tone was gruff, gruffer than he had meant it to be, the lump in his throat still impeding his speech. "Who else volunteered?"

"For the gig's crew, sir? Oh, they were all volunteers —the First Lieutenant picked them." O'Hara named his crew and Phillip heard, without surprise, that Williams and Jackson had been among the picked men and, of course, O'Leary. "I think O'Leary tried to swim to you, too, sir," the boy went on. "But I'm not sure—it was all a bit confused, you see. He didn't make it, did he, sir? But he's not here, so I hope the gig picked him up."

"So do I, Mr. O'Hara," Phillip said, tight-lipped. Dear God, he thought bitterly, if this affair had cost O'Leary's life, he would make Ambrose Quinn pay for it, if it was the last thing he ever did. He questioned O'Hara about the selection of his crew and, after telling him all he could, the boy added, "Oh, I almost forgot, sir. Your brother, Mr. Hazard—he's still laid up—but he sent for me before the gig was called away. He said that if we ran into trouble and were taken by the enemy, we'd be questioned about our signals and the ship's shift of anchorage . . . and possibly about you, sir, if they found you. But he said that if we told them that we'd lost a man overboard and were searching for him, then they couldn't claim that we'd broken the truce. They couldn't be sure what we were up to, even though we sent a boat into the cove. I mean, if we *had* lost one of our fellows over the side, we'd have been bound to search for him, wouldn't we, sir? Anyway, Mr. Hazard told us all to say that this was what we were doing, if we ran into trouble . . . and he told me what to say in Russian, if I can remember it." Screwing up his face in an effort to concentrate, the boy repeated what he could recall of the Russian words. "I had it pat but it's rather gone out of my head, I'm afraid, sir. But Mr. Hazard did say that it was most important not to let them think that we'd broken the truce, sir."

As, indeed, it was, Phillip reflected. Their liberty and perhaps both their lives might depend on their ability to convince their captors that there had been no violation of the truce. Graham's explanation was an ingenious one which, while it might not wholly be believed, could not wholly be disproved either. It even accounted for a gig's presence at the entrance to the cove and, if he claimed to have dived in, with O'Hara, in an attempt to rescue a drowning man, he might also be able to account for his own presence, without admitting that he had spent the past two days and nights ashore. He frowned, the newly risen sun in his eyes making his head throb, as he considered the possibilities.

The fact that his brother had briefed O'Hara so thoroughly suggested that he had realized that the gig's crew were risking capture by going in to pick him up but did it—*could* it—also mean that Graham had seen through Ambrose Quinn's elaborate attempt at deception? Had he, too, begun to understand the nature of the game the man was playing? Perhaps . . . although it seemed unlikely, since Graham could not have known of that almost fatal rock fall and, unless Williams or Jackson had remembered and talked of the matter to him, he would have had no idea how close it had come to being fatal, as far as he himself was concerned. And now there was no way of telling him. He bit back a sigh and, hearing this, O'Hara asked anxiously, *"Will* they question us, sir?"

"Yes, I fear so," Phillip answered. "They are bound to, in the circumstances. But don't worry, youngster—if we both stick like limpets to my brother's explanation, then it's possible that what occurred during the early hours of this morning may not be regarded as a breach of the truce. Let us hope it is not because, as my brother told you, it *is* very important—and not only for the sake of our skins. I have a report to deliver to our Admiral."

O'Hara stared at him. "A report on Odessa, sir?"

"Yes, that's what it amounts to, Mr. O'Hara. And curiously enough, it might well be very much to the advantage of the citizens of Odessa if I'm permitted to

195

deliver it, although unfortunately I cannot tell them so. But if you back me up, we may be able to persuade them to release us. Not a word of when you first set me ashore, of course."

"No, I understand that, sir."

"Good lad!" The cart lurched up a steep hill and Phillip raised himself on his elbow, to see the squat, stone-built fort directly ahead of them. "We are nearing our destination, Mr. O'Hara," he warned. "Prepare yourself; they may not receive us too kindly."

Their escort clattered through the main gateway and came to a halt, surrounding the cart in which the two British officers lay, when it jolted to a standstill in a small, square courtyard in the center of the fort. After a short delay, a tall, white-haired man in the uniform of a Colonel of Artillery, having received a report from the escort commander, approached the rear of the cart and, in excellent French, courteously bade them descend. Phillip endeavored to accede to his request but his legs buckled under him and he was compelled to cling on to the cart for support. The Russian Colonel apologized and motioned two of the escorting cavalrymen to go to his assistance.

"I will send a surgeon to you," he promised. "And when he has attended to you both, no doubt you will be good enough to explain your presence on our shore, Monsieur. . . . Perhaps I may know your name?"

"It is Hazard, sir, Commander Phillip Hazard of the Royal Navy and this is one of my officers, Midshipman Patrick O'Hara." Phillip spoke in English and the Colonel answered, a trifle haltingly, in the same language.

"I sank you, Commander. I am Colonel Piroff, commandant of this fort."

They bowed to each other stiffly and then, leaning heavily on the arms of his escort, Phillip entered the fort, shuffling barefooted down a long, dark corridor, O'Hara in a like state behind him. They were taken to a large, sparsely furnished room, the windows of which, set high

196

in the walls and barred, looked out on to a blank stone wall. It was a cheerless room but within a few minutes of their arrival a soldier kindled a fire in the empty grate and another brought them a samovar, from which he drew two steaming glasses of tea. They were sipping this gratefully when an officer of about sixty, with sparse grey hair and a close-clipped beard, entered with the announcement, in French that he was the surgeon. His French, like the commandant's, was fluent and his manner not unfriendly. He addressed each of them by name and his examination, courteously conducted, was thorough and painstaking.

"You were in the water—you were swimming, for how long, if I may ask, Monsieur Hazard?"

"I am not sure." Phillip told him truthfully.

The surgeon did not press him. He probed his gashed head and replaced the sodden dressing and then, to Phillip's relief, his attention was distracted by the old wound on his leg, concerning which he asked numerous interested questions. Phillip's replies were cautious but the surgeon appeared satisfied and, after bandaging the leg for him, he rose, smiling from one to the other of his patients.

"In my opinion, messieurs, you will both recover with few ill-effects. if you rest for the next day or two. Needless to say, you have both been exceptionally fortunate. We have believed, until now, that five minutes in our ice-bound sea at this season of the year is the most a man can survive. But you have given that belief the lie and I offer you my felicitations—to you, Monsieur Hazard, in particular. It says much for your tough English constitution that, despite this old wound of yours and the severe blow on the head you have suffered, that you are still able to stand upright!" He shook his head in puzzled admiration. "Colonel Piroff will require to make a report on you to his superiors, but I will request that he postpone his interview with you until you have eaten and slept. Au revoir, messieurs. I shall call upon you again this evening."

Soon after he had taken his leave, a meal was brought, on which both prisoners fell with sharpened appetites and afterwards, as the surgeon had advised, they slept, both of them exhausted. . . .

8

PHILLIP was wakened by a hand shaking his shoulder and, rising a trifle unsteadily from his bed, he saw that both his and O'Hara's uniforms, dried and pressed, had been laid out for them, together with two pairs of cavalry boots to replace their own. The soldier who had roused him indicated by signs that he was to dress but he left O'Hara undisturbed, for which Phillip, glancing down at the boy's white, exhausted face, was grateful.

He donned his uniform and the borrowed boots and two wooden-faced soldiers, both artillerymen, escorted him to what was evidently an ante-room to the commandant's quarters. Here he was kept waiting for about five minutes and then a young officer, with a scarred face and an empty sleeve pinned across his tunic, requested him in remarkably good English to accompany him to the commandant's office.

This proved to be a spacious room, furnished with bookcases, a desk and several padded leather chairs, and with a view across the bay from its single window, through which he was able to see the *Gladiator* and her squadron, still lying at anchor. He was permitted only a glimpse before being conducted to a chair placed with its back to the window, but this was enough to enable him to see that his own ship had returned to her original anchorage and he breathed a relieved sigh.

"And now, if you please, Commander Hazard," Colonel Piroff invited, with faultless courtesy, speaking in French, "I should be obliged if you would give me an explanation of your actions during the early hours of this morning—

yours and your ship's. You may give your account in your own language—Captain Schiller will act as interpreter." He gestured to the young officer with the empty sleeve and added, a faint edge to his voice, "He has recently returned from the Crimea."

Phillip gave as convincing an account as he could, aware as he told it that his story had a number of discrepancies in it. He did his best to gloss over these and saw that the commandant was listening with furrowed brows, as Captain Schiller translated what he had said.

"And that is all you have to tell me?" his interrogator demanded, in French, when he had done.

Phillip bowed. "Yes, sir, that is all. I can only ask you to believe me."

Colonel Piroff turned to his interpreter and spoke to him at length in his own language. The young German shrugged, his face expressionless.

"Commander Hazard, the Colonel finds your account of your actions very hard to believe. He requests me to point out to you that if you attempted to land on this coast for the purpose of spying, your offense is punishable by death, and he asks if you understand this?"

"I understand it, yes. But I assure you, sir, I am not a spy. I am an officer of Her Britannic Majesty's Navy and in command of one of Her Majesty's ships-of-war——"

"Which ships-of-war, sir," Schiller put in sharply, "are at anchor inside Russian territorial waters, under a flag of truce, are they not? To say the least, your actions were in serious breach of the truce, if your account of them is true."

Phillip could feel the palms of his hands go clammy with perspiration as he clenched them. "I can only offer my apologies if anything I have done is in breach of the truce," he said. "That was not my intention . . . but when a man is lost overboard and in danger of drowning, as his commander, I am bound to do all in my power to find and save him. That was my purpose in lowering a boat."

Schiller translated his reply and then said, "Colonel Piroff wishes to know why your ship was signalling with

200

lights, sir, for almost half an hour before you lowered your boat. Did you expect to find your missing sailor alive, after half an hour's immersion in a sea from which the ice has only recently melted?"

Phillip silently cursed Ambrose Quinn for his signals but he answered, as calmly as he could, "The signals were to two other boats I had lowered, which were also searching the area for my seaman. I was anxious to recover his body, even if I could not recover him alive."

Schiller, still without a change of expression, translated this hastily extemporized reply for the commandant's benefit and the interrogation continued. Phillip stuck obstinately to his story, conscious that almost every word he said was making his case sound less and less convincing but doing his utmost now to ensure that O'Hara, at least, was exonerated, on the grounds that he had simply obeyed orders.

"My junior officer is only a boy. If there has been anything to which exception can be taken, please tell Colonel Piroff that the fault is mine, not his."

"The Colonel is well aware of that, sir," Schiller assured him. "It is *your* actions that we are concerned with, Commander Hazard and frankly, sir, the Colonel does not find your explanation at all satisfactory."

"I am very sorry," Phillip returned, with conscious irony. "But it is the only explanation I can offer him."

He had expected an equally ironic retort but, to his stunned amazement, Captain Schiller presented him with a more plausible story. "Is it not a fact, Commander, that the English Navy has many disaffected sailors, who desert their ships, even in time of war?" the young German suggested and, before Phillip had recovered from his surprise, he added forcefully, "I would understand your anxiety to lower boats and make signals if, for example, some of your men had attempted to desert your ship and seek sanctuary with us here in Odessa. Some, I say— not just one! And if these deserters had stolen a boat, in order to make their escape, then neither I nor, I am sure, the Colonel would find your explanation hard to believe."

Taking Phillip's look of stupefaction as tantamount to an admission that he was right, Schiller turned to the commandant and, a note of satisfaction in his voice, evidently repeated his suggestion in Russian.

"And what, monsieur," Colonel Piroff asked, addressing Phillip in French, "what have you to say to Captain Schiller's suggestion that your sailors are disaffected and that some of them attempted, during the hours of darkness, to desert your ship?"

"Sir, I. . . ." Phillip hesitated, still bewildered by the accusation and searching for the right answer. His instinctive reaction was to defend his ship and his Service from so damning a slur but, over-riding this was the awareness that he must convince the commandant, if he could, that the truce had not been broken. Finally, deciding that, even if there had been any basis of truth in Schiller's accusation, he would have been in honor bound to deny it, he shook his head emphatically. "There is no disaffection among my ship's company, sir. Nor is there in Her Majesty's Navy, I assure you."

Both Russian officers smiled. This, clearly, was the answer they had expected him to give and almost certainly neither believed him, although he was at a loss to understand why. Schiller said, his tone disparaging, "There *are* desertions from your ships. I have heard it on good authority, Commander Hazard. But naturally you cannot admit that it is so."

Before Phillip could accept his challenge, the Colonel rose and moved across to the window. A telescope lay on a table beside it and, picking this up, he invited Phillip to join him at his vantage point and put the glass into his hand. "With the aid of this instrument," he stated gravely, "We are able, as you can see, to observe much of what is going on aboard your ships. This morning, not long after the return of your boat, we witnessed what I think you call a punishment parade on board *that* ship . . . which is yours, is it not?" He pointed unerringly to the *Huntress*.

Phillip nodded, feeling the color drain from his cheeks. For a moment, he was so shocked and angry that he could not speak and the Colonel went on, "Three of your sailors were flogged, monsieur, ceremoniously and before the eyes of their comrades . . . for the crime of attempting to desert, perhaps? This is Captain Schiller's interpretation and he knows your country and your people well as, I think, his command of your language proves. For myself, while I try to keep an open mind, I confess that I am inclined to agree with him."

Much of what he said was lost on Phillip and, sensing this, Schiller repeated it in English, his tone now unashamedly triumphant. "I am right, am I not?" he demanded.

Anger caught at Phillip's throat, directed not against the young German mercenary but against Ambrose Quinn. He could guess which seamen his second-in-command had flogged—Williams and Jackson would, no doubt, have been two of the three and the third—God help him —might well have been O'Leary. Sick with bitterness he knew that, whatever lies he had to tell or allow his interrogators to believe, he must somehow persuade them to release him, so that he might return to his ship and deal with the man who had usurped his command. At that moment nothing else mattered to him and, when he made no reply to Schiller's taunting question, the German turned to his superior, unleashing a spate of words, the meaning of which was clear enough, although Phillip could not understand the actual words. He was immeasurably relieved when Colonel Piroff summoned his escort and requested him, politely, to go back to the room he was sharing with O'Hara.

"I shall make a full report to the Deputy Governor," were the Colonel's parting words, swiftly translated by Schiller. "It would seem not improbable that His Excellency may decide to order your release, Commander Hazard, with that of your young officer. I will, of course, inform you of his decision in due course."

This was the outcome he had wanted, Phillip thought and, forcing himself to speak calmly despite the tumult of conflicting emotions within him, he thanked his captors and returned to his room. O'Hara was still sound asleep and, wanting a chance to think, he did not waken the boy.

He spent a miserable evening, battling with his conscience and even the arrival of an excellent dinner failed to rally his flagging spirits. O'Hara, roused at last from sleep, came pink-cheeked and hungry to the table, where he did full justice to the food, but Phillip had no appetite. He told the boy as much as he felt he could concerning his interrogation and saw the bright, intelligent eyes widen in dismay when he was compelled to admit that he had not decisively denied the accusations levelled against him by Captain Schiller. But Patrick O'Hara was loyal; he offered neither reproach nor criticism, the look of pained disillusionment in his eyes the only indication of his real feelings.

"If they ask me the same questions, sir, am I to back you up?" he inquired, with such obvious reluctance that Phillip could not find it in his heart to ask this sacrifice of him.

"No," he returned shortly. "You must answer as you see fit, Mr. O'Hara. All I do ask of you is that you make no admission that might lead them to suspect that we *did* infringe the truce. If they should have reason to believe we did, our chances of getting out of here will be slight."

"I understand, sir. But . . . did we infringe the truce, sir?"

"*I* did," Phillip answered.

"But on orders, sir?" the midshipman persisted.

"Yes, lad. But they were secret orders and I cannot use them to justify any infringement of the truce." Phillip smiled at him wryly. "It was not my intention to be taken by the enemy but unfortunately that's what happened, so . . ." he shrugged. "I'm not left with much choice—I must either lie or take the consequences. However, I fancy that you'll be released—the Russians are not inhuman and, in view of your age, I don't think they will hold you. Tell me"—as O'Hara started to voice an indignant protest—"did Mr. Quinn, did the First Lieutenant give any reason that you're aware of for making

204

those flashing light signals and for the shift of anchorage?"

The boy shook his head. "No, sir, not that I'm aware of, but Mr. Grey was instructed to make the signals and *he* understood that you had left orders to that effect, sir. He remarked to me at the time that you seemed to be taking rather a chance and that . . ." he broke off, reddening, as if suddenly realizing that he had said too much.

"Well?" Phillip prompted. "And that, Mr. O'Hara? I'd like to know, if you please. What else did Mr. Grey say to you?"

"Well, sir"—O'Hara's eyes avoided his—"only that I might have a sticky time with the gig, sir, when I picked you up. He—that was why he volunteered to come with us, sir. He said there was a lot going on that we didn't know anything about and . . . well, sir, I fancy he thought there'd be the chance of a scrap with the enemy, sir."

Phillip controlled himself with an almost visible effort. So that was how Ambrose Quinn planned to keep his sheet clean, was it? *He* was to be blamed for orders he had never issued and certainly had not entered in the log. He smothered a sigh. Quinn could have added to the logged orders, of course, and almost certainly had added to them by this time.

"Sir," O'Hara ventured, "*did* you leave orders for those signals to be made?" Phillip affected not to have heard the question and the boy hesitated for a moment and then added diffidently, "If they—if the Russians question me, I'll back you up, sir."

"Thank you, Mr. O'Hara," Phillip acknowledged, with restraint. "I'm grateful to you."

O'Hara, however, was not questioned and, after an uneasy and virtually sleepless night, it was again Phillip who was summoned to the commandant's office the following morning. But now there was a subtle change in the atmosphere, of which he became conscious within a few moments of entering the room. Gone was the courteous friendliness that Colonel Piroff had displayed towards him yesterday and Captain Schiller, he realized, was regarding him with undisguised mistrust, his manner, when he spoke, coldly hostile. There was a third officer in the room this time, a man in a dark uniform he did not recognize, who sat in silence, watching him from beneath beetling black brows. He was not introduced and offered no greeting and he remained seated when Colonel Piroff led Phillip to the window and, gesturing to the British squadron lying at anchor far below them, observed flatly, "Your ship, monsieur, has sailed without you, it would appear."

"Sailed . . . but——" taken completely off his guard by this unexpected news, Phillip stared down at the anchored ships. The *Gladiator*, with Lieutenant Risk's small, sturdy *Wrangler* and the French frigate *Mogador* lay as they had lain the previous evening but, search for her as he would, he could see no sign of his own *Huntress* and his heart sank. When and why had she gone, he asked himself, and where? He could only surmise that Captain Broke had ordered her to rejoin the Fleet, an action he would surely not have taken unless he had reason to suppose that her commander was dead, which meant—he drew in his breath sharply . . . which meant that Quinn must have reported him drowned or killed—and O'Hara with him—and could also mean that Broke would make no inquiries, no representations for their release. Indeed, the *Gladiator*'s Captain might be preparing to sail himself, with the rest of the squadron, in order to avoid any accusations of breaking the truce. In his place, Phillip thought, he would have been on tenterhooks, hourly waiting for an official protest to reach him from the port authorities and. . . .

"You are surprised?" Captain Schiller suggested, with a faint sneer. Phillip said nothing and he went on, with the obvious intention of goading him, "That proves my point, does it not, Commander Hazard? There is disaffection among your men and so your ship has been sent away. Or could there be some other reason, some reason which you have omitted to tell us?"

The questions went on, becoming more searching and harder to counter than they had been on the previous evening. As he endeavored to reply to them, Phillip was conscious of the cold, steely eyes of the officer in the unfamiliar dark uniform, fixed on his face in unblinking scrutiny, as if their owner were attempting to read his thoughts, rather than listen to his answers. But the man put no questions of his own and, after almost an hour he rose, bowed to Colonel Piroff and took his leave, still without having said a word, apart from one or two whispered asides to the commandant in his own language. Following his departure, Captain Schiller summoned an escort and Phillip, to his relief, was taken back to his room.

For the next six days, this became the unvarying pattern. Each morning he was escorted to the commandant's office, sometimes with O'Hara but usually by himself, and Colonel Piroff continued to question him through the medium of the young German interpreter. The questions were as unvarying as the routine, but once, producing a pair of sodden boots from behind his back, with the dexterity of a conjurer, Captain Schiller stated that they had been found on the beach where he and O'Hara had been apprehended and invited Phillip to deny that they were his.

"I imagine they were washed ashore," Phillip returned, thankful that they did not appear to have found his signal lamp which, being heavier than the boots, had probably sunk beneath the incoming tide. He added, with a confidence he was far from feeling, "I kicked them off when I was swimming—we both did. No doubt the tide will bring in Mr. O'Hara's boots also, in due course."

Schiller looked disappointed and reverted to his original line of questioning and the daily interviews went on as before, always it seemed to Phillip, with the object of wearing down his resistance and trapping him into an unguarded admission through sheer weariness. For the rest, however, both he and O'Hara were treated well enough, he had to concede. Their meals were regular and ample, their days—if long and empty—undisturbed. With warmth and sleep, the minor ill-effects they had suffered as a result of their immersion in the icy water soon cleared up.

The surgeon visited them each day and, on his advice, they were permitted half an hour's exercise on the drill square of the fort, under guard, morning and evening, and it was he who, as an expression of personal goodwill, lent them a chess set to help occupy their time. But there was no word of their release; the commandant did not mention it again and the surgeon, when Phillip inquired from him, simply smiled. "You are fortunate that I have prevailed upon our port health authorities to allow us to keep you here," he said cheerfully, "since, if they had their way, you would be confined in the *lazaretto*, monsieur, for the period of quarantine normally imposed. Believe me, you are a good deal better off where you are!"

Phillip did not doubt this but, although for O'Hara's sake, he maintained the outward appearance of optimism, he came close to despair when the second week of their imprisonment began without any indication that the Deputy Governor had reached a decision in their favor. His only consolation was the fact that the three ships of Captain Broke's squadron still lay at anchor in the bay where, each morning as he entered the commandant's office, he was able to catch a fleeting glimpse of them. On the morning of the ninth day after his arrival at the fort, even this consolation was denied him for, with Captain Schiller's hand firmly on his shoulder, he was made to seat himself with his back to the window, this time directly facing the black-uniformed officer whose silent scrutiny he had previously found so hard to endure. A trifle to his surprise, the officer broke his self-imposed silence, addressing him in correct but harshly accented French.

"Do you know who I am, Commander Hazard?" he demanded and, when Phillip shook his head, he smiled, the smile arrogant and oddly repellent. "I am Colonel Golitsin, Chief of His Imperial Majesty's civil and military police in this province." He paused and then added, his voice suddenly cutting like a whiplash, "You were here in Odessa before, were you not? You were one of the prisoners taken when we sank your English battleship the *Tiger!*"

The question, uttered accusingly, took Phillip by surprise but, since there seemed little to be gained in denying a fact which, in all probability, his accuser could easily prove, he inclined his head. "Yes, Colonel Golitsin, I was."

"You were wounded and your life saved by the skill of His Excellency the Governor's own physician, Dr. Vassily, who attended you at His Excellency's behest, is that not so?" There was a note of subdued triumph in the harsh voice and again Phillip answered him truthfully.

"That is so, sir. I willingly concede that I owe my life to Dr. Vassily's skill, as well to His Excellency Baron Osten-Sacken's kindness in lodging me in his own house and permitting his servants to care for me. I was treated, not as a prisoner but as an honored guest by His Excellency and all his household." He saw Colonel Piroff's brows rise in an astonished curve when Captain Schiller hastily translated what he had said and the German, turning to him, asked sullenly, "The Colonel wishes to know why you did not tell us this before, Commander Hazard. Explain your reasons to him, if you please."

Phillip shrugged, with simulated unconcern. "I was not aware that the fact that I was a prisoner-of-war here, over eight months ago, could have any bearing on the present situation or, of course, I should have mentioned it. In any event, sir, I was never asked."

Schiller looked as if he were about to dispute this statement but the Chief of Police waved him imperiously to silence.

"You claim, monsieur, to be the Captain of an English ship-of-war and not a spy," he said, addressing Phillip. "But I have three witnesses who saw you in the Cathedral here, in this city, the morning *before* you were apprehended by Colonel Piroff's troop of cavalry, supposedly landing on our coast! Is this how you repay His Excellency the Baron Osten-Sacken to whom, on your own admission, you owe your life? Mother of God, I am glad that His Excellency is with our victorious armies in

209

the Crimea for, if he were here, it would distress him immeasurably to learn of your treachery!"

His tone was exultant now and Phillip's blood ran suddenly cold. This, he recognized with bitter resignation, was the end. In spite of the lies he had endeavored to tell, Golitsin had proof that he had broken the truce and every reason to accuse him of spying . . . for which, as Colonel Piroff had reminded him, the penalty was death. He attempted to speak but the words died in his throat as Colonel Golitsin rose and, with a dramatic gesture, flung open the door into the ante-room, calling upon its occupants to enter the inner office.

They did so, in obedient procession. The first two were, as Phillip had feared, the black-bearded man who had stood behind him in the Cathedral and one of the ushers and then, to his stunned dismay, he saw that the third witness was Boris. Colonel Golitsin pointed to him and then spoke to the three newcomers, obviously inviting them to identify him which, almost with one accord, they did, the black-bearded man volubly, the usher with an emphatic "Da, da!" and Boris—incredibly—with a beaming smile of pleased recognition. Phillip stared at him, frozen into immobility and trying vainly to think of some defense to offer which would not, however indirectly, involve Mademoiselle Sophie when, to his amazement, the giant footman stepped up to him and bowed. From a gold embossed leather pouch, he took two envelopes, both adorned with heavy, crested seals. Still beaming, he gave one to Phillip and turning, almost contemptuously, put the other into Colonel Golitsin's outstretched hand. After a brief hesitation, Golitsin returned to his chair and opened the envelope he had been given.

Phillip, still unable to move, watched him in shocked fascination and saw a glittering object fall from the envelope into his palm—an object he instantly recognized as the emerald ring, with the Imperial double-headed eagle, which Mademoiselle Sophie had presented to him on leaving the *Trojan*. Oh dear God, he thought in bitter self-reproach, why had he not anticipated that Mademoiselle Sophie would make an attempt to save him? And why, in heaven's name why, had he not pleaded guilty to the charges against him days ago, when he might have avoided this catastrophe?

Boris touched his arm and gestured to the letter he was holding, as yet unopened, in his hand, murmuring something unintelligible in his own tongue. He looked calm and unruffled, even pleased and, seeing this, Phillip took fresh heart. He nodded, his throat still dry and, taking great care to hide the fact that his hands were trembling, he broke the seal and spread the letter across his knee where, controlling his apprehension, he forced himself to read it.

"My dear Phillip," Mademoiselle Sophie had written. *"I have only recently heard of your arrest. Why did you not tell me? Why did you not call on me for help? Dear Phillip, I am not without influence in high places and I could have spared you the anxiety and the discomfort which, I fear, you have had to endure for the past week or more.*

"Do not worry . . . I have spoken to the Deputy Governor on your behalf and told him how you most gallantly risked your life in order to bring to me here the ring my beloved husband entrusted to you when he died on the field of battle. I have told him also how well and nobly you served me when I was a passenger on board your ship the Trojan *and I have given him, in confidence, an account of some of the matters we spoke of when we were together last Sunday.*

"At my request, he has written to Colonel Golitsin, to whom both my letter and his instructions will be delivered at once and I shall, in due course, inform my Uncle the Tsar of his zeal in my service. His Excellency has assured me that your release and that of your brave young midshipman, Mr. O'Hara, will be arranged and you will both be conveyed to the English squadron, when the reply from the neutral Consuls—now being prepared by the Spanish representative, Senor Franco Baguer y Ribas—is sent out to them. For reasons which I need not go into, your re-

211

*turn to your ship will be arranged in secret and no official
mention of this, or your presence here, is to be made.*

*"My truly grateful good wishes go with you. It is a
matter for regret that I cannot come in person to bid you
farewell but my time is very near and I must shortly be
brought to bed, so I crave your forgiveness for this omis-
sion."*

The letter was signed with the single name *Sophie* and
Phillip felt unmanly tears come to sting at his eyes as he
folded the letter and put it carefully into his pocket,
relief and gratitude flooding over him. When he looked up,
he saw that the two witnesses from the Cathedral were
being hustled out by Schiller and that Colonel Piroff was
now studying the contents of the envelope Boris had
delivered to the Chief of Police, the emerald ring lying
on the desk in front of him. Boris himself, continuing
to beam with genial goodwill on friend and foe alike,
crossed to the desk, where he waited expectantly until
Colonel Golitsin picked up the ring and gave it to him.
The tall footman bowed, restored the ring to its case and
replaced both in his crested leather pouch and then, to
Phillip's surprise, took from it a small package which,
bowing again, he held out invitingly.

The package bore his own name, Phillip saw, as he
took it. Inside was a gold pocket-watch with the Imperial
Russian cypher engraved on the case and attached to it
was a card, on which was written, in Mademoiselle
Sophie's small, neat hand, *"This, too, was my Father's
. . . I send it to you with my gratitude."*

Colonel Golitsin eyed the gift, an expression of almost
ludicrous bewilderment on his gaunt, bony face as he
glimpsed the cypher and then observed stiffly, "It would
appear that I have done you an injustice, Commander
Hazard. Permit me to offer you my apologies . . . and
also to point out that you could have saved us all a
great deal of trouble—and yourself the injustice—had
you told us, at the outset, why you came here. But . . ." he
shrugged. "I presume you have been made aware that,
thanks to Her Imperial Highness's gracious plea on your

behalf, His Excellency the Deputy Governor has ordered that you be released?"

Phillip rose and bowed to him stiffly. "Thank you, sir, I have," he acknowledged, without waiting for Schiller to complete his translation. "When may we expect to be returned to our squadron?"

"Within a few days, monsieur. In the meantime, it is necessary that you remain here but you will both, of course, be Colonel Piroff's guests." The Chief of Police returned his bow and, with a brusque word of dismissal to Boris, went out, the smiling giant obediently at his heels.

"The Colonel-Commandant," Captain Schiller announced, avoiding Phillip's gaze, "would be honored, sir, if you and Mr. O'Hara would dine with him this evening."

"Thank you, Colonel, that will give us both much pleasure. But now . . ." Phillip looked from one to the other of his erstwhile interrogators without rancor, "have I your permission to retire to my quarters? I am anxious to inform Mr. O'Hara of our impending release."

"Within these walls, you are free to come and go as you please, monsieur," Colonel Piroff assured him. "As Colonel Golitsin told you, both you and Monsieur O'Hara will be my guests and we shall arrange for your release as soon as it is possible."

He was as good as his word. On the morning of 6th February, with a delighted O'Hara scarcely able to control his exuberance, Phillip rode back along the coast road to Odessa for what, while the war continued, he fervently hoped would be the last time. The church bells started to ring out as they neared the main boulevard leading to the Imperial Harbor and, hearing this, Colonel Piroff reined in his horse to enable Phillip to draw level with him. He was smiling as he said, in his careful French, "Your departure is well timed, Commander Hazard! You hear the bells? You will, I feel sure, be happy to know they signify that an heir has been born to the House of Narishkin."

Once again Phillip saw Mademoiselle Sophie's small,

sweet face floating before him, just as he had seen it when the icy waters of the cove were closing over his head, like a vision from another world. As indeed, he thought, it was . . . and, his heart suddenly full, he breathed a silent prayer of thankfulness. The son he had so much wanted had been born to poor, dead Andrei Narishkin. . . .

"I am happy for Her Imperial Highness," he managed to say aloud and Colonel Piroff laid a friendly hand on his arm.

"And your boat is waiting, monsieur, as you can see—which, no doubt, will also make you happy."

At the head of the stone steps leading down to the Mole, they dismounted and descended the steps together, O'Hara and two of their escort clattering after them. The Colonel took his leave when they reached the Mole and, accompanied by a solemn-faced Harbor Master and a naval guard, Phillip and his small midshipman were marched to the waiting boat. The church bells were ringing in their ears as the boat put off and was rowed out into the bay to meet one from the *Wrangler* which, under a flag of truce, came rapidly towards them. Lieutenant Risk was himself in command and, as his gig came alongside the Russian boat, Phillip glimpsed his look of astonished disbelief when he recognized the two passengers. He maintained a dignified silence while the Consuls' note was delivered but, when Phillip joined him in the stern-sheets of the gig, he could restrain himself no longer.

"Welcome aboard, Commander Hazard!" he exclaimed and wrung Phillip's hand warmly. "I trust you will forgive my astonishment but I feel as though I were looking at a ghost, and that's the truth! Your First Lieutenant reported you and your midshipman drowned, sir. He made no mention of your being taken by the enemy."

"My First Lieutenant did not wait to make sure, Mr. Risk," Phillip answered grimly.

Risk stared at him. "That's odd, sir—he told Captain Broke that your death had been witnessed by a whole boat's crew and asked permission to rejoin the Fleet, so

214

that your—er—your loss could be reported to the Commander-in-Chief immediately. So the *Huntress* is no longer with us, I'm afraid but . . . I'm extremely glad that the report was wrong, sir, needless to tell you. I'll take you to the *Gladiator* now, shall I, so that you can convey the welcome news of your survival to Captain Broke in person?" Receiving Phillip's assent, he added sympathetically, "I imagine you'll be anxious to get back to the Fleet yourself at the first opportunity, won't you?"

Phillip nodded, tight-lipped. "Yes, Mr. Risk," he agreed, thinking of the floggings and then of the mission with which he had been entrusted and his long delayed account of Odessa's defences. "Yes, I'm very anxious indeed to get back to the Fleet because I, too, have a report to deliver."

"We shall probably sail for the Katcha tomorrow," Risk informed him. "With the Consuls' letter, leaving the *Gladiator* and the *Mogador* to maintain the blockade."

"Then may I beg passage with you?"

"I shall be more than pleased to accommodate you, sir —and your mid. A well plucked 'un, isn't he?"

"He is indeed," Phillip confirmed, smiling across at O'Hara. "He's worth more than many a man of twice his size."

Fog delayed the *Wrangler*'s sailing for two days but she set course for the mouth of the Katcha River at first light on 9th February. Phillip occupied his enforced leisure by committing his report on Odessa to paper and when the *Wrangler* dropped anchor at the end of a line of steam frigates, he sent the bulky document he had compiled to the *Agamemnon*—still flying the flag of the Commander-in-Chief—together with Lieutenant Risk's dispatches. Unable to see the *Huntress* anywhere among the anchored ships of the Fleet, he fretted impotently until a letter from Frederick Cleeve, the Admiral's Secretary, was delivered to him.

It was brief, telling him only that Admiral Lyons was about to leave for Balaclava in order to attend a conference at Lord Raglan's Headquarters on the Upland, with both the British and French military Commanders-in-Chief. The receipt of his report was acknowledged and Cleeve assured him that it had been placed in the Admiral's hands.

"The Admiral wishes you to attend him immediately on his return to this anchorage," the letter ended formally, but Lieutenant Cleve had added a postcript, signed with his own initials, which read: *"Welcome back! We had feared you lost. Your Huntress is at Eupatoria, in case you have been looking for her in vain, and the Banshee will be proceeding to that port within the next two days, with despatches for Captain Hastings."*

The following evening, Phillip was summoned aboard the *Agamemnon* and Sir Edmund Lyons received him with gratifying warmth.

"My dear Phillip, I cannot tell you with what pleasure and relief I welcome you back from the dead! Yours was a loss I could ill have sustained, believe me, my dear boy. And this"—the Admiral's tired blue eyes lit up, as he gestured to the report, lying open on his desk—"this report of yours came in the nick of time. I was able, with its aid, to convince even General Canrobert that a second naval bombardment of the port of Odessa would be a waste of powder and shot, while serving no useful purpose in the prosecution of the war with Russia."

"I am glad of that, sir," Phillip answered, all his fears concerning the delay set at rest.

The Admiral smiled at him. "And so, I assure you, my boy, am I! My proposal for a spring offensive against the enemy's lines of communication in the Sea of Azoff has been put forward by Admiral Bruat and myself. We propose its occupation by a flotilla of vessels under our joint command and we have requested military co-opera-tion, to the extent of twelve thousand men, for a limited period of, perhaps ten days or a fortnight. We have even set a date, early in May, for the expedition to sail . . . and General Canrobert has promised to give the matter his careful consideration. I fancy he will have to agree, now that we have—thanks to your most comprehensive

report—robbed him of Odessa as a possible alternative."
He talked on with enthusiasm, despite his evident weariness, of his plans for the spring offensive and then said, with a swift change of mood, "We expect another attack on Eupatoria, Phillip. Your *Huntress* is there and I shall send the *Lynx* and the *Arrow* and possibly also the *Curlew* and *Dauntless*, to reinforce Captain Hastings' squadron, if necessary."

"May I be permitted to rejoin my ship at once, sir?" Phillip asked anxiously.

"Of course, my dear boy. Your passage shall be arranged aboard the first ship to leave this anchorage," the Commander-in-Chief agreed readily. "And touching on the matter of your First Lieutenant . . . you requested his replacement some time ago, didn't you?"

Phillip reddened. This was the question he had been dreading, yet had known that he would be called upon to answer. He had dealt with Quinn's part in his capture very ambiguously in his report, aware that—whatever accusations he might make—he had no proof and had made up his mind, resignedly, that he would deal with the man himself when he resumed command of the *Huntress*, in the best way he could. But now, it seemed, the Admiral was offering to replace him and he hesitated, aware that he could not let Ambrose Quinn go to any other ship with a clean sheet. "Sir," he began, "I regret to say, sir, that Lieutenant Quinn is——"

Quietly, the Admiral cut him short. "Lieutenant Quinn is, at this moment, under arrest and awaiting court martial on two very grave charges, Phillip."

Phillip expelled his breath in an astonished gasp. *"Two* charges, sir?"

"One of causing the death of your predecessor as Captain of the *Huntress*, Commander Francis Willoughby, and of giving false evidence at the court of inquiry into his death," Admiral Lyons told him distastefully. "And the other of mastheading a cadet of yours, whose name eludes me, but Frederick Cleeve can give you chapter and verse. I understand that Surgeon Fraser of the *Trojan*, who attended the lad, was a witness to his fall and that both he and the cadet will give evidence on this second charge. The other witnesses are two seamen, who deserted the ship in Constantinople and claim. . . ." The Admiral sighed. "It's not a pleasant story, Phillip, and as I said, Frederick can give you the sordid details. But it would appear that when the two deserters were picked up, they claimed to have jumped ship because of threats made against them by your erstwhile First Lieutenant, which put them in fear of their lives. Both say that they were on deck when Francis Willoughby was supposedly washed overboard—or fell overboard—whilst in a state of insobriety and both state that the unfortunate fellow was perfectly sober. The charge they are to bring against Lieutenant Quinn is a capital one and it seems that the cadet—ah, yes, I recall his name now—Cadet Lightfoot is to support their testimony. He, too, witnessed the unhappy incident but was afraid to say so, until now. It's a bad business, Phillip, a thoroughly bad business, isn't it?"

"It is indeed, sir," Phillip agreed with restraint.

The Admiral laid a hand on his shoulder. "You are a good judge of character, my boy. If my memory serves me aright, you requested a replacement for Mr. Quinn over two months ago. Well"—he smiled—"I've granted your request. You have a new First Lieutenant, who is temporarily in command of the *Huntress* and I fancy the appointment will please you."

"I'm most grateful, sir. May I ask his name?"

"It is the same as your own, my dear Phillip—Hazard." The Admiral chuckled. "Contrary, I must confess, to my expectations—though not to my hopes—Their Lordships have graciously restored your brother's commission to him, his senority to date from when he rejoined the Service. Well . . . does that please you?"

"Nothing in the world could please me more, sir," Phillip assured him. "Permit me to thank you, sir, on my brother's behalf and my own. I feel sure that *your* recommendation must have influenced Their Lordships' decision and——"

218

Again Admiral Lyons cut him short. "You have both deserved well of me, Phillip—you most of all. After reading between the lines of your report on Odessa's defenses, I have some notion of what it cost you to compile. But I'm not going to ask you how you contrived to make so thorough an inspection, nor shall I expect to be told how you prevailed upon the enemy to release you. Like the orders I gave you, it shall remain a confidential matter, of which no official mention can ever be made. Before I let you go, however, there is one question I feel bound to ask you. Have you any charge or charges to bring against Lieutenant Quinn at his trial?"

Phillip hesitated only for an instant. "No, sir," he answered quietly. "None that, in the circumstances, I could substantiate, sir."

"The mills of God grind slowly . . ." Sir Edmund Lyons quoted. "But in Mr. Quinn's case, I fancy they will grind exceeding small." He held out his hand. "You may rejoin your command, Phillip. Good night and God go with you!"

Phillip drew himself to attention. "Aye, aye, sir," he acknowledged and added softly, "And God go with you too, sir."

From the Navy Records Society map.

BOOKS CONSULTED

ON THE CRIMEAN WAR
(General)

History of the War Against Russia, E. H. Nolan (2 vols., 1857)

History of the War With Russia, H. Tyrell (3 vols., 1857)

The Campaign in the Crimea, G. Brackenbury, illustrated W. Simpson (1856)

The War in the Crimea, General Sir Edward Hamley (1891)

Letters from India and the Crimea, Surgeon-General J. A. Bostock (1896)

Letters from Headquarters, by a Staff Officer (1856)

The Crimea in 1854 and 1894, Field-Marshal Sir Evelyn Wood (1895)

The Destruction of Lord Raglan, Christopher Hibbert (1961)

Battles of the Crimean War, W. Baring Pemberton (1962)

The Reason Why, Cecil Woodham Smith (1953)

Crimean Blunder, Peter Gibbs (1960)

The Campaign in the Crimea, 1854-6: Despatches and Papers, compiled and arranged by Captain Sayer (1857)

Letters from Camp During the Siege of Sebastopol, Lt.-Colonel C. G. Campbell (1894)

The Invasion of the Crimea, A. W. Kingslake (1863)

With the Guards We Shall Go, Mabel, Countess of Airlie (1933)

Britain's Roll of Glory, D. H. Parry (1895)

Henry Clifford, V. C., General Sir Bernard Paget (1956)

Biographies

The Life of Colin Campbell, Lord Clyde, Lt.-General L. Shadwell, C.B. (2 vols., 1881)

A Life of Vice-Admiral Lord Lyons, Captain S. Eardley-Wilmot, R.N. (1898)

(Naval)

The Russian War, 1854 (Baltic and Black Sea), D. Bonner-Smith and Captain A. C. Dewar, R.N. (1944)

Letters from the Black Sea, Admiral Sir Leopold Heath (1897)

A Sailor's Life Under Four Sovereigns, Admiral of the Fleet the Hon. Sir Henry Keppel, G.C.B., O.M. (3 vols., 1899)

From Midshipman to Field-Marshal, Sir Evelyn Wood, V.C. (2 vols., 1906)

Letters from the Fleet in the Fifties, Mrs. Tom Kelly (1902)

The British Fleet in the Black Sea, Maj.-General W. Brereton (1856)

Reminiscences of a Naval Officer, Sir G. Gifford (1892)

The Navy as I have known it, Vice-Admiral W. Freemantle (1899)

A Middy's Recollections, The Hon. Victor Montagu (1898)

Medicine and the Navy, Lloyd and Coulter (Vol. IV, 1963)

The Price of Admiralty, Stanley Barret, Hale (1968)

The Wooden Fighting Ship, E. H. H. Archibald, Blandford (1968)

Seamanship Manual, Captain Sir George S. Naes, K.C.B., R.N., Griffin (1886)

The Navy of Britain, England's Sea Officers, and *A Social History of the Navy*, Michael Lewis, Allen & Unwin (1939-60)

The Navy in Transition, Michael Lewis, Hodder & Stoughton (1965)

Files of *The Illustrated London News* and *Mariner's Mirror*.
Unpublished Letters and Diaries.

The author acknowledges, with gratitude, the assistance given by the Staff of the York City Library in obtaining books, also that given by the Royal United Service Institution and Francis Edwards Ltd.

Pinnacle Hits!

HANNIE CAULDER, by William Terry. A new Western—wild, rugged, sexy! Soon to be a major motion picture from Paramount starring Raquel Welch. **No. P094—95¢**

GOLD WAGON, by Chet Cunningham. Guns blaze as love, hate, and intrigue erupt in this original, exciting and different western. Forget the cactus and cattle—it's gold! **No. P096—95¢**

AFGHAN ASSAULT, by Alan Caillou. In #4 of the Private Army of Colonel Tobin series, the toughest little army in the world challenges an army of ferocious Indian warriors. **No. P097—95¢**

EXECUTIVE YOGA, by Harvey Day. An exercise book—exclusively for men! Reduce risk of heart trouble, conquer fatigue and stress, gain efficiency—the yoga way. **No. P098—$1.25**

THE ELECTION, by Sherwin Markman. The timeliest and most suspenseful novel of the year! What happens when an exciting presidential election is tied, and the final decision is thrown into the House of Representatives. **No. P100—$1.50**

OVER THE WALL, by Duncan Thorp. A novel that captures the spirit and excitement of a revolution; the heat and passions of the Caribbean, and the tension of a do-or-die jailbreak. Romance, sex and action for the most demanding adventure fan! **No. P101—95¢**

RISE WITH THE WIND, by A. C. Marin. Espionage and intrigue in a fiery new novel! The ghastly shadows of WW II hover over the little Central American republic where the Agency sends their man—to find fifteen million dollars or ?. **No. P102—95¢**

THE DESTROYER: MAFIA FIX, by Richard Sapir and Warren Murphey. It's #4 in our series about the superman of the 70s, Remo Williams! This time Remo and his Oriental mentor have to find the biggest heroin shipment to hit the U.S. shores. **No. P104—95¢**

BLUE MARSH, by Thelma Rene Bernard. A Great Gothic Novel. A young and orphaned girl travelling alone meets a handsome young man, and soon becomes involved in a sinister plot. Pinnacle's large type. **No. P105—95¢**

A CROSS FOR TOMORROW, by Mona Farnsworth. This gothic suspense novel tells the strange and mysterious story of Margaret Alden's experience with a Spanish family in New Mexico. She becomes enmeshed in violence . . . and murder. In large type. **No. P106—95¢**